Charles Freshman

The Autobiography of the Rev. Charles Freshman

Late Rabbi of the Jewish Synagogue at Quebec....

Charles Freshman

The Autobiography of the Rev. Charles Freshman
Late Rabbi of the Jewish Synagogue at Quebec....

ISBN/EAN: 9783337116088

Printed in Europe, USA, Canada, Australia, Japan

Cover: Foto ©Raphael Reischuk / pixelio.de

More available books at **www.hansebooks.com**

AUTOBIOGRAPHY

OF THE

REV. CHARLES FRESHMAN.

Yours very truly
C. Treshman

THE

AUTOBIOGRAPHY

OF THE

REV. CHARLES FRESHMAN;

LATE RABBI OF THE JEWISH SYNAGOGUE AT QUEBEC, AND
GRADUATE OF THE JEWISH THEOLOGICAL
SEMINARY AT PRAGUE;

AT PRESENT

GERMAN WESLEYAN MINISTER AT PRESTON,
ONTARIO.

" Thou shalt remember all the way which the Lord thy God led thee."
Deut. viii. 2

TORONTO:
SAMUEL ROSE, WESLEYAN BOOK ROOM
KING STREET.

1868.

TORONTO :

PRINTED AT THE WESLEYAN PRINTING ESTABLISHMENT,

KING STREET.

PREFACE BY THE REV. W. JEFFERS, D.D.

BELIEVING that the story of his life might be useful, the Rev. Dr. FRESHMAN has given us—in this Autobiography—a story of more than common interest; and I cheerfully consent to contribute a few prefatory remarks.

The extraordinary series of providences by which God led him savingly to embrace the true MESSSIAH, and prepared him to become an ambassador of Christ, as well as the peculiar struggles of his spirit against doubt and every kind of difficulty, until a victorious faith fired his soul with zeal to preach the CRUCIFIED to his fellow-men, cannot but interest all serious readers, and arrest the attention of the thoughtless.

The youthful years of Dr. Freshman present a remarkable instance of " the pursuit of knowledge under difficulties." The thought of becoming a Rabbi—which he esteemed the highest honour on earth, and which was never for an hour absent from his mind—was the source of his ambition to become a scholar.

With an earnest reverence for religion, from his earliest years, he saw nothing so desirable as the office of a minister of religion — and learning was to him of value chiefly as a qualification for that office. Having once resolved to get an education, he persevered through every obstacle.

With little encouragement or assistance from friends, he worked his painful way through difficulties and discouragements, many of which would have made an ordinary student despair.

The romantic incidents of his youthful career awaken our sympathies ; while his perseverance and success present an example and encouragement to all young men.

This Autobiography introduces us to a state of society—to social and religious sentiments and customs — altogether different from what we have been familiar with. We seem in a strange world, when among those Jews. All their thoughts and ways are very different from ours. All their religious prejudices, superstitions, and fables; their sacred reverence for trifling traditions and useless ceremonies and customs,—give us a new idea of the excellence of the religion of Christ, and tend to produce a livelier desire for the conversion of these descendants of the once chosen people of God. Their ignorance of Christianity makes it easy for their bigotry to find a reason for hating it, and with an intensity that is hardly conceivable. As travellers while they gratify their curiosity in strange lands feel thankful for the better things at home; so may Christians, while becoming acquainted with other religious systems and societies.

Can anything awaken a more sympathetic interest than the history of an earnest soul, when well and truly written? An earnest soul, seeking after truth and rest—after happiness and hope; wrestling with doubt or confused by glimpses of the truth; trying to prove all things, and looking every way for help; searching into this mystery of life and despairing of relief; the impatient slave of prejudice, yet only a hesitating follower of wise counsel; yearning to know, longing for deliverance; making new discoveries, feeling new emotions; interested in everything, satisfied with nothing; finding everything in the Bible but its one great saving truth,—till at last he finds in CHRIST all he wanted, and then finds all things made new!

To watch the sublime conflicts and victories within the soul of an Augustine, a Luther, or a Wesley; to read of the events that take place in the world of the inner nature; the progress of the revolution in the kingdom of the heart, fixes the attention and awakens the sympathetic anxieties of the imaginary spectator, more than any story of outward adventure or muscular achievement.

But where remarkable inward and outward events and achievements go on together, the outward is ennobled by its moral significance. We have here a life which was one constant inward and outward conflict, until Christ became its rest and victory.

As Dr. Freshman was the first Wesleyan Missionary to the Germans of Canada, the beginning and progress of the German Missions give another special interest to his biography.

The missions among this industrious and thriving part of our population have already borne a large amount of precious fruit. In the United States, where the German Missions were commenced by the Rev. Dr. Nast, the author of a noble Commentary on the New Testament, the success has been astonishing, and has led to the establishment of many prosperous Missions, and the commencement of a great work of grace in Germany itself. Indeed, this work, in its numerous relations and results, already promises to become one of the most important religious awakenings of modern times. This portion of our population is quite large in Ontario, and is every year increasing.

Dr. Freshman has prosecuted his work in this department with all the energy and faith that characterize him in most 'of his undertakings. In the face of many difficulties he has followed the intimations of Providence, and by a wise and prompt improvement of opportunities, and the faithful and fearless preaching of the Gospel, he has gradually conquered prejudice, and commended himself to the consciences of many in the sight of God.

The great fault of most books of biography is, that they are four times too large. They contain so little fact and incident; so little of those whose lives they profess to give; and so much of the author's sermonizings and moralizings, that it is a task to read

them. That is not the case here. This story, which
we hope will prove the story of only half of a life,
contains more of interesting occurrences and events,
more of actions, experience, and adventures, than
many larger biographies.

He has purposely refrained from introducing the
peculiarities of Judaism, which many of his readers
will no doubt expect, as he intends, in a short time,
to publish a volume of Lectures on the " Manners
and Customs of the Jews," which will contain all
possible information on the subject.

Although, as a late Rabbi, he has the title of
" D. D.," still Dr. Freshman had no desire to have
it annexed to his name on the title-page.

This frank and unaffected narrative is well calculated to inspire confidence in the religion of God our
Saviour, to encourage seekers after salvation, and
to stimulate all workers for God to increased dili-
gence.

CONTENTS.

CHAPTER IV. *Page*

CHAPTER V.

CHAPTER VI.

CHAPTER VII.

CHAPTER VIII.

CHAPTER IX.

CHAPTER X. *Page*

CHAPTER XI.

CHAPTER XII.

CHAPTER XIII. *Page*

CHAPTER XIV.

CHAPTER XV.

CHAPTER XVI.

CHAPTER XVII.

CHAPTER XVIII.

AUTOBIOGRAPHY

REV. CHAS. FRESHMAN.

————•————

CHAPTER I.

Birth and Parentage—Impossibility of proving Tribeship—Incidents
of Childhood—Ceremony of the Fringes—First Scripture Lesson
— Earliest Recollections — Tendency to Pride — Strictness of
Early Training—Contempt for Christ and the Christians—Ar-
ticles of the Jewish Faith—Traditions—Stimulants to Pride—
Miraculous Escape—Coincidence—Omen.

I WAS born in the year 1819, in Micklosh, a city pleasantly
situated on the river Waag, in the kingdom of Hungary.
My parents were both natives of Hungary, and very strict
adherents to that form of belief peculiar to the Jewish religion. My grandfather on my father's side was a Rabbi of
the Synagogue in Miskolz, a city in the southern part of
Hungary. My grandfather on my mother's side was the
sexton of a Jewish synagogue all his lifetime. I was the
eldest of thirteen children with whom my father was blessed,
only four of whom survive at the present day. My father
was an only son; but for some cause he left his father's
house when very young, and removed to Italy, the land of
bright skies and balmy breezes. There he remained until

1

he grew to man's estate; but although he enjoyed considerable prosperity in his business, he felt that it was not good for man to be alone. None of the fair daughters of Italy seem to have suited his fancy, for he returned to his native land and settled in St. Micklosh, where he shortly after married my good mother, who was at that time the handsomest maiden in the Jewish congregation. Here he resumed his business, subject to the usual vicissitudes of fortune, during a long lifetime. He never was rich, but always honest, and scrupulously exact in the discharge of his religious duties. He died triumphant in his faith, at the ripe age of seventy-one years. Peace to his ashes!

According to a tradition handed down by our forefathers, our family is descended from the tribe of Benjamin. But this can never be proved. No Jew now living in the world is able to say to which of the twelve tribes he belongs. The greater number of them have not even a traditionary knowledge of their tribeship. Even the Levites, who retained this knowledge for the longest period, cannot at the present day be relied on; and no doubt many lay claim to be descended from that tribe without the slightest foundation for such claim. This power to prove their connection with the various tribes was destroyed when Herod the Great burned all the manuscripts containing the genealogies. His object in doing so was to prevent any one from proving, as they could have done, that he was a usurper of authority to which he had no rightful claim.

When quite an infant I was said to be such a pretty child that people came from far and near to see me. It is very hard for me to believe this now, if I am to rely on the testimony of the looking-glass! All children are said to be beautiful; and many people act upon the principle that the

easiest way to gain the favour of the mother is to flatter
the baby, and perhaps I got more than my share. When
but three years old I was taken to school by a Gentile servant, whose duty it was to carry me on her shoulders there
and back. In subsequent times I have often thought, how
strange that a Gentile should be the first to bring me to a
place of instruction! There I commenced to learn the
Hebrew alphabet, which is invariably the first lesson which
a Hebrew child receives on entering school.

The first religious instruction I received was in connection with a ceremony called צִיצִית *The Fringes*. This was
performed by my mother, and consisted in putting upon me
a little garment having four fringes,—one at each corner.
This garment I was thenceforth to wear continually; and
every morning before breakfast, as soon I suppose as I could
talk a little, my mother made me ask a blessing and kiss
the fringes. This ceremony is considered of great importance among the orthodox Jews, and is in compliance with
the command of God unto Moses (Num. xv. 38), "Speak
unto the children of Israel, and bid them that they make
them fringes in the border of their garments throughout
their generations, and that they put upon the fringe of the
borders a ribband of blue." The design in wearing this
garment was, that every time we looked upon the fringes
. we might "remember all the commandments of the Lord
our God and do them;" and perhaps it contributed as much
as anything else constantly to remind us that we were a
"peculiar people."

The first scripture lesson which was imparted to me, and
which every father and mother in Israel tries to engrave
upon the hearts of their children, was as follows: "Hear
O Israel: The Lord our God is one Lord: And thou shalt

love the Lord thy God with all thine heart, and with all thy soul, and with all thy might."—Deut. vi. 4, 5. What a pity that the beautiful supplement of our Saviour, " and thy neighbour as thyself," was not appended! But, alas! we were taught to hate and despise our Gentile neighbours, as perfectly consistent with loving God with all our heart. The verses quoted above are used on almost all occasions as a part of our devotions; and invariably in the morning when we rise, and in the evening before retiring to rest. The words שמע ישראל *Schemah Israel*, which mean, "Hear, O Israel," are the Shibboleth of the Jews in the whole world.

My first recollections extend backward to the time when I was about four years of age. I distinctly remember that about this time my father made a great festival in his own house, which they call סעורה, *Sudah*. It is customary among orthodox Jews that as soon as their children can read the first chapter of the Old Testament in the Hebrew language, all the friends, relatives, and associates of the child, are invited to meet on a certain Sabbath-day in order to celebrate this festival. It usually consists of a plentiful supply of eatables,—such as rich cakes, plums, nuts, &c.,—together with a glass of pure grape wine. The little fellow in honour of whom this feast is made is presented with a new suit of clothes. This time I was the happy recipient of the coveted treasure; and oh! how my little heart swelled with pride as I looked down upon my vest glittering with a bright row of silver buttons down the front, and thought how much handsomer I was than any of my companions or associates!

Perhaps vanity or pride is an ingredient in the nature of fallen humanity; but never, I think, did any poor mortal receive such a large share of it as fell to my lot! If the science of Phrenology is to be relied on, I must have been endowed with a large development in that part of the cranium where self-esteem is located, for while it is with humility I confess it, still, I must acknowledge that from my earliest recollection until the time when God in his infinite mercy converted my soul, I cherished that evil principle which had been seen so early showing itself at the festival. Perhaps, however, this was not altogether owing to any peculiar natural proclivity or development, so much as to the prejudices of education. I had never been taught to consider it a sin ; on the contrary, I grew up in the belief that it was a virtue which God gave to the wise and the rich,—and as I meant to be either a wise man or a rich one, I thought it necessary to cherish it. I hope, however, since I have been enabled to put off the "old man with his deeds," that I have laid this aside among the rest.

My early religious training was strict in the extreme. I was not allowed to taste a drop of water or a piece of bread without first asking a blessing upon it. It would have been considered an unpardonable crime to partake of food with my head uncovered, as this was held to be a great violation of the Jewish religion. In fact, any habit or custom prevalent among the Gentiles was hated and despised by every sincere Jew. As soon as I was able to read the Hebrew with fluency, I was obliged to pray out of the prayer-book every morning and evening. This required about an hour for the morning and half an hour for the evening. Besides this, if I chose, I might gain additional merit by reading a psalm or two. But this was at my option. The other was as inflexibly required as the sternest enactments of unyielding law. No matter how hungry I might be in the morning, it was no use to think of breakfast until I had finished my prayers, for previous to that it could not be obtained. I cannot help here making the reflection how much it would conduce to the spiritual welfare of the Christian world, if love to the Saviour would induce them to do what a mere sense of duty enjoined upon us. But the interior, or more private, duties of our religion, were not the only ones in which the utmost strictness was enjoined. In regard to the outward observances also I might say, " according to the straitest sect of our religion I lived a Pharisee." In fact such duties were forced upon me, —as, for instance, to eat such things only as were prepared by Jews; strictly to observe the Sabbath-day (Saturday); to fast every Monday and Thursday until dinner-time; to obey the Ten Commandments; never to enter the place where Gentile worship was held; never dare to read the New Testament, nor even the Old Testament in the German language—for this was at that time considered a sin among the Jews. I was not permitted to associate with Gentile boys; as we were taught to believe that the Jews were the only people of God, and that all the rest of the world would go to hell. Thanks be to God for the clearer light of a better dispensation, which teaches us that all may be saved and come to a knowledge of the truth! May the time speedily come when the blessings of this glorious gospel shall be universally diffused, so that not only the " savage hordes " in " lands remote " may feel its influence, but the Israelite also, who for so long a time has been rejecting the true knowledge of the only wise God, and Jesus Christ whom he has sent, may realize that there is mercy with Him that he may be feared, and plenteous redemption that he may be sought unto!

If I could charge the Jewish religion with nothing worse than its dry formality and attention to form and ceremony, how willingly would I now cease to write! But alas! it is not so. Memory will not be silent. I was taught from my earliest childhood to hate and despise both Christ and the Christians, and to do all in my power against them. Even in my prayers I was obliged to insert certain words of blasphemy against Christ. These words I had to learn off by heart; for, as already mentioned, I had to pray from a prayer-book in which the blasphemy was not inserted. As often as I passed the image of our Saviour on the cross (of which there are many to be seen in my native country, where the Roman Catholic faith predominates), I was taught other words of blasphemy again to repeat, as also to spit out three times, in token of contempt or utter abhorrence. We were taught to believe that Jesus, whom the Jews call הָלוּי, the *Talo*, that is, the man who was hanged, was a bastard, and that because he made himself a God they crucified him. Prejudices against a גוי *Goy*, that is, a Gentile, were early inculcated, and became deeply rooted. We all learned to look upon them as idolaters, and hence unworthy of sharing a part of heaven with us—the chosen people. The remembrance of all this is very grievous unto me; but I trust it leads me to magnify the grace of our Lord Jesus Christ, whom I now see to be the fairest among ten thousand and the altogether lovely.

At a very early age I was taught to repeat the thirteen articles of the Jewish faith. These articles affirm the Unity of God, but a unity of a peculiar nature. They do not believe in the doctrine of the Trinity, in our sense of that term; and yet there is a kind of plurality which they ascribe to God, not inconsistent with His unity. To this one

God they ascribe the various attributes found in the Old Testament, and substantially the same as Christian theology teaches. They also affirm the genuineness, authenticity, and inspiration of the books of Moses and the Prophets, as also that of the *Hagiographa*, or writings, including the Psalms, Ecclesiastes, &c. These articles also affirm the resurrection of the dead, and the doctrine of future rewards and punishments. Also, that a Messiah should come, more deserving than all the kings who have ever lived. That although he thinks proper to delay his coming, no one ought on that account to question the truth of it, or set an appointed time for it, much less produce scripture in proof of it, since Israel will never have any king to rule over them but one that should be of the line of David and Solomon. Thus it will be seen that there was a great similarity between their creed and that of the Christian ; as in fact they might expect, since both are deduced from the same volume of Inspiration.

In reality, however, the commandments of God were rendered of none effect through their traditions. One of these, which asserted that by virtue of God's covenant with Abraham, every Jew was certain of everlasting life, was early taught, and firmly believed by all ; and this without a word being said about faith or obedience as a condition. I must confess, however, that notwithstanding this the pious orthodox Jews practised a very strict morality, which they considered in the highest degree meritorious. It is true, also, that many were to be found, who, considering their salvation as a fixed fact, abused the doctrine by giving way to their carnal passions. Even some of the learned among the Jews, in ages subsequent to our Saviour, were found to be the most profligate. It was enough for such to reflect at any time, "We have Abraham for our father," and immediately conscience was still again, and they went on as before.

Many of the silliest and most childish traditions were incorporated in the Talmud, and held as of equal authority with the written word of God. It would no doubt be highly amusing to some of my readers if they could enter a Jewish Synagogue, and hear a learned Rabbi reading the tradition about Eve, who is said to have had a body fifteen yards in length, and symmetrical in proportion; and then hear him gravely explain the philosophical necessity for this unusual size, as she was to be the mother of all living, and it was desirable to people the earth as speedily as possible. These, and many such things, I was taught at a very early age; consequently, when I reached my eighth year I was pretty well prepared to enter upon the study of the Talmud, a book which contains the laws of God, mixed up with many traditions and superstitions, together with the comments and explanations of their most learned Rabbies on both the word of God and the fables of men.

I have before adverted to my natural tendency to pride of heart. I found many things, even at this early age, to stimulate it, and keep it alive. Let an instance or two suffice. When I commenced to study the Talmud we used to go every Sabbath to a Rabbi to be examined in our weekly lesson, and receive his blessing on our dismissal. When it would come to my turn he used to say, laying his hand on my head, "May the Lord make you a great Rabbi in Israel," which of course stimulated my desire to learn, but I fear increased my pride.

Another circumstance which contributed not a little to the same result, was the following :—I had a very pious

1*

grandmother, whom I used frequently to visit. On such occasions she was always highly delighted, if, on my way home from school, I would drop in to see her, especially when I would bring some tradition and explain it to her, or translate something for her from the prayer-book. Here it must be observed, that although most of the Jews pray in the Hebrew language, yet very few of them understand what they pray or read. The women especially know hardly anything, I might say nothing, about what they pray for or read. I spent almost every Sabbath with my grandmother. I was indeed very glad to do so, for she used to give me the best pies and cakes to eat that the city of Micklosh could produce. She never would call me by my proper name, but generally her תאני *Tana*, i.e., teacher. This pleased me so much, that in one of my school books I actually signed my name after the same fashion. All this tended to make me more ambitious than ever, and pride, which seemed to be my besetting sin, was thus early striking its roots deep into my heart, and sending out branches in every direction to destroy every other good quality.

About this time a very serious accident happened to me, which, but for the kind interposition of a merciful Providence, would have suddenly terminated my career. It occurred in this way. I with some other boys of my own age went down to the river Waag to play. The time of the year was in early spring, during the celebration of the passover, which generally takes place in the month of April, and corresponds with our Easter. We played quite a while on the edge of the river, till at last we all agreed to gather as many chips and pieces of wood as we could find, and send them down the river to the city of Pesth, as lumber. This branch of industry (only on a much larger scale than we attempted it) forms the principal part of the business done there. I had collected my little raft, and was just bending down close to the water's edge, for the purpose of pushing it off, when suddenly I lost my balance, fell into the water, and was carried away by the strong current. Not for a moment did I lose consciousness. I could think, feel, and reason. I distinctly remember that I was not at all afraid to die, but only sorry that I could not be buried in the city, and have a grand funeral. But the principal thought which seemed to absorb all others was this:—Where now are the many blessings of my good Rabbi and grandmother! If I am to find a watery grave at this time, surely I cannot become a great Rabbi in Israel. However, down I was carried, much quicker than I have been able to pen these lines, about a quarter of a mile, still in the possession of perfect consciousness, when suddenly my head struck violently against an iron post, and from that moment until some hours after, when I found myself in the house of a friend close by, I was utterly oblivious of everything that occurred. I learned afterwards that a young man (a Jew) who was standing on the bridge and saw me, heroically risked his own life in the attempt to save mine. He jumped down into the river, grasped me by my long hair, which I wore in curls then, and rescued me from a watery grave, just as I was on the point of being carried by the current under the bridge, where I should have been beyond the reach of mortal aid. When I again opened my eyes the whole thing appeared like a dream, and to the present day I have a mark on my head, which serves as a constant remembrance of my miraculous escape from a watery grave.

Here I may be allowed to mention a singular coincidence. My son Jacob, who is now a minister of the gospel, met with a similar accident, at about the same age, but was rescued by a Roman Catholic. How wonderful are the ways of God! and how comforting after such experiences are the declarations of that Saviour whom I used to despise : "Even the very hairs of your head are numbered," and "Ye are of more value than many sparrows!" Since I have learned to love Him I feel that I owe my life to Him, and my constant determination is to devote it to His service.

My grandmother considered this event as a great omen, or indication, that there was some important work for which my life was spared, and used to say repeatedly, "I am sure you will be a הגדול תנאי *Tana gaddel,* viz., a great Rabbi. This seemed to be her highest idea of what human nature could attain to, and she was sure I would reach the top of the ladder. My good father, instead of giving me the same blessing, gave me a sound whipping, which was the first and the last I ever received from his hands. Perhaps this was a mistake on his part; but if so, it is such a mistake as, I am sure, most children can easily forgive, the testimony of such a respectable authority as Solomon to the contrary notwithstanding.

CHAPTER II.

Soon after my recovery from the effects of the accident just mentioned, I again resumed my studies; but now my Rabbi was changed. The progress which I had already made rendered this necessary. I was now promoted to the study of the Talmud; but while I was almost exclusively confined to this, my preliminary studies had been as full as usual. It was, however, very unusual for one so young to have made sufficient advancement to warrant his commencing the Talmud. I was then only eight years of age, and yet I could read Hebrew well, and translate every word without difficulty, and very seldom would I require a lexicon. I could also repeat from memory many choice passages of the Old Testament, and whole Psalms in the Hebrew language. Even of the Chaldaic I knew a little. I had also been taught to read and write the Armenian language. In fact I never found any difficulty in accomplishing anything on which I had fully set my mind.

Just at this time my mind became fully possessed of the one determination—that of becoming a Rabbi—not an ordinary Rabbi, such as one meets with every day, but a great Rabbi, such as those who had immortalized their names and imprinted their thoughts upon the pages of the Talmud. Perhaps it was with a view to facilitate this result, that I began to have a most intense desire to know everything about a book called "Sohar," containing the "mysteries" or cabalistic symbols, many of which could only be understood by the highly learned. But the Rabbi would not allow me to think of such a thing,—not even to take it in my hands ; for he said it was only fit for very holy men to read, and not for such a little boy as I was. Prohibited from satisfying this desire I went on with the study of the Talmud both day and night, for a Rabbi I was determined to become, and I knew that many long years of close study and intense application were necessary before I could be qualified to become a *Tana gaddell.*

Some of my schoolmates were not particularly gifted with natural ability as students, or else lacked the ambition which acted as a stimulant on me, and incited me onwards. Certain it is that they would often be found lagging behindhand with their studies. On such occasions they would come to me, and beg of me to assist them. This I was generally very glad to do, as they would mostly reward me with a kreuzer, (cent.) Besides, this recognition of my superiority over them was very gratifying to me, and incited me to still further efforts to excel. Thus pride and ambition worked hand in hand, and separately stimulated me to strive for higher victories over my schoolmates, and greater conquests over the difficulties which presented themselves in my studies. Even the Rabbis encouraged me in this, and so furthered my pride.

Things went on in this way until I was eleven years of age, when, as far as I could judge from the precepts and examples of the Talmud, I attained the highest pitch of perfection attainable on earth. I used to read and pray a great deal in secret, fast very often, and be very strict in the performance of the minor points of our belief. Of course a great deal of tradition and superstition was mixed up with the pure doctrine; but even now, when I look back to that time, I actually believe I loved the Lord with all my heart. Certainly that heart was a proud heart, and now I could not love the Lord if I cherished it; but at that time I did not know pride was a sin. On the contrary, I thought the more holy a man is the prouder he ought to be; proud of his holiness, and consequent superiority over his fellow creatures. There were times, however, in which I was humble, but it was only while in secret prayer, in the presence of that mysterious Jehovah whose wonderful name no Jew is permitted to pronounce without the greatest reverence. Yet as soon as I would finish prayer, I would again be myself, with pride as my king. I do believe those who flattered me so much in those days contributed greatly to develop this evil propensity. I used to be often told by my teacher that I was the best boy in the school, and I always considered myself as superior to any of my school-mates. I even used boastingly to declare to some of my class-mates that I knew more than the teacher himself. But alas! "pride goeth before destruction, and a haughty spirit before a fall." How soon was I to prove the truth of this!

I was now entering upon my twelfth year; but an unaccountable change came over me at this time. I not only became mischievous, but I fear positively wicked. I left off praying, commenced to desecrate the Sabbath, to read bad books, and even attempted to read the New Testament in secret. I read until I came to the passage, "I and my Father are one," which so exasperated me that I hurled the book across the room, and from this time I hated Christianity more than ever. Still my mind was ill at ease. Though young in years I reasoned and speculated with a maturity far in advance of my years. I felt a want of something which I already knew Judaism could not furnish me with, and perhaps this will account for the change in my habits and conduct. Whether this will account for it or no, certain it is that such a change had taken place. In addition to what is mentioned above, I also neglected my books, played truant from school, and when anything would occur to ruffle my temper I would give dreadful vent to my feelings in violent expressions of most ungovernable rage.

Perhaps a circumstance, in illustration of my mischievously wicked proclivities, may not be out of place just here. On a certain occasion I was punished in the presence of the whole school by my Rabbi, for playing truant. The punishment itself was no more severe than usual, nor was it more than I knew I deserved; but my proud spirit could ill brook the idea of being humbled before the rest of the students. The idea that I, the best boy in the school—I, who knew as much as my teacher—that I, who was some day to become a grand Rabbi—should be punished like an ordinary schoolboy! It was not to be entertained, it was grinding, humbling; so I fully determined on being revenged. I had never been taught the precious words of the apostle, "Recompense to no man evil for evil." The law which I had been taught and which I now resolved to follow was, "An eye for an eye, and a tooth for a tooth." So I went home at noon, supplied myself with matches and sealing wax, came.

back in the afternoon, and waited for my opportunity. I had not long to wait. It was customary for the Rabbi, who was a very old man with a very long beard, to take a nap every day during recess. This afternoon I waited till he fell asleep in his usual position, with his head resting upon his desk. I then jumped in through the window, lit the matches, melted the wax, and sealed him to the desk by his beard. He slumbered on unconscious, and I left him to enjoy pleasant dreams, and wake to an unpleasant reality— a thing which often falls to the lot of poor mortals, whether Jew or Gentile, in this world.

No doubt while I was contemplating my revenge it may have been sweet enough, and while in the act of consummating it I may have thought myself exceedingly clever; yet no sooner was it done than I would have given anything to have had it undone : but afterthought often comes too late. He never discovered who did it, but my own conscience punished me more severely than he could possibly have done. In years long after it would grieve me to the heart to think of the trick I had played upon that pious old Jew, and never while memory holds her seat will I be able to efface his image, as he lay there in the unconsciousness of innocence, with his beard sealed to his desk. I hope the good old man is now in heaven, and I trust his naughty pupil is on the way thitherward.

Soon after this I left school altogether, and scarcely anything worth recording occurred during the remainder of the year. I got into habits of idleness and distaste for further study. Having nothing to do but to loiter around and get into mischief, that part of my life is a blank which I can take no pleasure in looking back upon, and hence may be excused for dismissing it with this short paragraph. But I may say that so low had I sunk, and so much unlike myself had I become, that I no longer had any more desires to become a Rabbi.

Towards the close of the year my father met with a misfortune in his business which involved the loss of everything. So clean a sweep did it make of his property that, when it blew over, we had scarcely bread enough left in our house to satisfy our present demands. This circumstance, however adverse it seemed, proved a blessing to me in the end. It furnished me with something to do, and was the means of bringing me to the resolution again to try and be a good boy.

One evening he came to me and said : " My son, I am going to leave home for a few weeks, as I have some friends in Galicia who will no doubt assist me when they hear of my misfortune. I shall have to leave you and mamma to take care of the children (seven in number,) during my absence, and upon your exertions their maintenance will principally depend. Take this powder (ink powder) and help mamma to make some like it every day. This you can sell, and procure as much bread by this means as will suffice for your maintenance till my return." This circumstance made such an impression on my mind, that I thought it was on account of my wickedness this misfortune had come, and I firmly resolved to commence praying again. I promised God that if he would only help us out of this difficulty, I would again try to become a good boy. As if to encourage me in my resolution, as I was walking in the street the same day, to my great joy I found a groshen, worth about five cents. This I considered a direct answer to my prayer, and from that moment I resolved not to be mischievous any more, but to become a pious lad again. I believe this was the turning point in my life ; and if I had not improved it I might have become one of the worst of men, and perhaps ere this have found a dishonored grave.

In a few weeks, according to his promise, my father returned. His very presence brought again joy and gladness into the home circle. He had seen his friends, and for several evenings furnished us with amusement and instruction, as he related some of the incidents of his visit ; but better than all, he brought back with him a snug little sum of money, which he invested in business again, and so things looked pleasant once more.

In pursuance of my good resolution, I now went to school again under more favorable auspices. This time I had a private teacher to prepare me for confirmation. I was now in my thirteenth year at which time the Jews confirm their children, or rather their boys—for girls among the orthodox Jews are not considered proper subjects for any religious ceremonies until they are married. In fact some of them do not even allow their daughters to go to synagogue until that time. It is very evident that Miss Lucy Stone and those other "strong-minded women" who talk about "women's rights," as well as that other large class who are now advocating "female suffrage," were not trained in any of the Jewish institutions !

The confirmation of a Jewish boy consists in teaching him how to use the phylacteries. These phylacteries consist of two pieces of parchment, on each of which is inscribed a passage of Scripture. These parchments are enclosed in leather cases and bound with thongs, one on the forehead, the other on the left arm. The practice of using these was not from the beginning, but was probably introduced among later superstitions. It is founded upon a literal interpretation of that passage where God commanded the Hebrews to have the law as a sign on their foreheads and as frontlets between their eyes.—Ex. xiii. 16.　Our Saviour does not appear to condemn the practice, but only the abuse of it which prevailed in the days of his flesh, and which consisted in making broad their phylacteries for purposes of ostentation, while the original intention was merely to preserve the law in their memory.

It requires considerable practice before a person can know how to use these properly.　But as they come into daily requisition this is soon acquired.　Every Jew who has been confirmed is required to use them every morning during prayers, except on Sabbath and festival occasions.　Every candidate for confirmation, who intends to become some personage of importance among them, is required, besides acquiring a facility in the use of these phylacteries, to read publicly in the synagogue a chapter of the Bible in Hebrew, and to address the congregation.　Apart from this there is nothing solemn connected with the ceremony except when the father of the boy pronounces the words,—"I am relieved from the responsibility of my son."　This gives the boy to understand that from that time forth he will have to be answerable to God, and before the whole world, for his own moral and religious character and life.

As may be expected, I looked forward to this time with anticipations of the liveliest delight.　I would then cease to be a child, and if not become a man, at least make a rapid stride in that direction.　But, alas! when the time came, so long waited for and so anxiously anticipated, I could not be confirmed ; for my father was again so poor that he could not even spare me enough money to purchase the phylacteries, and I had no nice clothes in which to appear before the congregation. This was humiliating in the extreme, and drove me to the resolution of leaving my father's house and going to some distant city, where I thought I could easily enter some Jewish theological institution. I had, however, only twenty kreutzer in my possession; but a single smile of fortune encouraged me to proceed. It was the following, which will serve to illustrate how boyish I still was in my ideas, notwithstanding my desire to be a man all at once.

I had for a long time coveted to be the owner of a penknife, all my own. Just as I was about to leave home some of my companions came to me and said they were going to have a lottery for a penknife, and if I would only give a kreuzer I might possibly win the knife. To this I agreed, but at the same time retired apart by myself to pray. I prayed for nothing but the penknife, and I believe the Lord heard my prayer; at any rate I won the penknife, so I had a knife and nineteen kreuzer (about 24 cents) to start with on my journey.

With a sad heart I took leave of my parents and the rest of the family. My mother was loving and affectionate, and it almost broke her heart to contemplate this first breach in her family. My father was strict and very honest, not less affectionate, but less emotional. He would have seen his family in want sooner than defraud a creditor of a farthing. He could give me nothing but his blessing, which I did not value half as much as the 20 kreuzer given me by my good grandmother, or the penknife procured with one of them. However, I was not to be deterred from my purpose by seeming difficulties; so bidding them all good bye, I started out into the "wide, wide world,"—alone.

The day was beautiful. The road on which I travelled was the highway, so that even after I got beyond the limits of the city, the constant traffic of those passing to and fro in pursuit of their usual avocations prevented me from feeling at all lonely. The Carpathian mountains, with their cloud-capped summits and colossal proportions, lay to my right; and the river Waag, bespangled with fishing boats and pleasure crafts, to my left. Often have I wondered, as I looked towards those mighty mountains in the distance, what sort of a world lay beyond their rugged peaks and mysterious recesses. But this was not the time for specula-tion. All was real around me, and stern necessity demanded action. I had chosen my pathway, and now I must pursue it. Perhaps it was natural that my first sensations on leav-ing home, and realizing that I had escaped from parental restraint, and was now my own master, should have been pleasurable rather than otherwise. But as I travelled on-wards, mile after mile, I began to realize the extreme loneli-ness of my position. The mountains with all their grandeur, and the river with all its beauty, began to lose their charms for me. As every step took me farther away from home, and brought me in contact with objects less and less familiar, I began to think it was not so bad after all to have *a home*, even if my father was not in circumstances to procure my phylacteries; and, if my resolve to leave it had then to have been made, I do not think it would have been made at all. Even the people whom I met, and the traffic which was passing on the road, did not relieve my loneliness; for I soon discovered that all these people acted upon the motto adopted by Young America: "Look out for number one!" So engrossed was each in the prosecution of his own affairs, that they seldom condescended even a passing glance at the poor young traveller, with his bundle on his arm, pursuing his lonely journey.

These feelings were, after a time, overpowered by the prevalence of a stronger one—the sense of hunger. Thanks to the forethought of my good grandmother, I was supplied with a large piece of cake to allay this appetite when it occurred. On this I regaled myself, and continued my journey, but being unaccustomed to walk so far at a time I soon became very tired. My bundle also, light enough at first, now became almost unendurable. However, there were plenty of stones by the roadside, and whenever I got very tired I would sit down on one of these and rest myself. But now the shades of night began "falling fast," and I had nowhere to stop, so, weary as I was, I resolved to continue my journey all night. I ran no risk by this resolve of losing my way, as at every cross-roads fingerposts were erected pointing out where the various roads led to, and the distance to such places in German miles, each of which is equal to about four English ones. It was about the first quarter of the moon, so that I could have no difficulty in deciphering the inscriptions on these guides, as they were no doubt intended to prove to the stranger who might require such assistance.

If I were at all poetical I might try to give a description of my native land by moonlight; but as I am not, I must ask my readers to draw on their own imagination, as I can only give a poor idea. The River Waag meandered close by the roadside, in places calm and placid, each little ripple sporting as playfully with its beams, and murmuring so gently in the stillness of the night, that no one would have thought it capable of so nearly depriving any one of life as it had done to me a short time before. The rest of the country lying around, diversified with hill and dale, and now with light and shade. Some of those shaded caverns in the sides of the mountains, now enveloped in deep gloom, would suggest thoughts of hiding-places for hordes of bandits, or coverts for those supernatural appearances with which from time immemorial superstition has invested this earth. As I allowed my thoughts to go out in this direction, I could almost fancy I saw their weird forms and unearthly aspects emerging from the gloom. These feelings were not at all diminished when I suddenly came to a part of the road on which two men had been beheaded some time before. Without thinking of my fatigue, I immediately took to my heels, and, without looking behind me, ran till I was completely out of breath. Fortunately I discovered a waggon a little in advance, and mustering what little strength I had left, I pushed on until I overtook it.

I accosted the driver in the blandest manner I could assume, and requested him to give me a ride ; but a hoarse " Ugh" was all I got in response. Thinks I to myself,—Is he a hog ; can he do nothing but grunt in response to such a polite question ? But on closer inspection I saw he had been imbibing rather freely of something stronger than the redoubtable " lager," or else an unusual quantity of that. However, I thought the company even of a drunken man was preferable to that of the goblins, and the decapitated men whose spirits I had fancied loitering around ; so I jumped in, and glad enough was I to rest my weary limbs, and have some one by my side who I knew was possessed of real flesh and blood, even supposing he was no company. But, alas ! for all mere earthly delights—they are short-lived at best, and this one proved no exception. We had not gone very far when, owing to his carelessness or incapacity to drive, he went too close to the edge of the road, the waggon upset, we were thrown out, and my bundle—which contained, among other things, the remainder of my cake—rolled down into the Waag.

I was sorry for the loss of my cake, but the loss of my bundle was a real relief, as I had enough now to do to carry myself. I soon began to get very hungry again; but as it was now near midnight the houses were all closed up, and the inhabitants asleep. Even if they had not been, my national prejudices were so strong that I believe I would have starved to death sooner than touch a morsel of food from a Christian, for fear it might be contaminated by that abominable PORK. I would not, *now*, consider the man either worthy of death or of bonds, who would place a barrel or two in my cellar every winter. But in those days my prejudices extended farther even than *pork*, for everything pertaining to the Christian religion we held in abomination. On my journey, whenever I came to a *cross*, I used to exhibit my contempt for the crucified One, by repeating the curse common to the Jews, viz., "May his name and memory be blotted out." O how thankful I have been in after years, since my eyes have been opened, that *my* name and memory have not been blotted out for my many acts of impiety and blasphemy! But I know it is only because "His mercy endureth forever."

I plodded on my journey till towards early morning, when it seemed as if tired nature could endure the fatigue no longer; and glad was I when I came to a little tavern by the roadside, kept by an old Jew, who was already beginning the labours of the day in order to be prepared to accommodate the early passers-by on their way to market. I was fain to crave from him a bite to eat; after which I enjoyed a few hours of sweet repose on the soft side of a plank, ranged along the wall, which served the double purpose of

2

seats for the company and a bed for such unfortunate wights as I, who could not afford to pay for a better. Notwithstanding the noise and bustle usual in such a public place, I slept well, and rose in two or three hours greatly refreshed. I rewarded him with three of my nineteen kreuzers, and started again on my journey, which I prosecuted during the whole of the day, and at night I reached my destination,—a place called Namensdorf, just two days before I would be of the proper age for confirmation, at which time I would become *Bermizweh*, which means, " A son of commandment," and accountable to God and the world for my own moral character and conduct—my parents being released from all responsibility in that direction.

CHAPTER III.

On my arrival in Namensdorf, I made enquiry for the house of a Jew, a dealer in butter, whom I had met in St. Micklosh, and with whom I had some slight acquaintance. The Jews are very particular in regard to butter, as well, indeed, as every other article of diet ; and will purchase from no one but an established dealer in that commodity, who is himself very careful in the purchases which he makes to see that it is prepared in strict accordance with the strictest injunctions of the Rabbies, and especially that it be not defiled with anything which may have had the most remote connection with their detested *pork*. This good man was surprised to see me, but made me welcome to the best which his house afforded—which, by the way, were no great things. A dish of steeped peas, without sauce or condiment of any kind, was set before me. I did not hesitate to commence, for those who have been in circumstances to prove it, must have realized that hunger gives a peculiar relish to even the coarsest fare, and, coarse as it was, I had the satisfaction of knowing that there was nothing objectionable in its mode of preparation, without which knowledge I would hardly have dared to touch the best pies or cakes which could have been set before me. I remained with him during the night, and in the morning enquired my way to the Jewish Theological Seminary.

This I found without difficulty, and on presenting myself before the Rabbi, was received very kindly. This Rabbi was a very pious old Jew, who would not allow any of his students to study anything except the Talmud. He examined me in regard to my proficiency in study, with which he seemed well satisfied. On ascertaining my financial position and prospects, he sent me to the Gabi (president) of the Jewish Charitable Association, for assistance. On hearing my story he gave me thirty kreuzer (about half a dollar). I next had to look around for a place to board and lodge in. If I had possessed a fortune, adequate to my own opinion of my deserts, I would immediately have rented a suite of rooms in one of the first-class hotels. But to a poor student with only thirty kreuzer in his pocket, and but a very uncertain prospect of supply when that was done, this project was out of the question. So 1 had to seek for accommodation in some humbler position. With great difficulty I at length procured a house in which I might obtain my meals three days in the week gratis. It was a Jewish family, of course, but they could not furnish me with a sleeping apartment. This, however, after some search, J procured. But such a place! It furnished me with a partial shelter, it is true; but no bed, nor any thing as a substitute for one, except a bundle of straw shaken down in a corner, and sometimes not even that. I had not even the consolation of reflecting that, "if lonely, I had peace;" for during the night the rats and mice would dispute with me the possession of my apartment. Besides this, a troop of light infantry, too numerous to mention, would commence an attack from all points as soon as I began to think of repose. They would not even give me the consolation which our Canadian mosquitoes so considerately furnish, that of " singing a song before taking a bite!"

I, however, resolved to study all the harder, knowing that in this way alone I could become a great Rabbi—and then all my troubles would disappear. In my new school I met with a number of Jewish students from Poland, a set of ignorant, superstitious, and dirty fellows, with whom I never could make up my mind to associate. For, poorly as I fared, I always managed to maintain an air of respectability in my appearance, which was owing, perhaps, to my natural pride. I maintained myself in this way :—I fasted two days in the week ; three, I was supplied gratis with my meals ; on the sixth, I used to procure a roll of bread for a groschen (penny) ; and on the seventh, all the poor students of the Institute were provided for among the different members of the Jewish congregation. As to washing and mending, I had all that to do for myself. Still, I was comparatively happy, and always learned my lessons well. One thing, however, troubled me : I had not yet any phylacteries, nor did I see any prospect of obtaining them while I remained here, and I was now of proper age for confirmation. Hence I resolved to leave the place and go to Poland, where colleges, for the training of young Jews, in great repute, were to be found. So off I started, without apprising my parents, or even bidding good-bye to my friends.

On the first day of my travelling, which of course was again on foot, I came towards evening to a village not far from the city of Crakow. Here I fell in with a Jewish family, where I remained over night. The master of the house, on learning that I was a theological student, proposed for me to remain in his family and teach his children, for which he would give me fifteen dollars and board for six months. This I readily agreed to, as by this means I would be enabled to procure my long desired phylacteries, and other necessary articles of which I was then in much need. Accordingly, I was duly installed as tutor in his household, and for a few days all things went on very smoothly and agreeably. But what was my astonishment when, one morning, he ordered me to take the cow to pasture, and then go and help to dig potatoes! But the end was not yet. When I returned from the performance of these requirements, he coolly informed me that the horse was in the stable, which had not been cleaned for a long time, and I had better go and attend to it at once. There I stood, poor candidate for a " grand Rabbi," obliged to submit to such a menial avocation! However, I executed this command also, as well as I could; but when night came, and I lay on my bench (for this was my ordinary bed), my thoughts were not of the most exhilarating character. The world seemed so dark, and my pathway so hedged about with difficulties, that death seemed preferable to life. The moon was shining down in all her splendour into the room where I lay, and as I watched her quiet and majestic motion, my thoughts became more tranquil, and I thought the best thing I could do would be to leave the place. Accordingly, without another moment's reflection, I raised the window, jumped out into the moonlight, and was off again.

I continued my journey all night. When morning dawned I found myself on a high hill, where lived an isolated farmer, into whose house I went to rest myself, and read my prayers;

and here I may mention that, for the first time, I broke the Jewish law, and ate bread with a Gentile. I had always such a horror of Gentile food, that it was with the utmost reluctance I commenced my repast. After I had swallowed a few mouthfuls, however, I began to think that Gentiles knew what was good for them as well as Jews. Certainly it was much more savoury than the swelled peas of my Jewish host a short time before.

After thus partaking of his hospitality, I wandered on, weary enough, and often very hungry, until I came to a city called Bialla. With the curiosity, natural, I suppose, to all on arriving in a strange place, I wandered through the streets, reading the names and inscriptions above the doors. While thus engaged, I discovered on one of the firms the name of a person who I supposed was from my native country ; so I ventured to go in and see him, if I could. On entering the establishment, I immediately recognized a young man with whom I was well acquainted, but who was a Gentile, and had come here to learn the jewellery business. While conversing with him, the owner of the establishment also came in, and, on learning who I was, immediately said : "I know your father well—he is an honest man ; it is a pity you are a Jew, but if you would like to become a Roman Catholic priest, I will send you to college where you can prepare yourself, and by that means you may become a rich man, and so be able to help your poor father." I at once commenced to cry, and begged of him not to baptize me, as I never could become a Christian. "Never mind, then," said he, "I will not force you ; don't be afraid." He then gave me five gulden (about a dollar),[*] and told me I

* At the present time, five gulden would be worth $2.50.

might now go away if I wished—a permission of which I was not slow to avail myself, as I considered it a most miraculous escape from being swallowed up by the Christian church.

On finding myself in the street again, my first thoughts were of my *phylacteries*. I had now the means of procuring them, which I lost no time in doing. Indeed the thoughts of them had scarcely ever been out of my mind since leaving home. The pair I procured were not of that description condemned by our Saviour. They were not very broad, and not very expensive ; but they were phylacteries, and I was as happy as any prince when I had them on. I looked upon the money with which I had procured them as a special reward from God for my firmness in resisting the great inducements which had been offered me, if I would become a Romish priest ; and I was more resolved than ever to adhere to the religion of my forefathers.

I now laid out a plan to go to the great Jewish College in Moravia. To resolve was to act. I had, in those days, no trouble harnessing my horse ; nor did I give myself any trouble to study the time-tables of the railroad. I started when I pleased, went where I pleased, and did, in a limited sense, what I pleased : but sometimes I would have been pleased to eat my dinner, when I did not do it ; sometimes I would have been pleased to sleep on a bed, when I did not do it ; but with these, and kindred exceptions, I was delightfully free. And so I was free to start for Moravia when I resolved to do it, and free to continue my journey during five long and weary days, till at last I arrived at the famous College of Hellesbau. Here I very opportunely met a young student from my native city. He was very kind to me, and assisted me in procuring a home where I could reside during my stay in that place.

In my new home were two young ladies, who desired very strongly to learn the Hebrew language. I readily agreed to teach it to them in consideration for my board and lodging, a compensation with which they and their parents were much better satisfied than if I had agreed to pay for it. This I again looked upon as a divine interposition in my behalf, and I resolved to study harder than ever. In consequence of this resolve, I had not been long at the college before I distinguished myself as a good *Bucheral*, (student).

But the money which my friend in Bialla had given me was now all gone, and I began to feel very much in need again. In my extremity I wrote home for some. My grandmother and my good mother united their fortunes and sent me five gulden, which was the first and the last that I ever received from home during my college life. However, my wants were few. I had formed none of those expensive habits which "Young America" permits her sons so readily to adopt. Havannah cigars, oyster suppers, gin cocktails, &c., were things of which I had been kept in blissful ignorance, and I am not sorry that it was so; for how seldom do we see those "precocious" students, who are "mighty to drink wine," or addicted to any of the fashionable follies of the age, attain to any useful position in after-life! On the contrary, how often have we seen the mightiest intellects debased, and a career which might have been one of the greatest usefulness, cut short, owing to the prevalence of habits in after-life, carelessly formed while at college. "*Facilis descensus Averni*"—("The descent to Hades is easy"), is a well known saying of an old Roman poet, but he has not deterred many from proving its truth.

2*

Perhaps the method by which I maintained myself while there might not prove uninteresting to those young men who have the purse-strings of their rich fathers at command, every time they desire to scribble a few lines home. Of course I had no anxiety on the score of board, as I have already explained my good fortune in that respect. But for the rest, I managed in this way :—The Jews have a custom of reserving the greater part of their charitable contributions to various benevolent objects until a particular time of the year. This occurs in the month *Ellel*, nearly corresponding with our September. About eighteen of us used to take advantage of their charitable dispositions at that time, and go around collecting supplies. We used to take clothing, money, or whatever they felt disposed to give, and would usually be absent three or four weeks on our tour. After all, we did not get very liberally supplied, and had to practice the most rigid economy in order to keep up appearances at all. I remember I used to have to sew my boots when they would wear, with a white thread, and then blacken the seam with ink, to give it a more respectable appearance. This may excite a smile in some ; but in this age of shams, when people wear false hair, false teeth, false eyes, false legs, false faces, and false characters, it will surely be pardoned as a harmless expedient, even though it appears a little hypocritical !

Here I remained over two years, gaining honourable distinction as a student. But I began to get tired of college life, or, rather, tired of such a constant struggle to make a living and get an education at the same time. Besides, it was now a long time since I had seen my parents and early associates, so I resolved to return home. My little preparation to do so was soon completed, and, after taking kind leave of my good Rabbi and host, I commenced my journey, which occupied nine long days, travelling on foot as usual.

My parents were very glad to see me ; but after the first greetings were over I discovered that they were not well satisfied that I had left college. However, I had been such a length of time my own master that these things did not affect me a great deal. I had discovered that "The best way to do is to do as you please," and my pleasure at that time was to commence teaching school, as I thought it would furnish me with more secure means of support than the precarious method I had to adopt while at college. Accordingly, after a little effort, I obtained a small school of about twenty children, near the city of Micklosh, in which the earliest years of my life had been spent.

But I had now become so accustomed to roving about that I could not content myself very long in this situation. I began to reflect that I was now growing up into manhood, and still without any profession. I never felt any inclination for any other profession than that of a Rabbi, and this I knew I could never become while I remained a mere school teacher, which I looked upon as little superior to a common labourer, and was, besides, little to my taste. So, with the determination of completing my education, I again left home, resolved to go to the great city of Prague, where facilities of the highest kind existed to learn every thing necessary in order to become a *Tana Gaddell*.

I need not detail the incidents of this journey, for, however interesting they may have been to myself, they might not prove equally so to my readers. Suffice it to say, that I reached my destination after "many a long and weary day," by my usual mode of travelling. I enjoyed the most robust health, and my mental faculties were reinvigorated by my short recreation, for another vigorous seige at my books.

On arriving in the city, I was amazed at its greatness, and I thought, "Surely I will never be able to find my way among all these streets and houses to the Jewish College!" However, I knew that the Jews resided by themselves in a separate part of the city,* and I enquired of a man whom I met where the Jews quarter was located. He proved to be a Gentile, and he replied: "Throw a stone from your hand and it will be sure to strike either a dog or a Jew," intimating by that the numbers which existed both of the one and the other, and also conveying the idea that both were held in equal contempt. This I afterwards discovered to be the prevailing sentiment among the Gentiles of that place. However, there was no love lost between us, for we looked upon the Christians as worse than dirty water; if they considered us as bad as a dog, we looked upon them as little better than a hog, which had always been in our estimation the essence of abomination.

Prague is a very ancient city—the capital of Bohemia. It has for several centuries been celebrated for its seats of learning, which are equal to the best in the world. The Jews there were very numerous, and some of the most celebrated Rabbies in the world are to be found in Prague. But although many of them occupy the highest positions in the intellectual and social world, still there is no place in the world where they have been subjected to so many and so great persecutions. They have several traditions among

---

* At the present day, however, it is not so. They mix up among the other inhabitants.

them to account for this. Among them the following :—A long time ago, some bad man, becoming offended at something which had occurred, resolved to have revenge. For this purpose he abjured Judaism and became a Christian, not from any love he had for the Christians, but the better to carry out his purpose. He took a bottle of blood and put it secretly into the ark in the synagogue, among the sacred things which are there preserved. He then professed to reveal some of the secrets of Judaism. Among other things, he told the civil authorities that, when celebrating the Passover, the Jews were accustomed to make use of a bottle of Christian blood, as a proof of which he offered to go with any of them and point out the place in the ark in which it might be found. A day was appointed, on which some of the bishops, civil authorities, and *gens d'armes*, were to accompany him. The whole thing was kept a profound secret from the Jews. But on the very night previous to that on which the examination was to take place, Rabbi Ezekiel, who was a very holy man, dreamed that something was wrong with the ark, and he should go and examine it. On doing so the next day, he found the bottle above mentioned, and at once removed it, so that when the authorities came to make their investigation they found nothing amiss. This is their tradition ; and although it exculpates the Jews from all blame, still they lay for a long time under the imputation of using Christian blood in celebrating the Passover, and hence the persecutions.

To show the manner in which this enmity among the Christians exhibited itself, let me relate another tradition. But a few words of explanation will be necessary. During the celebration of the Passover, no Jew is permitted to eat bread baked with leaven, nor even to have it in his house, for seven days. After this long abstinence they endeavour to make up, as much as possible, by purchasing leavened bread, pastry, cakes, &c., in abundance, and having a regular feast of good things the very next day. Of course they are obliged to purchase these things from Christians, as no Jew could furnish them without violating the last day of the Feast of the Passover by preparing them—a thing which they would not do. The Christian bakers take advantage of this, and do a very large business on the first day after the Passover.

And now for the tradition. A certain Christian baker, a great enemy to the Jews, but a secret enemy, prepared, on the last day of the Passover, several thousand loaves of bread to sell to the Jews the next day. These he impregnated with some deadly poison, and contemplated the wholesale destruction of those who would partake of them. But his design was defeated in a miraculous manner. On the last day of the Passover, it was revealed by an angel to the Rabbi * * * *, another very holy man, that the Passover must be prolonged during another day. This was accordingly done, and by that time the poisoned bread, not having a fresh enough appearance, could not find a purchaser; and thus God had interposed to preserve them from their enemies.

On arriving in Prague and enquiring for the Jews' quarter, I did not throw the stone as I had been directed to do, but I did not realize much difficulty in finding them notwithstanding. There were at that time about 40,000 Jews in the City of Prague alone, and these could not all be stowed away in a corner. It seemed the more they were persecuted the more they increased, which is often found to be the case. I of course sought out the best college in the city. It was one of the colleges in connection with the *Alt-Neu Schule*—(Old New College). Certainly it seemed old enough ; but I could discover no new features in its external appearance. It was said to be the first Jewish synagogue built in Europe, after the destruction of Jerusalem, and it is standing to this day, if that can be said to be standing which is almost buried beneath the ground. I could not convey an adequate idea of its appearance to an American reader, if I should try my utmost. I will only say that the greater part of it is so deeply sunk beneath the surface of the ground, that candles and lamps have to be kept burning day and night all the year round. This circumstance, no doubt, preserved it from total destruction during the troubles through which it has passed. It is also favourable to the vigorous prosecution of study, as is shuts out the noise and bustle of the outer and upper world to a very great extent. Of course it would be very expensive supplying all this light so constantly, while sunlight was so much cheaper, and this would no doubt prove a weighty objection to this style of architecture. But a good Providence provided, as usual, for this emergency, at least if we may believe the following tradition.

About two hundred years ago, a Roman Catholic princess, very wealthy, was driven by political disturbances from Portugal, her native land. She toook refuge in Prague, and, falling in among the Jews, was so well treated by them that she renounced Christianity and embraced Judaism, in which faith she died. On her death-bed she bequeathed to the Jews of Prague the whole of her property, which was to be appropriated towards keeping those everlasting lights burning in this and other Jewish Synagogues in Prague. I had not been long there before I heard the story, and was told, besides, that in consequence of her generosity, there was a perpetual miracle to be seen by any one who would visit her tombstone, viz., a large spot on the stone from which oil came continually oozing out. I visited the tombstone a short time after, and discovered a large grease spot as large as my head ; but to make sure that it was not illusion I placed my hand upon it, when a large portion of the oil adhered to my fingers.

The first service I attended in Prague I was struck with a certain peculiarity in their mode of worship. The Sabbath service is always opened by reading the 92nd Psalm, but in Prague this Psalm is twice repeated. On enquiring the reason, I was told that it was in commemoration of an event which had happened a long time ago. The story goes that the Rabbi * * * * had, by means of his skill in cabalistic mysteries, constructed a man of clay, whom he obliged to perform his manual labour during the week. On one occasion he forgot to take the cabalistic words and signs, which kept the man at work, out of him, on the evening of the sixth day, and so his man was found at work on the evening of the Sabbath. Those who discovered him at work came in great haste to the Rabbi, and found him engaged in opening the service, just after he had finished reading the 92nd Psalm. On learning what had annoyed them, he immediately destroyed his man ; and, again turning to his congregation, said, "The service has not yet been commenced," and again proceeded to·read the Psalm. Ever since that time it has been read twice in the same synagogue ; and I have myself, in after years, read it the second time when worshipping there.

All these things, and many more, some of which I am

half inclined to believe in to this day, tended to make me very superstitious although perhaps I had my share of that in my early years, as my conduct on my first journey from home plainly evinced. Whether true or false, they were as firmly believed in as the most authentic history they had amongst them, and I could not be expected to be wiser than my masters.

I had not been here very long before I again began to feel the pressure of hard times. There was there, however, a young man who had taken quite a fancy to me, and felt disposed to do all in his power to assist me. Seeing that my pants were getting the worse for wear, he urged his mother to let him lend me a pair of his to wear on the Sabbath. His mother, who was a bad dispositioned woman, would not listen to his request, and even scolded him for making it. But he was determined to assist me in some way, and so the poor fellow collected for me one gulden and twenty-five kreuzer among his friends, and, handing it over to me, told me I could for that procure a pair in some of the places where cast-off clothing was for sale. The Jews who keep these places are rogues and sharpers of the worst description, who would cheat their own fathers if they had a chance. I had not much experience in making purchases for myself, never having been overburdened with spending-money. However, I went to one of these places, told the man what I wanted, and showed him my money. It was just getting dark, on the evening before the Sabbath, and his practised eye no doubt discovered in me a fitting subject on which to exercise his roguish propensities. So taking me into the inside of his shop, where it was still even darker, he showed me an article partially folded, which he

declared was just the thing which would suit. I felt the
cloth, and examined it as well as the imperfect light would
admit, without, however, unfolding it; and as I was not
very scrupulous, thinking anything would be an improvement on the pair which I wore, I concluded to take them.
He immediately scooped my money into his hand, bundled
up the pants, and sent me off. What was my surprise
when, on trying them on the next morning, I discovered
they had only one whole leg, the other having been ampu-
tated at the knee!

This circumstance furnished me with one lesson in the
great department of knowledge, called human nature, which
was, after all, worth perhaps as much to me as I paid for it.
However, it did not prevent me from being taken in on a
second occasion in a similar manner. As winter approached,
I wanted something to keep me warm when I had occasion
to go abroad, and accordingly purchased myself a mantle
to throw·over my shoulders, which hung loose around my
person. On my first appearance in this garment, I could
not tell why all the smaller boys commenced to laugh, and
the countenances of the larger ones to assume that peculiar
expression characteristically denominated a "broad grin."
I soon discovered it was not at my mantle they were laughing, but at the appearance of my face and hands, both of
which were blackened very much in those places where my
mantle had touched them. On a closer examination of my
new-made purchase, I discovered that it had been originally
white. Some miserable dye had been daubed upon it, in
order to colour it, which would last long enough to give it an
appearance till it was sold, but was never intended to stand
service or wear. This was, in human nature, lesson No. 2.'

But I need not recount the progress which I made in this department, especially as it was not embraced in my college course.

On the whole, I had much better times at Prague than ever I had enjoyed away from home before. The young students paid me, often very liberally, for assisting them in their studies. I was a general favorite among them, and was also much beloved by the Rabbi Rappaport, who was the head of the college at that time. My studies in this place were not by any means confined to the Talmud, but were principally devoted to the acquisition of languages and the pursuit of scientific knowledge, history, philosophy, &c. For this, great facilities were offered us, as those of us who desired to do so were permitted to attend lectures in other parts of the city, in Christian institutions, embracing subjects not taught in our own college.

During my fourth year in Prague a sad calamity befel me. My mother had been ailing for some time, but no one apprehended anything serious as the result. All unexpectedly I one morning received a letter stating that my good mother was no more. Perhaps if I had been prepared for it, this intelligence would not have produced such an effect as it did ; but it was poignant and bitter in the extreme. Little did I think, when leaving home, that it was the last time I should look upon her dear face. I hope she has got safe home to glory, and, if so, it shall be my constant endeavour to be found worthy to meet her in that upper and better world, where all distinction between Jew and Gentile will be forever obliterated.

This circumstance did not, however, deter me from going on with my studies, as I was now in a fair way to attain the goal of my ambition—to become a Rabbi. I continued to prosecute them with the utmost vigour until the end of my fifth year in Prague, when my education was pronounced completed. I received my diploma, and other credentials of the highest class, and returned home as proud of my position as a young peacock the first time it spreads out its eye-spangled tail to the sun. Every step of my homeward journey I seemed to set down my feet with an air of greater importance, and carry my head higher than ever before. I was now a graduate of one of the most celebrated colleges in Prague—the great city of Prague, world-renowned for its wisdom. *I was now a Rabbi*—and a Rabbi in my own estimation of no mean importance. Henceforth, every Rabbi who was not educated in Prague must stand aside, and give place to me as to a superior order of creation.

Here I may observe, in concluding this chapter, that, unlike the practice in Christian churches, no ordination, nor ceremony equivalent, is required previous to entering upon the duties of a Rabbi. As soon as he has completed his education, and arrived at the required standard of attainments, he receives his diploma to that effect, and is thenceforth competent to enter upon the discharge of his duties, as soon as he can procure a congregation.

CHAPTER IV.

Now that my education was completed, and I possessed all
the qualifications so long desired for becoming a *Tana Gaddel*, my next business should have been to look around for
a congregation. But people are not always found doing
what they ought to do, and I was no exception. I had read
somewhere in a good old book, " He that findeth a wife,
findeth a good thing" (Prov. xviii. 22), and that passage
began to work itself uppermost in my mind. I believe the
man who wrote it got "too much of a good thing;" but
with all my ambition, I was not ambitious to follow his example in that respect. If I could get one good one, I would
be satisfied. After all, perhaps, this was not a purely selfish
desire, for I was informed by my friends that without a wife
I should not so easily get a congregation. Many of the
young ladies of St. Micklosh were proposed to me, but there
was some drawback in the case of each. One was too young;
another not handsome enough; a third not rich enough;
a fourth had not received education enough to be the wife

of a Rabbi from Prague; a fifth was all right in every respect, but—I would not suit her; and so I spent a whole year in looking out for a wife, as a preliminary essential to procuring a congregation.

My father's circumstances at this time had undergone a very great change for the better, so much so, that he was now considered among the more wealthy Jews; while a short time before he was not able even to send his son a dollar while at college. But such are the vicissitudes of life. This circumstance only tended to increase my pride, and make me all the harder to please in selecting a companion. Perhaps if I had been left entirely to myself, I might not have been able to find one to this day, who came up to the standard of perfection of which I thought myself worthy. But things in those days, and in that country, were very different from what they are in the present day. The parents generally used to dispose of their daughters as they pleased, and the daughters would generally fall in with the arrangement without a murmur. So, after I had wearied myself looking around, and trying to make a selection, I found another who kindly took the task out of my hands. It occurred in the following way :—

One New Year's day I was invited to go and dine with a rich Jew and his family, about an hour's walk from home. He had heard me officiate several times in the synagogue, in the capacity of Rabbi, and, my vanity led me to suppose, had discovered in me some marks of superiority above my fellows. I was very glad to accept his invitation, for the wealthy and the learned could always command my attention at any time. While at dinner a conversation took place to the following effect : "Well," said Mr. A——, the father of the family, "I suppose you want to get married!" "Yes," said I, "if I can only find a wife to suit me." "If you are not too hard to please," said he, "perhaps you would not object to my daughter!" "Where is she?" said I. "Why, right there next you," he replied. Up to this point I had not observed who was sitting next to me. As I turned to look upon her, I beheld a fair young creature covered with blushes, who had suddenly discovered something interesting on the floor, at which she was intently gazing. Although she was strikingly beautiful, I thought to myself, "You will never do for a Rabbi's wife, you are so young and so very small." Still I made no audible reply.

After dinner I went out into the garden for a walk, but could not dismiss the subject broached at table from my mind. I began to contrive some plan by which I might see her, and have some conversation with her alone. As good providence would have it, she came, after a while, into the garden—by chance of course—(such things always happen by chance). I immediately went up to her, and opened a conversation. I found her to be intelligent beyond her years; educated, pious, handsome, very interesting in every respect; and, to crown all, the daughter of a rich Jew. Taking all these things into consideration, and weighing them against her extreme youth and smallness of stature, I thought, after all, "she is just the one I have been wanting;" and she appeared to have no objection to me. So after four weeks we two happy creatures were made one.

I believe there is a proverb in English to this effect: "Marry in haste and repent at leisure." If that is what they do in England, I am glad I did not go there to get married. I have now had twenty-four years of leisure since

the knot was tied, and have never spent a single moment of
that time in repentance. If she were not likely to see what
I write, I could say a great many handsome things about
her; but, without at all fearing to make her vain, I must
say she has been a faithful helpmeet, a devoted wife, a good
mother, and now, I am happy to say, a pious Christian
mother.

In this connection let me relate an amusing incident.
When about ten years of age, I went, in company with my
grandmother, to spend a day out in the villa, some distance
from Micklosh, where one of our relatives resided. It so
happened that we stopped on our way at the residence of
Mr. A——, who in after years became my father-in-law.
While there, I distinctly remember seeing a beautiful little
girl, about four years old, and did not hesitate to express my
admiration of her to her mother. "Well," said she, "if
ever you become a good *Bucheral* (student), you may perhaps get her for a wife." Strange to say, so it fell out.
Miss A—— became Mrs. Freshman in the month of November, 1842. May she long be spared to discharge the responsible duties of her exalted trust!

My father-in-law and his wife were both very strict, pious,
orthodox Jews, and no doubt glad enough to secure a Rabbi
for their son-in-law. Still they could not think of a separa-
tion from their beloved daughter immediately, and prevailed
on us to remain with them for a time after our marriage.
I was very glad to comply with their request, as I was very
comfortable with them, and knew I should have everything
provided for both of us, without any care or anxiety on my
part. We remained with them over a year after our marriage. During that time, spent in ease and plenty, I became

careless, lost all desire to find a congregation, or practice the profession of a Rabbi. My desire was now to go into business, a desire which my father-in-law did not attempt to discourage. On the contrary, he contributed of his wealth to give me a start, and used his influence to establish me. But all was of no avail. In less than a year I had lost all my capital, and was, besides, deeply involved in debt.

Nothing daunted, however, my father-in-law paid my debts, and again set me up in another business, I, meanwhile, officiating occasionally as Rabbi in some of the small neighbouring synagogues, whose numbers and wealth would not warrant them in keeping a stated pastor. There were many of these throughout the country, in villages and small places. These had to depend on casual occurrences and chance circumstances for a supply. In these, then, I used to officiate occasionally, while engaged in business; but I soon found I could not do two things at once. I again failed in my business as before; and this time I resolved I would not be induced to commence it again. So I started forthwith away from home, in quest of a congregation.

Hungary was at this time a free country, and was known as a land of refuge to foreigners, especially to the Jews. Accordingly, the great body of Jews in Hungary were composed of various nationalities, in respect to the land of their birth; therefore, when the revolution broke out in 1848, it was to be expected that many of the Jews would stand up for liberty and freedom. In this the celebrated Kossuth encouraged them, by his presence and his patriotic speeches. Many of the Jewish Rabbies and Protestant clergymen went along with him, heart and soul. The congregation which I obtained were unanimous in opposing the encroachments of the Austrians. I soon became very popular amongst them,

3

as I lost no opportunity, in public or private, to condemn the policy of the Austrian government. The whole country was at this time in a most critical position. Even after the termination of the war, although a partial adjustment of affairs was made, no one of those who had opposed the Austrians could repose with any feeling of security. After a time, spent in great insecurity, and in a very unsettled state of mind, I resolved to leave the country. As I had heard wonderful stories of the civil and religious liberty of the New World, I resolved to make that my future residence. Thus the good providence of God brought me, with my good wife and five children, to this country, in the month of July, 1855.

On coming into this New World, the first difficulty we experienced was, that we could not speak a word of English; the second, that we had very little money left after our long voyage ; and the third, to obtain a situation as a Rabbi.

The first difficulty, however, seemed the most formidable. I thought I never could learn the English language. The first time I heard it spoken, was by a gentleman in the railroad cars, in my own native land. I suspected it was English as soon as I heard it, but, in order to make sure, I turned to a fellow traveller, and asked him, " Ist das die Englische sprache ?" (Is that the English language ?) He replied in the affirmative. " Well," thought I, " such a hissing, hoarse, jumbled-up conglomeration of sounds without meaning, I am sure I can never learn." This, however, did not deter me, and I pushed onwards, every hour removing me farther from the scenes and hallowed associations of my youth.

On arriving in Montreal, C. E., I went immediately to see Dr. DeSola, the Jewish Rabbi of the Portugese congregation.

in that place. On producing my testimonials from the chief
Rabbi of Prague, and credentials from the other colleges
which I had attended, he at once received me cordially.
He gave me a letter forthwith, recommending me very
strongly to the Jewish congregation of Quebec. On the
strength of this recommendation, I took my family to Quebec, where, after a meeting of their official board had been
called, Mr. Benjamin being president, I was duly approved,
and installed as their Rabbi, a position which I continued
to occupy for about three years, until the light of the blessed
gospel began to shine into my poor and benighted, though
proud and Pharisaical heart, and I became a follower of the
meek and lowly Jesus, whom I had formerly rejected and
despised.

> "Oh, happy day that fixed my choice,
> On Thee, my Saviour and my God !"

My congregation in Quebec was composed of mixed
nationalities of Jews, but chiefly German and English.
I used to officiate in the Hebrew and German languages.
It was not until I had been a long time among them that I
tried to conduct a service in English. I had, however, over
estimated my own powers, and miserably failed. The Rev.
Mr. Marsh, of Quebec, who was present, notwithstanding
my failure, gave me every encouragement to proceed in the
effort to master the language, telling me that if I would
study the language more, he had no doubt I would be able
to excel many of our native-born English preachers in power
and effect. Without believing implicitly in his prophetic
inspiration, his encouragement stimulated me to persevere,
and took the edge off of the mortification which I felt on
becoming sensible of my failure. Although I have now

attained considerable fluency in the use of the language called "plain English," the tones of my own dear "mutter sprache" possess a charm, and have a power of setting my soul on fire, especially when I speak about Jesus, of which I can give but a faint conception through the medium of the English language.

One thing struck me as very strange,—this I observed in connection with my charge in Quebec, almost as soon as I had entered upon the discharge of my duties there : it was the little regard which the Jews paid to their Sabbath-day (Saturday). Many of them, after the services of the synagogue were over, would repair to their usual places of business, or go to the pursuit of their usual pleasures, apparently unmindful of that command so strongly set forth in the law : " Remember that thou keep holy the Sabbath-day." I was horrified at their impiety, and remonstrated with many of them, reproving them severely for their conduct. Their excuse was, that the observance of the Christian Sabbath was enforced by law, and they could not afford two whole days in the week from their business. Besides, they had to compete with the Christians in business, and if they would not accommodate their Christian customers on that day, they would withdraw their patronage, without which they could not make a living. These, of course, were weighty objections, but I succeeded in a few cases in over-ruling them, and enforcing strict observance of the Sabbath, according to the requirements of the Mosaic law. But my success in this respect was not very marked or extensive.

I used to spend the Christian Sabbath in visiting my congregation, as they mostly spent that day in idleness or recreation. Often, as I would pass through the streets, and see the large congregations thronging towards the various

Christian churches, or streaming homewards from the services, my mind would be variously exercised regarding them.
At one time I would think, "What a pity that such a
multitude of people will so easily believe a falsehood, and
blasphemously worship a bad man!" But, again, I would
reflect, "Here are men of intelligence, men of education,
men of a profound acquaintance with human nature, men
who have the Old Testament Scriptures as well as I have,
men who are accustomed to exercise their reason and judgment in regard to their worldly affairs, and men who, I am
sure, do not place implicit confidence in the Christian religion without some strong foundation upon which to base it.
What if, after all, I have only examined one side of the
question? What if, after all, they should be right, and I be
wrong?" These kind of thoughts I usually dismissed with
an effort, as a temptation of the devil, but they would frequently recur again, in spite of myself. Thus was the spirit
of God working upon my mind, and leading me step by step
towards that great change which He was so soon about to
work in me.

Before entering, however, on a detailed account of that
wonderful chain of circumstances which led to my conviction and conversion to God, I may be permitted just here
to recall a circumstance which happened in my own native
land, as an appropriate conclusion to this chapter.

One night during the progress of the revolution to which
I have adverted, I happened to be remaining at a hotel in
the city of Cashaw. While there, a Jewish missionary, employed by the Scotch Church, was passing through Hungary,
selling very neatly bound editions of the Old and New
Testaments, very cheap. He came to the hotel at which I

was stopping, and offered me one of his books. I told him I did not want any, as I had copies enough of the Old Testament; and as for the New, I would not give a kreuzer for one. But he was not to be put off so easily. He said to me, " If you do not want the New Testament, cut that part out, and sell it to some poor Christian ; you will then have the Old, and besides, I have no doubt, make something by the transaction." There was something so persuasive in his manner, and his whole address, that I felt myself drawn towards him. Of course I did not know he was a converted Jew ; if I had, I should not even have conversed with him. As it was, I felt very much inclined to purchase one of his books. I thought to myself, as he offered me a beautiful gilt-edged one, handsomely bound, for a gulden (fifty cents), " why, it is very cheap ;" so, without more ado, I purchased it—not that I felt any desire to read it, but because the pleasant colporteur almost forced it upon me. I have been thankful to God for that purchase, many a time, since the light of the Holy Spirit has shone into my heart !

I took it home with me, but never even looked into it. I left it lying among my books somewhere, and when I was coming to this country I left a number of my books in Hungary, which would only have been an encumbrance, and I thought I had left this among the number. What was my surprise, therefore, on arriving in Quebec, and unpacking my books, to find among them this Bible, with the New Testament in it ! I mention this circumstance here, because this little Bible plays no unimportant part, under God, in that wonderful chain of events by which I, a poor benighted Pharisee, was brought out of darkness into light. I had not then discovered its value, as was very evident by my conduct ; for, as soon as I discovered it among my books, I took it and locked it up among my private papers, lest my own wife or children, or some of my congregation, should find out that I had such a book in my possession. I felt like a guilty person because I did not destroy it at once ; but I believe God, in an inscrutable manner, directed the whole transaction, to bring about the final result. But I must not anticipate.

CHAPTER V.

I now begin to approach the most important period in my history, and my own idea of its importance must be my excuse for going into considerable detail. I will also, just here, take occasion to beg the liberty of making use of the names of some who, under God, were instrumental in bringing me out of darkness into the marvellous light of the Gospel of Christ.

Before entering upon the account of my conversion, however, a detailed account of that wonderful chain of circumstances which led to my conviction of the errors of Judaism may not be out of place.

Towards the end of my third year in Quebec, I have explained how my mind used to be exercised in regard to the Christian religion. On such occasions, I have felt strongly tempted to look into that New Testament which I still kept locked up in my private desk. I generally resisted the temptation, after a brief mental conflict. But on one occasion, after preaching to my congregation about the restoration of the people of Israel, my mind became more beclouded than ever, and I felt I did not fully believe all I had told my people. In this state of dissatisfaction and perplexity, I went to my desk and carefully unlocked it, all the while trembling as if I were about to commit a great crime. Taking out my Bible, I went into my library and locked the door, so that I might not be disturbed. When thus secure from interruption, I opened the New Testament, and commenced hastily to read a few pages; but, after a very short time, I threw it away in disgust, thinking all the while I had been reading, "This cannot be!" "That is impossible!" So disgusted did I become, that I believe if a fire had been in my room at that time, I would have thrown the book right into it. Soon I took it up again—read a while, and again threw it from me. So I continued for about an hour. At last I became so excited, that on again taking up the book and reading awhile, I threw it on the floor with such violence that several leaves were torn from their places. In a moment afterwards I was seized with remorse for what I had just done, and, gathering up the loose leaves, I placed them in their proper places, carried the book to its former hiding-place, and locked it up, with a firm resolve never to look into it again.

Evening came, but my mind was so greatly disturbed that I could scarcely perform my routine duties in the synagogue; and even when night came I could get no rest. Still, I did not know exactly what was the matter with me. The next day being the Christian Sabbath, I went as usual to visit among my congregation. I first called upon Mr. Jacobs, the president of our synagogue. As soon as he saw me, he enquired what was the matter with me, "for," said he, "you

3*

do not look well." I, however, kept my own counsel, and made no reply. He then said to me, "Rabbi, you will have an opportunity to-day of witnessing a very strange spectacle, the like of which, perhaps, you may never have seen before." He referred to a grand procession which was to pass through the streets.

In a short time it came along, and it was indeed an imposing spectacle. All the Roman Catholic priests of the city, dressed in their full canonical costumes, according to their various orders, with the Host elevated before them, passed in front. These were followed by a numerous retinue, among whom were exhibited, in great variety, banners, crosses, and images. As I looked upon them, I fancied the priests of olden time must have presented a somewhat similar appearance. I watched them disappear in the distance, unable to repress the mental exclamation, "How long, O Lord, how long shall we poor Jews be deprived of our glorious restoration!"

All this only tended to increase my mental perturbation. "How strange," thought I; "the sermon yesterday, the affair with the Bible, and the procession to-day—all contributing to keep the Christian religion continually before my mind." All this I looked upon as an omen of evil. Still, I made no remarks on the subject, but went home, resolved more than ever to lead a strict and pious life.

From this time an all-controlling desire arose in my mind carefully to study the Prophets, especially those having reference to the coming of the Messiah. While engaged in this occupation, a Jewish Rabbi from Palestine,* who had been sent out to America to collect money for the poor Jews of

---

* His name in the Hebrew is נחום הכהן Nachum Hakohen. He is probably still alive.

Jerusalem and Damascus, happened to be in Montreal, where I was on a visit at the same time. I met him at Dr. De-Sola's. He could only converse in the Hebrew and Arabic languages, so that very few except the doctor and myself could have any conversation with him. After he had collected something among the Jews in Montreal, he asked me whether I could do anything for him among my congregation in Quebec. I readily agreed to do all in my power, thinking at the same time, I should have a fine opportunity of conversing with him about those different traditions and beliefs which now characterized our religion in different parts of the world, and also of hearing from him something about those sacred curiosities, so dear to the mind of a Jew, which are to be found nowhere else but in his native land. But chiefly I wished to converse with him about that person whom the Christians worship as " Jesus of Nazareth."

I was, therefore, much pleased when he informed me that, being tired of travelling, he would gladly rest with me a few days. He accordingly accompanied me to Quebec, and during the time he remained with us we were never separate, for he would not even take a meal of victuals anywhere but in my house, for fear they might not have been prepared in strict accordance with the requirements of the Jewish religion.

I shall ever be thankful to God for this visit at that time. It seems to me altogether providential that, just at that period, when my mind was so unsettled, I should have the privilege of conversing on these perplexing subjects with one who lived, I might say, in the very place where these wonderful things detailed in the New Testament had transpired. We used to sit up until after midnight, conversing .upon various topics, all very interesting to me. On these occasions, many questions which I had never before thought about would spring up in my mind, when I would immediately ask his opinion in reference to them.

On the evening before his departure, the subject of conversation was the "Messiah.' I asked him what the Jews in Jerusalem thought about the coming of the Messiah. "We are looking for him every day," said he. "And what," said I, " do our people there think about *Talu?*" for at that time I did not venture to call him Jesus, since the Jews call him, as already mentioned, *Talu*, that is, the "crucified impostor." "Of course," said I, "you, who are living almost on the very spot where he lived and died, must have some more reliable tradition respecting him than we have here!" He then gave me the tradition which the Jews in Jerusalem hold. This I found altogether different from the one which I had received while at college in Prague. Upon this I asked him how it happened that we, as a people, taken all the world over, had not one and the same tradition on a subject of such great importance? "We had at one time," said he, "but since we have had to suffer so much persecution about it in different countries, we never published it in any of our books ; and so in many places, the true tradition has been lost ; but we in the Holy Land preserve the true account to this day." Here I may mention that the tradition is of such a blasphemous nature, that I must be excused from publishing it even here. My opinion is, the sooner it dies out the better.

"And do you actually believe," said I, "that there is nothing in the Old Testament which refers, in any way, to Him in whom the Gentiles believe as their Messiah?" "No," he replied, "not a word." "Then how in the world does it happen," said I, "that the prophets, in whose inspiration we all believe most firmly, and who have foretold every event,

great and small, in reference to our nation, should so over-
look such a great catastrophe, as not to mention a word
about it! Even if he were an impostor, they would, at
least, have said something to warn us not to follow him;
especially since it is written, 'Surely the Lord will do nothing, but he revealeth his secret unto his servants the
prophets?'"—Amos iii. 7.

The poor Rabbi stood there as if struck dumb. This was
a new idea to him, the glimmerings of which had never
entered his mind, and of course he had no reply to make.
After a few moments deliberation he said: "As soon as I
get home I will take your question—which is, I admit, of
great importance—into earnest consideration, in company
with other learned Rabbies; and whatever result we may
arrive at, I shall let you know as soon as possible." He
left the next day, but from that time to this I have never
heard a word from the good Rabbi. I hope the Lord may
make his enquiry and research result in his conversion!

After he had gone, leaving my question unanswered, in
this manner I thought to myself,—"If a Rabbi from Jerusalem cannot answer this question, it cannot be answered,
and there is something wrong with our belief—a screw
loose somewhere." From this time my mind became more
aroused and agitated than ever, and my inclinations to the
opinion that the Christians *might* be right, stronger than
ever. I even commenced to speak my thoughts aloud to
some of my congregation, upon the subject that lay so close
to my heart; and, notwithstanding all my former resolutions not to read the New Testament, I again found myself
perusing its pages, not only in the German, but in the
English also, in the study of which I had made considerable
progress.

I had a very pious Christian neighbour, a Mr. Hinton, with whom I used to spend hours in conversing on religious topics, and who assisted me very greatly in mastering a reading-knowledge of the English language. After such conversations with him, I used to feel what a miserable position I occupied; for I felt in my heart that I was no longer a Jew, and yet I revolted at the idea of becoming a Christian. I now neglected all Jewish ceremonies, except the mere routine duties of my profession; and when I stood up in the synagogue to conduct the service, I felt that I was a hypocrite.

Still, I did not believe in the authenticity of the New Testament, so that my position was altogether a most unenviable one. I had no rest by day. Even the silent watches of the night refused to bring

"Tired nature's sweet restorer—balmy sleep"

to my poor wakeful eyes. Many a time have I spent the whole of the night, searching in the Bible, and among Jewish writings, for matter having a direct bearing upon the all-absorbing question of the Messiah. Still, conviction came not. Sometimes I would even think the whole Bible was a work of fiction. Again I would doubt the good providence of God, in causing me to be born a Jew. But sometimes I would become all but persuaded of the truth of Christianity, and then I would reflect,—"What will become of my poor wife and family, if I should renounce the faith of my fathers, and become a Protestant?" (For I never had much opinion of Roman Catholicism). Thus would Satan, the tempter, continually harass my mind with difficulties, which contributed to hinder my progress in the search after truth. I believe now that my greatest mistake during that period was, that I would not entrust any one with the secret which burdened my mind, and was wearing out my life.

The Jewish Passover was approaching, and, as usual, I had to prepare a special sermon for the occasion. Never had I experienced more difficulty in doing so than now. I now neither believed in the Jewish religion fully, nor yet was I convinced of the truth of Christianity. This being the case, I thought the most honourable course for me to adopt, would be to resign my Rabbiship at once. But here greater difficulties than ever began to accumulate. My good wife, to whom I broached the subject, was altogether against it. "How will you support your family?" she would ask me, "and, as for myself, I will never become a Christian. No, never!" I was thus in a measure forced to practice hypocrisy, and I accordingly commenced, with a heavy heart, to prepare a sermon for the Passover.

The text I chose was—"The sceptre shall not depart from Judah, nor a lawgiver from between his feet, until Shiloh come; and unto him shall the gathering of the people be."—Gen. xlix. 10. During my preparation of this subject, doubts would continually spring up in my mind: —"Where is now the sceptre and the lawgiver? Where are now the morning and evening sacrifices? Where are now those distinguishing marks of our religion which characterized it in the days of its glory and magnificence? Where is even the tribe of Judah itself, much less the sceptre swayed by that tribe?" These and kindred questions, all unanswerable, would start up in my mind; and it is not to be wondered at, that when my sermon was completed, I determined not to preach it. This sad state of things could not long continue; so I called in my wife, and told her that I could not on any account preach Judaism any longer, giving as my reason my firm belief, thus expressed for the first time, that the Messiah had already come in the person of Jesus of Nazareth, in whom the Christians all believe. This was enough to break her down. She commenced to weep bitterly. This soon attracted my elder children, who, on learning the state of affairs, joined in with their mother, and we had a house filled with lamentation and mourning. I must confess I had to weep myself.

Being unable to endure the sight of the misery I had thus brought upon my family, I left my home and repaired to a solitary place beyond the barracks of Quebec. Here no human eye could witness my misery, and, in an agony of soul, I threw myself on the ground, and cried mightily to God. It was a strange prayer, not to be found in our prayer-book, but befitting the occasion; and that cannot always be said of printed prayers. Still, relief came not. I had in my heart renounced Judaism, but I had always an unspeakable shrinking, whenever I thought of acknowledging its errors in public. With a heavy heart and a dim eye, looking, I suppose, as wretched as I felt, I retraced my steps homeward. There I found my family just as I had left them, still bathed in tears. Without saying a word, I went into my bed-room, where I remained awake until after midnight, reading my Bible and praying. At last nature became exhausted, and I fell asleep in my chair. While there I had a very strange dream. I thought I was in some great trouble, out of which no one was able to deliver me, and was just about to resign myself up to despair, when I beheld an image of the Saviour on the cross, over whose head were inscribed the words, " I am thy Saviour."

I immediately awoke, and, after pondering upon the strange dream awhile, came to the firm resolution that I would not be called a Jew any longer. But, alas! the flesh is weak. When I came to give in my resignation, my moral courage failed me, and so I put it off again.

On the day before the Passover, I took my Bible, and with a true praying spirit I approached the mercy-seat of the mysterious Jehovah, and prayed that he would lift upon me the light of His countenance, and show me the right way. While I was thus engaged, Mr. Hinton called in to see us, of which my wife duly informed me; but I would not see him, as I desired to be alone and undisturbed. I still pondered on the text which I was to have preached from on the morrow, little dreaming when I selected it, that it would thus have been made the means of my awakening. In connection with this verse, I also opened at the fifty-third chapter of Isaiah, and taking down a commentary, I read until I was as fully convinced of the fact that Jesus Christ is the expected Messiah, as I was of my own existence: and never have I doubted it since that time.

Without the least hesitation I then proceeded to write out my resignation, and sent it to the president of the congregation the next morning.

But now the storm burst upon me in all its fury. My wife and children wanted to celebrate the Passover as usual, while I, poor miserable sinner, was an unbeliever! I had no objection to their doing so, but as for myself, I gave up everything that was Jewish. The ceremonies I felt no longer binding upon me. I put away my prayer-book, but substituted nothing in its place. In fact, I had no desire to pray at all. Of course I believed now that Jesus was the true Messiah, " of whom Moses and the prophets did write;"

but that was all. I knew nothing about justification, or faith in His name. My heart was still as proud as Lucifer; and if any one had told me just then that I was a poor lost sinner, I should have felt inclined to send my slipper after him, or, perhaps, if I had been a woman, tried the virtue of a broomstick.

In this state I continued several weeks. The matter soon became noised abroad in all parts of the city. My principal Jewish friends forsook me. Others avoided me as if I had the plague, and most of them became my most bitter enemies. One even went so far as to come to our house and try to persuade Mrs. Freshman to leave me, and return to her father's house, promising if she would do so to provide all her expenses. "The Rabbi," said he, "is insane, and it is dangerous to live with him!" Others, again, said that I wished to become some great bishop among the Christians; while others gave currency to a story, that I had received ten thousand dollars for renouncing my faith in Judaism. These and similar stories were propagated everywhere, which had not even hay and stubble for their foundation, but still found many among our people who believed them.

During all this disquiet and commotion, I was trying with all my power to convince my wife and elder children (especially my son Jacob, who is now a minister of the Gospel), that Jesus was indeed the true Messiah, and that we should no more have to look for his coming, until we saw him coming the second time, "without sin unto salvation." My son Jacob, who was a very intelligent boy for his age, readily appreciated my reasoning, and felt the force of my arguments, but would turn with instinctive confidence to his mother, in whose judgment he always placed (and does to this day) the most implicit reliance ; and early prejudices in her were not easily eradicated. I do not wonder that I was so slow in convincing them, for I now see that I was still in bondage myself.

I could now read the English Bible almost as well as the Hebrew or German ; but though I read it in one language or other almost incessantly, still I did not get a clear conception of my condition as a sinner in the sight of God, nor of the necessity of a change of heart. I thought,—"If I believe that Jesus Christ is the true Messiah, that is all that is necessary to constitute me a good Christian ;" and yet, although firmly persuaded of the truth of that, I still was not satisfied. I felt my need of something else ; I could scarcely tell, or even imagine, what that something was. I had not yet begun to see "men even as trees walking."

But the Lord would not long leave me to grope at noonday as in the night. He sent me light out of darkness, in his own good time. A Mr. Clapham, a worthy member of the Wesleyan Methodist Church, who lived but a short distance from us, having heard of my condition, came to see me, accompanied by the Rev. James Elliott, who was at that time stationed in Quebec, in charge of the Wesleyan Church in that place. He was the first Christian minister who ever visited our house, and I may say, brought salvation into it at the same time ; for it was from his lips I first heard the proclamation of the gospel of peace. I must confess that I received him coolly, and felt in no humour to converse with him. After a partially unsuccessful attempt on his part to engage in conversation with me, he turned to my family, and spoke so kindly to them, exhibiting so much the spirit of his Master, that I commenced to like him immediately. Before he left us, he engaged in prayer, in all

the while sitting in my chair and looking on, half amused
at the whole performance. I thought his prayer a very
strange one. He prayed that God would enlighten my dark
mind, show me my position as a sinner in His sight; that
He would trouble and then wash my troubled heart in the
atoning blood. I thought to myself, " I guess I have trouble
enough, without you praying for any more ; and, as for
being a sinner, I am as good as you are, and perhaps a little
better. Then, about my dark mind, I wonder whether you
know that I was educated in Prague ?" Still he continued
to pray—unconscious of the thoughts passing through my
mind. As he laid hold upon the promises of God, and
pleaded them with such fervency and earnestness, I could
not help receiving the impression that he had access to God,
and a power with Him which I did not possess. After his
prayer I liked him all the better, and went the very next
Sabbath to hear him preach.

I cannot well describe my sensations on finding myself
for the first time amongst a Christian congregation, engaged
in the solemn act of worshipping God. I thought every eye
was riveted upon me from the beginning of the service
until its close ; and every word from the pulpit seemed to
have some reference, immediate or remote, to my special
case, and intended for my special benefit. Not-caring to be
looked at, and talked at, for such a length of time, I was
very glad when the service was brought to a close, and I
found myself outside the church again. But I had received
a favorable impression of the Christian mode of worship,
and began already to see faint glimmerings in outline of that
wonderful scheme of redemption, by which God can be just,
and yet the justifier of him that believeth in Jesus.

I walked home with Mr. Clapham, who asked me, among other things, whether I would have any objection to accompany him to a class-meeting on the following Wednesday evening. I replied, "Not in the least." He accordingly called for me on the evening appointed, and we went in company.

As I had never been at such a meeting before, everything appeared curious and strange. I looked with wonder and astonishment upon men and women who would stand up, and, with tears in their eyes, confess their sins and bewail their unworthiness before God. I thought to myself, "What does this mean?" Still, I said nothing, until, on our way home, I took occasion to ask Mr. Clapham what it all meant. "Surely," said I, "these men must have done something dreadfully wicked, to make them weep and lament in the manner I have witnessed ; are they going to be sent to the penitentiary, or what is to be done with them?" He smiled at my ignorance, and told me that those men were amongst the most respectable citizens ; that their grief arose on account of the evil propensities of their hearts ; that their tears were tears of joy when they thought on the grace of our Lord Jesus Christ, who for their sakes became poor, that they through his poverty might be made rich. "But with all their morality," said he, "they realize that, if they had not repented of their sins, they must have perished everlastingly ; and they continually delight to magnify that grace which has averted the just penalty due to their sins." "Well but," said I, "I have never repented in this manner ; and I think if I believe that Jesus is the Messiah who should come into the world, that is all that is required." "Not so," said Mr. Clapham, "the devils also believe that much, and tremble."

Still, I fancied I knew better. "These Gentiles, after all, know very little; how should they?" And so I parted with him, almost laughing outright at his remark about the "devils trembling."

The next morning I called to see the Rev. Mr. Elliott. Our conversation naturally turned to the Messiah and his mission, embracing the redemption wrought out by Him, the doctrine of man a lost sinner by nature, and the necessity of being born again before he could inherit the kingdom of heaven.

There was I, a poor Nicodemus, considering, "how can these things be?" The words "born again," kept continually resounding in my ears; and, do what I would, I could not get rid of them. I asked a great many questions about the new birth, and received a great deal of light from Mr. Elliott. Still, I longed for more, but was ashamed just then to ask for it. I have no doubt if I had done so, he would have been pleased to answer me, and that satisfactorily. But I returned home only partially enlightened, saying to myself on my way, "A pretty fellow you are now, neither a Jew nor a Christian! even worse than a heathen, for they have their gods whom they worship, and a religion in which they believe; while here you are, without God, and having no hope in the world—if all be true that Mr. Elliott says."

Thus would the enemy work upon my mind, and often assail me with such thoughts as the following: "Only wait," he would say; "this is only the commencement. Your present difficulties are but little to what they will become. Only wait, and you will discover what a sad exchange you have made, and how difficult it is to become a Christian."

Notwithstanding this, the cords which had bound me to Judaism became effectually severed. However many difficulties I might meet with in Christianity, I never could again disbelieve in their Messiah. I had now begun to receive some dawnings of truth. I had some little acquaintance with the mode of worship and doctrine of one section of the Christian church. The remainder of the way in which God led me, until he converted my soul, and the providential manner in which he opened up my path, must be reserved for the following chapter.

CHAPTER VI.

UP to this time I had lived in blissful ignorance of those
minor sectional differences which characterize the Christian
church.   I thought all Christians were divided into two
great classes, Protestant and Roman Catholics, and that all
Protestants were alike in their beliefs and ceremonies.
This degree of ignorance was not long to continue.   I became acquainted shortly after with a very nice man, a member of the Baptist persuasion, who invited me to go to their
church on a certain evening, when they intended to have
a bible-class meeting.   I readily consented, and went.
While there, I was given to understand that every true
believer must be dipped under the water, as a preliminary
to his legitimate introduction into the Christian church,
"Indeed," thought I, "so this is also a part of Christianity.
is it ?   If so, I don't want anything to do with your new

birth, by being dipped under the water. If this is necessary, I wonder why Mr. Elliott never said anything to me about it, and I certainly think he is a very good Christian." At any rate, I thought I might be a good Christian without attending to that part of its ceremonies. I dare say I expressed my thoughts aloud, on returning from the meeting, for it was only a very short time after this, when the Rev. Mr. Marsh, the minister of the Baptist Church in Quebec, a very pious Christian gentleman, came to see me. He advised me to study carefully the Scriptures, and judge for myself whether immersion was not the proper mode of baptism. I had no particular relish for the study, as I felt a shrinking, whenever the idea would come into my mind, of being dipped under water in some cold and wintry day; but afterwards, when I began to realize that some form of baptism was necessary, I did commence to study the Scriptures, as I was determined to use my own judgment, let men say what they pleased.

I now began to receive visits from ministers of all denominations, among whom I may mention the names of Dr. Helmuth, a converted Jew, now Archdeacon of the Church of England, in London, Ontario. He came in company with the Rev. Mr. Clark, minister of the Presbyterian Church in Quebec. Both of them were very interesting in conversation, and very solicitous as to my spiritual welfare, and engaged in prayer with me before leaving. It would be tedious to detail the names of all who in this manner visited me. Suffice it to say, that I soon became acquainted with all the Protestant clergy of the city, and even with some Roman Catholic priests. Although all of these were very kind to me, and their conversations interesting and profitable, still I felt a peculiar leaning to the

4

Wesleyan Methodist Church, and to Mr. Elliott as its minister, which none of the other churches or their ministers had been capable of producing. Thus passed away the days of the week, visiting and being visited. My soul was athirst for information on those points in which my education had been defective. So, on Sabbath morning, I again repaired to Mr. Elliott's church, and heard him preach. The novelty which filled my mind, when present at the first service, had now partially worn away. I no longer felt that all were gazing upon me, and hence had better opportunity to attend to the discourse, to which I listened very attentively. Often during the discourse, I thought many of his remarks were intended for myself; but he preached with power, and with the unction of the Holy Ghost. As he unfolded the gracious scheme of redemption to his hearers, he would at times seem much affected; and several times I noticed the moisture gathering in his eyes, while many in the congregation were shedding tears. The Spirit of God commenced to operate on my own heart, and I must confess that I often wept myself, although I could hardly tell for what. After service I returned home, more serious and thoughtful than ever, but still unable to grasp the *"modus operandi"* of the simple doctrine,—" Believe on the Lord Jesus Christ, and thou shalt be saved."

In the afternoon a friend called at my house to take me with him to a Union Sabbath School. It was that famous school kept by the late Jeffrey Hale, Esq., a worthy member of the Church of England. While there, I could not help being struck with the neatness and decorum which everywhere prevailed. The good conduct and attention of the children, as well as the disinterestedness and devotion of the teachers, could not help making a favourable impression on my mind, especially when I found that all the instruction imparted there had a tendency to make them "wise unto salvation." Surely, thought I, in the days of my youth had I been privileged to attend such a place, I would not now feel such a difficulty in apprehending the way of faith, as taught in the New Testament, and believed in by the Christians! I felt, indeed, much surprised that a respectable and very wealthy citizen of Quebec should humble himself so much, as to kneel down and pray with the children, and take so much pains to point them to the Lamb of God, who taketh away the sins of the world. But when, at the close of the school, I heard them unite in singing some beautiful hymns, especially that one,—"I love Jesus," &c., my heart was much moved, and I thought how gladly would I exchange places with one of these little ones, if I had my life to live over again ; if by that means I could ever get to sing with as much confidence as these seem to manifest,— "I love Jesus." I determined, when I should return home, to tell my children what I had seen, and if possible influence them to go the next Sabbath. But I was saved this trouble, for the very next day the Superintendent of the Sabbath-school called at our place, and all my children liked him immediately so much, that, to my great joy, they readily promised him to go the next Sabbath to his school.

About this time the City Missionary, employed by the various religious denominations of Quebec, called to see me. I asked him if there were any German Christians in the city. "Yes," said he, "we have some, but they are not converted." "What do you mean by converted?" said I. (For at that time I did not know how a man could be a Christian, and not be converted.) He at once explained the apparent anomaly, and left with me a few tracts in the German language, which he said would fully explain the nature of conversion, and the means of its attainment. I was very much pleased with his conversation, and very glad to receive his tracts ; but when, a short time after, he took his leave without praying with me, my good opinion of him sunk several degrees below zero, and I was even inclined to call him back, but did not. Mr. Elliott came in shortly after, with a pious lady in company, who both prayed with us before leaving.

After they had departed, and I was again alone, I commenced to read the German tracts, in which I became very much interested, and which did me a great deal of good. Still, after all the light I could obtain from sermons and tracts, my mind continued very dull to apprehend that great "mystery of godliness,"—"God manifest in the flesh." So I again took my formerly-despised Bible, and read the New Testament, with such a burning desire thoroughly to explore its mysteries and understand its truths, that I even refused to take my meals. The epistle to the Hebrews was especially difficult. When I came to the ninth and tenth chapters, I could not proceed any farther, as I could not follow the apostle's reasoning, nor feel the force of his arguments. Accordingly I went to Mr. Elliott, my never-failing resort in times of perplexity, and he assisted me very much in clearing up the intricate points. He also gave me a commentary to assist me in the further explanation of this and other difficult portions of Scripture, which I had met or might meet with.

The great difficulty which now arrested my attention and occupied my mind, was in regard to the atonement. The Jews believe that on the day of atonement God pardoned the sins of Israel, when the High Priest, entering into the holy place with the blood of sprinkling, atoned, first for his own sins, and then for those of the people. Now, I thought, we have neither temple nor sacrifices, and how then are the sins of a Jew atoned for in the present day? Here the enemy would come in and whisper,—" You are no sinner, you have nothing to atone for ; only adhere to the faith of your fathers, and you are sure of the crown at the last." But when I would turn to the fifty-first Psalm, I would feel, and my conscience would tell me, that I was no better than David, who had written the psalm, and he evidently felt himself, at that time at least, to have been a great sinner. His penitential expressions in the psalm referred to gave evidence of a mind scarcely less disturbed than was my own ; and much bitterness of soul was my portion when I would reflect upon my position. To such an extent did these feelings prevail at times, that when under their influence I would sometimes feel akin to regret that ever I renounced my old faith, as then I had no mental disquietude or trouble about my sins. Now I had nothing but trouble. Not only trouble on account of my sins, but trouble also in reference to my temporal circumstances, and the means of supporting my family.

While in one of these unpleasant moods, my wife came into my study one day, and said to me, " My dear, what are we going to do now? The baker has just been here, and said he could not let us have any more bread until that which we have already received is settled for. We have not a loaf in the house, and the children had to go to school this morning with only a very slight breakfast. What will become of us ? We have not a cent in the house ; all our former friends have forsaken us ; rent will soon again be due, and nothing to pay it with." This was said all in a breath, and the whole concluded with a woman's most forcible argument—tears. Certainly, affairs looked desperate enough ; but instead of increasing my despondency, it only increased my trust in God. I now felt it to be my duty to encourage and comfort her, and said to her, "Never mind, my dear, God will provide for us." Perhaps this was my first distinct act of faith in God, and I was not disappointed. Hardly had an hour elapsed when Mr. Elliott came in to visit us, and left with me ten dollars, without even enquiring whether we needed it or not. "Surely," thought I, "he must know something about our affairs, and God has sent him to succour us." This tended greatly to increase my confidence in God ; and taking the money in triumph to my wife, "See," said I, "did I not tell you the Lord would provide ?" She, however, was more matter-of-fact than I, just at that time ; and instead of entering heartily into my views of the providence of God, again began her forebodings for the future. "How," said she, "will you support your family when that is gone ? And even this is but a pittance, doled out to us by the hand of charity, and rather would I die than live on charity." But although she was thus careful and anxious about many things, I had already begun to choose that good part, which, I feel thankful to God, has never since been taken from me. Since that time I have more fully been enabled to prove that our God is not only a God of grace, but a God of providence also ; and as I look back upon all the way in which he has led me, it is with feelings of the most unfeigned thankfulness for the past, and implicit confidence for the future.

My salary from the Jewish congregation was of course discontinued from the time I ceased to officiate as their Rabbi, now more than two months ago. Although the support which I had received from the synagogue was liberal (my salary, together with presents and other perquisites, amounting to much more than a Methodist preacher usually receives), still, at the time of my renouncing Judaism, I had not three dollars in the house, and my debts amounted to about thirty dollars. Hence the straitened circumstances detailed above. But this was not the worst. Other trials yet awaited me. The Jews, as already mentioned, as a natural consequence, became my most bitter enemies, and would do everything in their power to injure me. I had never taught them, when their Rabbi, to love their enemies, nor to return good for evil, nor any of those beautiful precepts of our Saviour; and now I must take the consequences. The house in which we lived belonged to a Jew, and, with a view to distress my family, we were peremptorily ordered to leave the premises immediately. It required the most unbounded confidence in God to endure these trials, so frequently repeated. And often (after all my confidence), as a picture of my children, forsaken and destitute, would loom up before me, would I find myself exclaiming, " How long, O Lord, how long ! " Still, though persecuted, I was not forsaken ; though cast down, I was not destroyed.

I now commenced to attend churches of different denominations, and although I found good, pious, Christian people in all of them, I did not feel so much at home in any as in that of the Wesleyan Methodists. I experienced the utmost kindness from the ministers of these various churches, yet none of them obtained such a hold upon my affections as Mr. Elliott. He it was to whom I could go in confidence, and lay open my heart in his presence. He it was who was always the friend in need, and has always since proved, the friend indeed. He it was whose ministrations I most

frequently listened to ; and he it was whose ministrations
and counsels were made, under God, the means of my
saving conversion to a knowledge of the truth as it is
in Jesus.   One distinguishing feature in his preaching had
struck me, in contrast with that of others to whom I had
listened.   In some of the churches which I had attended,
the ministers would have a great deal to say about the scriptural mode of baptism, and the necessity of immersion.
Others attached a great deal of importance to the apostolic
succession of their ministry, and the regeneration of infants
in baptism.   Still others would enforce a rigid morality, but
say very little about conversion.   Some, again, would preach
the necessity of conversion, but would so mix it up with
divine decrees as apparently to nullify the force of their
argument.   Mr. Elliott, on the contrary, was eminently
practical.   I do not remember ever to have heard him say
a word from the pulpit about the mode of baptism, apostolic
succession, infant regeneration, or the divine decrees.   His
great theme was, " Ye must be born again," " Except ye
repent ye shall all likewise perish."   So constantly did he
keep these truths before my mind while attending his Sabbath
services, and also in private conversation, that I resolved at
last, if there was any truth at all in conversion, that, by the
help of God, I would seek to know it.   From that time I
commenced to seek the Lord with all my heart.

On the same day on which I made this resolve, I was
visited by a very pious lady, a Mrs. McLeod, who, before
she left us, prayed very earnestly for the conversion of my
wife.   "Ah !" thought I, " if she only knew that I am still
unconverted, surely she would pray for me also."   However,
I prayed as well as I could for myself, and was always much
comforted after the visit of a pious Christian friend, be it

lady or gentleman. After she had gone, I noticed she had
left a favourable impression on Mrs. Freshman, for she came
to me and said: "I do believe that is a good woman, and
I wish she would often come and see us." The Spirit of
God was evidently beginning to work upon *her* mind also,
and planting those seeds which afterwards developed into
such an abundant harvest. We were frequently visited also
by a Miss Clapham, also a very pious young lady, who would
talk to us, and pray *with* us, and *for* us, and whose visits
were made a blessing to our whole family. I hope their
example may serve to stimulate many others to the exercise
of such works of faith and labours of love ; and in the day
of final rewards, these devoted Christian ladies may shine as
the brightness of the firmament.

Before this, I had sometimes been called upon to pray
when attending the prayer-meeting, which I lately had
made a practice of doing regularly. I had, however, always
declined, when called upon, for the simple reason that I
could not do it. But this evening, as I went to the prayer-
meeting, I resolved to pray in public, even if I should not
be called upon to do so. So great had my anxiety become
to experience the forgiveness of my sins, that I thought,
"If taking up my cross in public will assist me in procuring
deliverance from this bondage, I will willingly do it, or anything else, so that I may be free." When I arrived in the
lecture-room where the prayer-meeting was held, I found no
one present but the sexton. I waited anxiously until the
congregation assembled, thinking all the time about my duty
to pray in public. Mr. Elliott came in, and as he shook
hands with me, I tried to muster courage enough to ask him
to give me an opportunity to pray ; but I could not do it.
He opened with singing and prayer, and the meeting was

4*

continued as usual; but I did not engage in prayer. When it broke up, I felt condemned, and went home weeping. When I got home, I found all my family had retired, except my wife, whom I again found to be in trouble—but a trouble different from that which was distracting me. She met me with upbraidings. "What is the use," said she, "of your going to these meetings, night after night, and leaving your family to starve? Things have come to a pretty pass, when we have all got to be turned out of the house into the street to-morrow," and much more of the same import, all the while weeping bitterly. I could not answer her a word. This, which I would have considered a great calamity at any other time, was now sunk into the shade by comparison with the greater sorrow which sat nearest my heart. I feared not those who could kill the body, or turn it houseless into the street; all my trouble was in reference to Him who has power to cast both soul and body into hell. Filled with these thoughts, I went straight to my room, determined that this should be the last night. I felt that things had reached a crisis, and I was resolved, if I had to pray all night, I would not leave the throne of grace until deliverance came. I felt all the time persuaded that if God would only convert my soul, all would be well. I spent the whole of the night in crying to God in deep, earnest prayer, but the more I cried and prayed the more I felt the burden of my sins press grievously upon me. I saw myself more clearly as a lost sinner, unworthy of anything but condemnation and eternal banishment from the presence of God and the glory of his power. Oh! such a night of agony! I have thought since then, "If the torments of the finally unsaved are to equal in intensity the misery of that night, and be protracted throughout eternity, how diligent I ought to be, and how earnest in my endeavours, to save them from such a horrible fate." Truly, it was the hour and the power of darkness. All my pharisaical props and self-righteous supports were taken from under me. My sins came looming up before me, and piled themselves mountains high. The whole of the individual sins of my past life seemed to flash before my mind, and concentrate themselves in a single instant; and that instant was protracted through the greater part of the night. So imminent did the danger appear, of having condign punishment immediately visited upon me, that in agony of soul I cried out in very self despair, "Lord, save me or I perish;" "Jesus, have mercy upon me, or I am eternally lost." I saw there was no other hope, and I realized the sufficiency of that one; and at that moment "the clouds dispersed," the shadows fled, the Invisible appeared in sight, and rolled away the burden from my troubled soul. Prayer now gave place to praise, and I could select no language suitable in which to convey the raptures of my new-born soul, save "Glory to the Lamb!" "Glory to the Lamb!" I can no more doubt the reality of the change that was then wrought in me, than I can doubt the fact that previously I was a poor condemned sinner in the sight of God. Why, even the face of nature seemed to have undergone a transformation. As I paced my room, singing and shouting the praises of God, and as I looked out of my window upon the moon wending her pathway through the heavens, among those myriad troops of stars which everywhere spangled the firmament above, I could not but thank God for my very existence; and never before had I been so sensible of His goodness in placing me in such a beautiful world, surrounded by so many delightful and lovely objects. Even as my pen traces these sensations, I feel like exclaim-

ing, "What would I not give if I could only have, at least
once a week, such a foretaste of heaven upon earth as it was
then my privilege to experience." But never since them
except on one occasion, and that was when I heard my son
Jacob preaching the gospel for the first time, have I experienced anything like the same intensity of joy, although I
have had many, very many, sweet seasons of spiritual refreshing coming from the presence of the Lord. "Bless the
Lord, O my soul, and all that is within me, bless and praise
His holy name!"

Thus I spent the remainder of the night in blessing and
praising God for his goodness, and when morning came I
could not keep my happiness all to myself. I first thought
how happy the good news, that I had found the Saviour,
would make Brother Elliott, so I bent my steps in the direction of his residence. Every one whom I met on my way,
I told of the great things which the Lord had done for my
soul. Many seemed to think I was beside myself, and perhaps I did not act entirely according to the most established
and approved conventional usages of society; but my heart
was full of love, and it seemed to me that—

"If all the world my Saviour knew,.
All the world would love him too."

So on I went, practically complying with that injunction,—
"As ye go, preach." Brother Elliott was delighted to hear
the good news which I had to tell him; but I did not give
him much of an opportunity for remarks. My tongue was
let loose, and I did almost all the talking. This was on a
Friday morning, and I asked Brother Elliott to give me an
opportunity to preach on the following Sabbath. It seemed
as though I must preach; and if I had been standing on a

mountain top, with the whole world gathered at my feet,
I would have rejoiced in the opportunity to publish to them
all what the Lord had done for me, and exhort them to a
like precious faith in Christ. Brother Elliott readily
granted my request ; and on the following Sabbath I
preached in three different churches, telling everywhere
what God had done for me, and publishing the great truth
that Christ has power upon earth to forgive sins. It was
real preaching, too. If I ever preached an original sermon
it was on that eventful Sabbath. I believe I said little
else but "Come all ye that fear God, and I will shew you
what he hath done for my soul." Whether my congregations were affected or not, I myself was deeply moved, and
from this time my desire continued to increase to become a
preacher of the everlasting gospel which had done so much
for me.

I commenced with my own family. My wife, although
very slow of heart to believe all that the prophets had
written concerning the Messiah, still was no more opposed
to Christianity, and even consented to accompany me to
church. My son Jacob, who was brought up a pious lad,
now loved to attend the Sabbath-school, and read the New
Testament. My other children had also imbibed some of
the principles of Christianity in the Sabbath-school ; so that
when I commenced, after my own conversion, to preach
Christ to them, I found the ground in a manner prepared
for me. My own life and conversation also disposed them
to hear the word with gladness, for they saw there was a
great change for the better in myself as compared with
former times, so that I had no longer to meet with opposition from my family, but, on the contrary, had the happi-

ness to witness them gradually, one by one, falling in with the doctrines of the cross, as revealed from God, and taught in the New Testament.

The next Sabbath the city missionary came to inform me that a ship had just arrived from the old country, with German emigrants on board, and requested me to go and preach to them in their own language. This I willingly consented to do, being very glad to get such an opportunity. I never had heard the gospel preached in the German language, and hence perhaps it is natural that I felt a little strange while on my way to the ship, and thinking in what manner I should best express myself. The missionary had provided me with a prayer-book of the Church of England in the German language. This I made use of for a short time in the commencement of the service. After a moment or two praying from the book, I laid it aside, and commenced to pray out of the fullness of my heart. I suppose it was a very original prayer, for after the service, the captain called me aside, and said to me,—"That was a terrible prayer; to which church do you belong, sir." I told him,—"I do not know yet; I am a Christian." Here my old German Bible, which I have had occasion to mention before, came in very useful. It was it which I took with me to preach from, and, strange as it may appear, the lesson which I felt impelled to read to them, and make the basis of my remarks, was one of those very loose leaves which had been so violently torn from its place in the manner which I have before described.

After service was over, the captain called me into his cabin, thanked me for the sermon, and offered me a glass of wine, which, however, I respectfully declined,—and here

I may be allowed to mention that long before I became a Christian, I and my family became strict adherents to those principles usually advocated by those who are called, for whatever reason, "Teetotalers."

Thus was the Lord leading me in a way that I knew not, and opening up my way into that which afterwards became my providential path.

CHAPTER VII.

Now that I had not only espoused Christ myself, but had
begun to preach him to others, the subject of baptism began
greatly to occupy my mind. It seemed, however, as if every
individual step of my progress was attended with difficulties
of one kind or other, and this was to be no exception. The
principal difficulties in the way of my being baptized were—
1st, I had not yet decided on what mode of baptism I should
undergo. Immersion was always associated in my mind
with such a chilling, cheerless sensation, that I mentally
resolved to lay it on the shelf, until I had fairly examined
the scriptural doctrines in favour of other modes, adopted
by other sections of the Christian church. My second
obstacle was in regard to my family. I was desirous, whenever I was baptized, that my whole family should be prepared to receive the ordinance at the same time as myself.
As regarded my younger children, of course there was no
difficulty, as they were proper subjects already. But then
there was my wife and my elder children, whom I would
not attempt to coerce or control as far as their religious

views were concerned. It is true, I reasoned with them, and laboured all in my power to convince them of the truth of Christianity. But to command them to renounce Judaism and prepare for Christian baptism in obedience to my will, was a thing I would never attempt to do, even if they had not been baptized to this day. But while I was still undecided as to the mode, I could not make any definite calculations as to the time. Hence, I commenced in good earnest to study the law and the testimony on this seemingly important subject. I never, however, fell into the error of considering baptism a rite essential to salvation, because I knew it was perfectly distinct from conversion. I knew I had been converted myself, and felt persuaded I would go to heaven if I died, whether baptized or not. Still, as a rite, I looked upon it as a very important means of grace; and as a duty I esteemed it one which I could not avoid and remain guiltless.

I found on reading the New Testament that while John the Baptist and our Saviour, as well as the apostles, say a great deal on baptism, not one of them distinctly inculcates any particular mode. It is true I found passages where it speaks of those who were baptized going down into the water and coming up out of the water, but I had enough knowledge of the Greek language to know that the prepositions *εις* and *εκ*, rendered "into" and "out of," are often translated "to" and "from." Besides, in that very account of the Eunuch's baptism by Philip, where these expressions occur, the very idea of baptism must have been suggested by a passage out of the chapter in Isaiah which he had just then been reading, where it is said, referring to Christ, "So shall he *sprinkle* many nations." I found also various passages in which the word "sprinkle" is distinctly mentioned.

as Ezekiel xxxvi. 25 : "Then will I sprinkle clean water upon you and ye shall be clean ; from all your filthiness and from all your idols will I cleanse you." Various passages also spoke of the " blood of sprinkling ;" but nowhere in the whole Bible or Testament could I find the word "immersion." One consideration alone, in addition to the absence of an express scriptural command, deterred me from adopting this latter mode ; that was, my children would not be permitted to enjoy its benefits as well as myself, and I felt it a duty incumbent upon me to bring my children as well as myself under the provisions of the " new covenant," and thus consecrate them to God. So, after carefully studying the claims of the various modes, and comparing them with the practice under the old dispensation, and seeking divine aid and wisdom, I at last came to the conclusion that as soon as my wife and my eldest son would believe in the Messiahship of Christ, we should all be baptized publicly in the Wesleyan Methodist Church. In coming to this decision I received no influence from others, but acted perfectly free and unbiassed, according to my own judgment and convictions.

Old prejudices, and the effects of early training, could not be dissipated as far as my family was concerned. Kind friends, however, belonging to different religious denominations, used frequently to visit us and converse with my family. With their assistance, I succeeded in about a month in destroying the last barrier which prevented my family from falling in with my views, and obtained from them a confession that it was their duty to renounce Judaism. Here I do not wish it to be understood that they were already converted, but simply convinced that the faith of their forefathers, in not believing in Christ, was erroneous.

However, they were sincerely desirous of becoming acquainted with the way of saving faith in Christ. I shall ever have to acknowledge my indebtedness to the Sabbath-school for bringing about this result. My children still attended it regularly, and would often make the instructions which they had there received the subject of conversation at home, by which means, as also by means of the books which they brought home with them, Mrs. Freshman was gradually made acquainted with the fundamental doctrines of Christianity. She received a great deal of information and instruction also from the conversation of Miss Clapham, Mrs. McLeod, Mrs. Middleton, and other pious ladies, to all of whom she would acknowledge her everlasting obligations. But above all, it was the change which she observed in me, and the influence of the prayer-meetings, which she had begun to relish, that convinced her of the truth of Christianity, and brought her to the point at which she yielded a willing assent to be baptized with her husband and family.

Just at this time I had another great attack from the enemy of my soul. I suppose he saw he was now about to lose me, if he did not make a vigorous effort to turn the course which affairs were apparently about to take. I was in very straitened pecuniary circumstances, and would often revolve in my mind how I was going to support my family. As I was walking out one day, thinking over this subject, I met a Roman Catholic priest, who acted as secretary to the bishop of the same denomination. I had heard some time before of a vacancy in the Lavelle College (a Roman Catholic Institution), for which they required a tutor of Oriental languages. I thought at once, this would suit me very well, never thinking that any objection would be made in respect of creed or religious persuasion, nor any other credentials

required than those of proper qualification for the situation.
I mentioned the subject to the priest whom I met, and with
whom I was slightly acquainted. He informed me that the
situation was still vacant, and had no doubt I would receive
the appointment. I went at once to see the bishop, who
received me very cordially, as did also a number of priests
by whom he was surrounded.

Almost the first question put to me by these worthy suc-
cessors of the apostles was, whether I had yet connected
myself with any religious denomination. I replied in the
negative; and added that as yet I had seen no motive in
particular urging me to join one sect more than another.
"Well, but in order to be a Christian at all," said the bishop,
" you must be baptized." I replied that I had already considered that subject, and had determined that my family
and myself should be baptized in the Wesleyan Methodist
Church. This, I could see at once, did not contribute to
raise me much in the estimation of the good bishop and his
worthy satellites. In fact it was a point of such weighty
importance that they could not decide about granting my
request, but told me they would see about it. I suppose
they retired to consult the fathers, or the saints in their
calendar, whether it was lawful, or whether such a thing
had ever occurred as the appointment of a Wesleyan
Methodist to an office in a Roman Catholic Institution !
Whether they ever got any light on such a perplexing subject or not, I am unable to affirm. But if ever they did
" see about it," they never gave me the benefit of their
improved perceptive faculties.

Quick as lightning the rumour spread throughout the
city that the converted Jewish Rabbi was about to become
a Roman Catholic. Some of my friends came to see me

about it, but their anxieties were soon dispelled, when I told them the exact thing as it stood; but I could not go around correcting false reports to the extent to which they prevailed, and as the progress of truth is but slow, compared with that of error, the report continued to spread, and to gain credence as it progressed. The Jews especially took a great deal of pains to make a noise about it, and tried their utmost to make people really believe that I intended to become a priest. The whole thing was amusing in the extreme to myself; for there was Mrs. Freshman, the dearest little woman in the world, whom I would not have given up for a seat on the throne of St. Peter himself, or an elevation to the topmost place in the calendar of their canonized saints, much less for a paltry office, where my highest duties would have been to try and beat the contents of a Hebrew grammar and lexicon into the heads of boys and young men.

But this silly rumour had its result, independent of the amusement it afforded, and that result was to hasten my baptism. I thought my best course, in order to stop all such annoyances, would be to be baptized at once. Without more ado, I apprized the different Protestant clergymen of Quebec of my intention (having first secured the full consent of my wife and children); appointed a day on which I invited them to be present and take part in the service; and on Sabbath afternoon, the 2nd of September, 1859, myself, my wife, and seven children, were baptized in the Wesleyan Methodist Church in Quebec. The ministers who were present on the occasion were the following, viz.: Rev. J. Elliott, pastor of the church; Rev. Dr. Cook, of St. Andrew's Church; Rev. Mr. Clark, of the Presbyterian; and Rev. Mr. Puller, of the Congregational Church. Dr.

Cook preached a sermon suitable for the occasion.   Mr.
Clark, who was the senior minister, was appointed to
baptize myself and my good wife.   Mr. Elliott baptized my
family, and Mr. Puller assisted in the devotional exercises.*
I must not here forget to make kind mention of the Rev.
Dr. Helmuth, who had promised to be present, but was
prevented by unforseen circumstances from giving us the
pleasure of his company and assistance.   He had on several
occasions visited us and prayed with us, and proved, by
various acts of kindness to myself and family, that he was a
worthy and devoted labourer in the vineyard of his Master.
A friend in need to me, and a beloved brother in Christ
Jesus—" An Israelite indeed."   He has ever remained my
firm friend, and continues so to this day.   During the ser-

---

* A more detailed account is given in the following extract from
the *Gazette* :—

ADMISSION OF A JEWISH FAMILY INTO THE CHRISTIAN CHURCH.
—In accordance with forenoon notification from the pulpits of the
various Protestant churches of Quebec, an immense number of
persons attended at the Methodist Church yesterday afternoon,
for the purpose of witnessing the administration of the sacred rite
of baptism to Mr. Freshman, late Rabbi of the Jewish Synagogue
here, and his wife and family.   The service was opened by the Rev.
Dr. Cook, who preached a most impressive sermon, admirably
adapted to the occasion.   The Rev. Mr. Clark then gave a short
and feeling address, and afterwards proceeded to administer the
sacred rite.   Mr. Freshman and his lady stood forward, and amid
the most wrapt attention and profound silence, the sacred and impressive ceremony was performed, and " in the name of the Father,
Son, and Holy Ghost," that Hebrew man and woman were received
into the communion, not of any particular sect, but of the true
Christian church.   As we remarked, the attention of the audience
seemed strained to its utmost intensity during the performance of

vice the church was crowded to its utmost capacity. Even some of my Jewish congregation were present, attracted, no doubt, by a feeling of curiosity. A feeling of solemn awe seemed to pervade the vast assemblage, except some of the Jews aforesaid. If ever I pitied their ignorance, and felt to pray for light to shine into their dark minds, it was when I heard of some remarks they made while Mrs. Freshman was being baptized; and also when they saw me carrying my youngest child in my arms to receive the sacred rite. These remarks are not proper to be inserted; but they gave free expression to the opinion that now we were lost indeed, and could never be fit for anything but the bottomless pit to all eternity. Thus was this solemn service brought to a conclusion. It had been looked forward to with great anxiety. It was undergone with timidity, and

---

the ceremony : but, if possible, it was still more keen when the children of Mr. Freshman's family—seven in number, from the lad of fifteen or sixteen years of age, down in regular gradation to the infant in arms—were ranged up, and also admitted into the bosom of God's Church. The Rev. Mr. Elliott then offered a most fervent and impressive prayer, and the impeded utterance which at times marked his supplication, proved how deeply the solemn ceremony had impressed itself on the mind of the reverend gentleman. A short and effective address was then delivered by a reverend gentleman whose name we did not catch, but who attended on behalf of Mr. Powis, of the Congregational Church; and the doxology being sung, the congregation broke up, evidently much impressed by the solemn scene they had witnessed. The meeting also in another respect was a most important one; inasmuch as it presented the spectacle of all our Protestant clergymen ignoring distinctions of name or sect, and joining together in the true spirit of Christianity to celebrate the admission of this Jewish family into the Christian church.—*Quebec Gazette.*

concluded with a feeling of almost painful solemnity resting upon me. I was now fully the Lord's. I had promised to renounce the devil and all his works, the pomps and vanities of the world, and had taken the most solemn vows upon me. According to the testimony of my children, they were also pervaded with a similar feeling; and some reminiscences of their thoughts at that time are now amusing in the extreme, as they betray an egregiously erroneous estimate of the nature of the ordinance to which they had just been subjected.

From this time our Jewish customs and forms of worship, which had been partially abolished already, were entirely abandoned. This proved a greater hardship at first than my family had any idea it would be. Another form of worship now claimed our observance; another system of educating the children. All our old traditions to unlearn; new truths to study day by day. All meats were to be considered as clean and good for food, and this was perhaps the hardest requirement of all. A Jew would consider it a great sin to eat even the best of meat, such as is purchased in the market, prepared by a Christian butcher. When we first began to use this meat, some of my children, especially one of my daughters, would not touch it, and could not be prevailed on to do so for quite a length of time. They would rather live on vegetables than taste the most savoury dish of the "unclean thing," as they were pleased to term it. Even "*sauer kraut*" has not had a greater number of hard things said against it by the English, than good butchers' meat had to endure from my family.

Again, to give up the old Jewish Sabbath-day (Saturday), was another difficulty. They had no objection to observe the Christian Sabbath after our own, and perhaps no one ever was any the worse for observing two Sabbath-days in the week ; but when it came to renouncing one of them entirely, my family, especially for the first few weeks, did not know what to do with themselves. To engage in our usual employments would have appeared like sacrilege, or at least wilful desecration. Even to prepare our food on that day was a thing not to be thought of. We used to sit all together, looking at one another, and listening to the ticking of the clock, which admonished us of the passing away of time ; and the bustle and noise in the streets outside, indicating it to be the busiest day in the week among the large bulk of the population by which we were surrounded. Finally, I made a commencement, and broke the ice by desecrating that day, which, after all, we were not keeping holy, no matter how secluded we might remain. My family gradually followed my example, and in a short time no one would ever have known by our practices or mode of life that we had ever been anything but Gentile Christians. The New Testament became the book of books in my family ; and the instructions imparted in the Sabbath-school were taking root downward and bringing forth fruit upwards; and, after a time, I had the pleasure of seeing my wife and elder children bearing their testimony for Jesus.

One single exception in the use of Christian food still characterized us for a length of time ; and that was the use of *pork*. I shall never forget my sensations on partaking of the obnoxious food for the first time. It was after I commenced to travel as a preacher that a good brother in the ministry, who was then in Port Hope, and at whose house I was stopping over night, wishing, I suppose, to have the credit of being the first to introduce to me that dish which my forefathers had held in abomination, took advan-

5

tage of my ignorance, and introduced it upon the breakfast-table. I noticed the meat, nicely fried, with eggs in abundance upon the table, and was helped to it in a liberal manner. I thought, while eating it, I noticed a peculiar flavour; still I asked no questions, for conscience sake, and did ample justice to it and the rest of the good things which Bro. Warner had provided. After breakfast we had family worship, and we then went up to the library, when my kind host playfully asked me, with a bright twinkle in his eye, if I knew what kind of meat it was I had had for breakfast. I never suspected anything amiss, and replied that I did not know. " Why," said he, " that was pork !" " Pork !" said I, " impossible; you are joking with me !" " You may take it as a joke, if you please," said he, " but it was verily and truly pork, nevertheless." " I wished to break the ice," said he, " and give you a taste of that which no Englishman, nor any other man who knows what is good for him would despise—ham and eggs." Just then I began to feel a very queer sensation in my gastronomic regions— the sensation which is characteristically described by Young America as " all overish ;" but what had got safely down remained in its place notwithstanding ; yet, during the remainder of the day, everything I saw reminded me of pork—everything I tasted, tasted like pork ; even the good brother, whom I still esteem and love, seemed to be more "porkish" than ever he had appeared before. But, as he said, the ice was broken ; and soon after I returned home from this visit to Upper Canada, pork, with all its concomitants, was introduced into our house. If Bro. Warner will now come to see me, I can repay him in his own coin, and will be very happy to do so, and that with compound interest. May his shadow never grow less !

On the Sabbath after our baptism I preached my first prepared sermon in English. I have since had the privilege of preaching it in several places, and some of our brethren may be curious to know what it was like. I take the liberty of inserting it in this place. I may say, however, by way of explanation, that the first few times I preached it I had the manuscript before me, from which I did not once deviate in the slightest degree. The sermon here reported is a verbatim copy of that manuscript, which I would not alter in the slightest respect for a guinea. It is, I may also say, a dry sermon; and those who go to sleep in church during the service, will find it to their advantage to turn over the leaves and skip the whole thing. Dry as it is, however, it cost me not a little effort to prepare it, and if I bestowed the same amount on every sermon I preach, I fear my poor congregation, who greedily devour from me two each Sabbath-day, would starve to death before I could satisfy their craving appetites.

SERMON.

Our text, dear friends, you will find in the 1st Epistle of Paul to the Corinthians, the 1st chapter, and at the 22nd, 23rd, and 24th verses :—" For the Jews require a sign, and the Greeks seek after wisdom, but we preach Christ crucified, unto the Jews a stumbling-block, and unto the Greeks foolishness; but unto them which are called both Jews and Greeks, Christ, the power of God, and the wisdom of God."

God has always accompanied his revelations to man with strong evidence of their truth, and these evidences have always been greater and more impressive according to the importance of the revelation.

Thus the ceremonial law, which was a direct law from God, was given only on the testimony of Moses, accompanied with miraculous power. But when God revealed the moral Law, he said to Moses,—"I will come unto thee in the darkness of a cloud, that the people may hear me speaking to thee; and although the people saw not the Lord, yet they saw the terror of His glory—thunder and lightning, and a thick cloud upon the mount, and the voice of the trumpet exceeding loud, so that all the people that were in the camp trembled."—Exodus vii.

But now, in the revelation of the gospel, it is God himself who speaks face to face with man. No other testimony is needed. God, in the person of Jesus, is his own testimony. He not only spoke in the presence of thousands, but was visible to the eye. Here the people have not been charged by the voice of God from amidst the cloud of darkness; but heaven itself has poured forth its glorious light, to enable every person to behold the glory and hear the voice of the Lord. "We have seen and heard the truth itself; and that which we have seen and heard declare we unto you, for in Jesus it dwelt among us." But the Jews require a sign, and the Greeks seek after wisdom; and our purpose to-day is to inquire what is the nature of the evidences upon which Christianity rests, and ascertain whether these evidences are as powerful and conclusive as the importance of the subject, and our vital interest in it, justly demands.

If it be of the greatest moment for every man to distinguish between that which is true and that which is false—between that which is genuine and that which is counterfeit, in worldly matters;—of how much greater importance is it that he should distinguish between the true and the false, the genuine and the counterfeit, in spiritual matters! An error in the first leads but to a momentary loss, while in the second it leads to eternal ruin ; and if it is important for man to distinguish the truth, it is equally important for God to make it clear and plain to him—to make it so plain, that " he who runs may read."

We state our subject, then, thus :—It was incumbent on God, in revealing a plan of salvation to man, to give man such evidences of its truth as should be sufficient to convince every sincere and earnest mind. Now, we assert, that God has done this in his revelation of the gospel, and we proceed to indicate the nature and the force of these evidences.

The evidences of Christianity are of three kinds :—1st. Of Testimony; 2nd. Of Reason; 3rd. Of Experience. Under the title of the "Evidences of Testimony," we include several correlative evidences—such as prophecy and miracles—inasmuch as whatever evidence they afford in themselves, they again rest upon the evidence of testimony : we have neither witnessed the miracles nor heard the prophecies. Under this head, too, we include all the internal evidence.

Now, the value of testimony depends on two things : 1st. On the character and credibility of the witnesses ; 2nd. On their number, relation, and harmony. We say, then, first, that the characters of the witnesses to the truth of Christianity are unimpeachable. The greatest foes to the system acknowledge the perfection of Jesus, and the truthfulness and sincerity of his followers. They were manifestly, therefore, not imposters, and, unless they were self-deceived, their witness must have been true. And, second, from the occurrence of the events to the closing of the testimony concerning Christianity, there was a considerable lapse of time, during which several witnesses, at different times, announced its facts and truths unchallenged by the world. And those narratives, without being identical, are harmonious and consistent throughout.

The evidences of reason may be stated thus: That the things or truths attested shall consist with the reason and constitution of man,—that they shall do no violence to either; not that man shall be able to comprehend everything stated, but that, as far as he does understand them, they shall be reasonable.

The reason of man is often appealed to in holy writ:— "That ye may be able to give a *reason* to every one for the faith that is in you;" "Render yourselves unto the Lord a living sacrifice, which is your *reasonable* service;" "Come and let us *reason* together, saith the Lord." The soundest deductions of reason show that Christianity is true, as we shall prove after having stated our third kind of evidence— the "Evidence of Experience," which is faith. The evidence by experience, or experimental evidence, is that evidence which every man receives directly he becomes a sincere lover of the truth; so long as he hardens his heart and denies the truth, he is without this last evidence; he is like a man who, shutting his eyes, declares that he cannot see, and faith, or the evidence by experience, is just the opening of his eyes when he sees everything.

This evidence is the most satisfactory method of obtaining a knowledge of the facts, for it is the evidence of our consciousness; we do trust, and cannot help trusting, for it is an intuitive principle, the testimony of which no man can resist. It is indeed this evidence of our consciousness which, through our senses, is our only means of knowing

what passes in the world without us; and this wonderful
and irresistible testimony to the truth of Christianity any
man may have who will clear his heart of prejudice, and
give up his mind to the action of Christianity upon it.

Let us now briefly notice the superiority of this evidence
over every other, and we see it in two things—first, in its
greater weight and force; and, second, in the facility and
ease with which it may be procured.

However credible a witness may be, or with whatever
proofs he may come to me, if my experience and consciousness testify against him, it is impossible that I should believe
him, even if I am shown a thousand reasons which appear
strong and conclusive. They all fail to overturn my consciousness and experience. So we see the superior strength
of this evidence, although, as we have shown before, both
witness, reason, and testimony agree in this case, making
our evidence trebly strong.

Then see, secondly, the facility we have in getting this
evidence by experience! It may be had at once by the
poorest or by the most unlearned; by the child or by the
savage; in any place, at any hour; it rests entirely with
ourselves. But the other evidences can only be gained by
long study and large resources, as we have seen. It is
necessary to examine and test the truthfulness of the history
and of the historian, of the oration and the orator, before we
can trust them; and even the internal evidence of the truth,
and the fact that it harmonises well in all its parts, and is
corroborated by so many distinct sources of information, is
only gained by the careful student at considerable expense;
and all these minor evidences together, when obtained, still
leave the inquirer in perplexity. They only serve to make
visible to him the cloud of darkness and doubt that sur-

rounds him: at the best they are only the twinkling glimmer of a few stars through the night of unbelief.

But the evidence of experience is as the bright shining of the noon-day sun, and can no more be mistaken or doubted than the presence of that great luminary. For instance, is it said, "Ye must be born again?" If I have become the subject of the new birth, how can I doubt its truth? Is it said, "The blood of Christ cleanseth from all sin?" and have I washed my robes and made them white in the blood of the Lamb, how can I doubt the efficacy of that blood? Is it said, "Through faith in Jesus we have peace with God, and are adopted into His family?" and is this peace mine, and can I call God my Father, what other evidence do I need of the preciousness of that faith? And am I told that "faith worketh by love, and purifies the heart?" and has love to Jesus begun to purify my heart, what proof besides this do I need that "Christ is the power of God unto salvation to him that believeth?"

We have thus shortly stated what are the evidences of the truth, and we now proceed to explain the office and nature of faith.

We have already intimated that the evidence by experience and faith are the same, and we state our subject thus : Faith is the act by which the truth is made to an individual the power of God unto salvation. It might have been supposed, indeed, that the salvation which God has wrought out for man was a universal one, and that it redeemed our whole race. But we are taught that it is not so. Man is a free agent—is still left to accept it or reject it, as he pleases.

Salvation is not an external thing put upon him as a garment, and changing only his condition and appearance ; but it is an internal thing, put within him as a principle which changes his heart and nature, and Christianity has made a perfect provision for the spiritual destitution of man; but since there can be no change of circumstances without change of heart, we then say that the peculiar adaptation of Christianity rested in its power to effect this change of the heart and nature. Acceptance of the truths of Christianity implies, in a corrupt nature, a choice of a desire for holiness. Now in a free moral agent, no such change can be effected but by the concurrence of the will. It was necessary, therefore, that the first step to such a procedure should be an appeal to the choice. The offer of the truth to man is thus made the first appeal to his moral choice, and faith is that act of the will by which the truth is accepted and received into the heart, while unbelief is its rejection and exclusion from the heart.

Holiness, then, and therefore salvation, is unattainable except through the faith of the individual; and therefore it is, that "he that believeth shall be saved, and he that believeth not shall be damned." It must be so, and cannot be otherwise.

Having thus shown that faith is the first step towards salvation, let us go on to see how it brings the sinner into relation with God.

We know that man, by sin, is brought under condemna-tion of the law of God, and that Christianity is a plan for his rescue from this condemnation. We know, also, that this rescue can only be effected by the infliction of the penalty of the law upon an innocent person, who is able to represent the guilty. Now, Jesus Christ is the innocent person who has borne the penalty of the law against sin; and faith in Jesus Christ is the act by which our sins are

5*

removed from us and imparted to Him, and are so atoned for by His death. Faith effects this by transferring the sinner's moral being to Christ: the sinner is made one with Christ—in Christ he becomes created anew. The sinner has no longer a separate moral existence. His very being is merged in Christ; and if the law still demands satisfaction, it has to seek for the sinner in the Saviour, where it finds every claim fulfilled, as it is written,—" There is now therefore no condemnation to them that are in Christ Jesus."

But there is another respect in which faith holds an important place in the sinner's restoration to the divine favour. The sinner is not only guilty but impure, and, as an unholy thing, cannot stand accepted before God. The sinner requires something more than an atonement, and faith in Christ furnishes him with more ; as, by faith, the sinner's crimes are imputed to Jesus. So by faith, too, the Saviour's righteousness is imputed to the sinner.

Here, again, we recognize the transference of the sinner's moral being to Christ. In Christ the sinner is perfectly pure and holy ; and God seeing him there by faith, can be " just, and the justifier of him that believeth."

It will be seen that I hold the doctrine of justification by faith alone ; that I exclude all mention of works. I do it on several grounds, some of which I shall proceed to state. In the institution of the " ceremonial law," it was ordered that every offering should be perfect, pure, and spotless, without mar or blemish. Even the palm-branch, which the Jews use in their Feast of Tabernacles, must be perfect.

Now, from all these significant facts, we have the grand lesson that God can accept nothing but perfection. But all the actions of man are imperfect. The best deeds of Christians themselves are all tainted by unsubdued evil in their hearts : every act is touched with selfishness, mingled with impurity or marred by unfaithfulness. Therefore we say, that for man's justification, no act of his can be accepted by God, for he accepts nothing but perfection. It is true that in Christ, and for His sake, God accepts both us and our services ; but it is by the righteousness and perfect holiness of Christ that we are justified.

Again, there are two distinct ways in which justification is possible. One is by faith, the other is by the works of the law, as it is written " He that keepeth the law shall live thereby." But these two methods are perfectly distinct and separate from each other, and can in no way be blended. If we are justified by works, it must be by works alone ; faith is altogether out of the question. If we are justified by faith, it must be by faith alone. Works are excluded as a part of our justification. They are in this case impossible. To say that we are justified by faith and works at the same time, is to contradict ourselves. But faith, while it excludes the works of the law, provides for their fulfilment. Faith is a vital power in the heart. Like love, it commands all the passions : it moves to fear or awakens to hope ; it arouses to action or strengthens to endurance ; it excites to penitence, it kindles to love ; it is a living and acting principle within, as it is a faith working by love, and as love is the fulfilment of the law ; while faith stands alone for justification, it inevitably leads to holiness. Faith without works is dead.

It has been held by some, that human actions may possess merit, and that thus they may even not only satisfy the just requirements of God, but do more—even atone for sin. Now for an act to possess merit it must be in excess of duty ; but do we not feel that, for human action, this is impossible ?

The best service and obedience we can render fall infinitely short of God's holy requirements; they are not sufficient to justify, much less to atone. How different is the righteousness of Jesus! There we have not only a perfect fulfilment of the law, but all this is excess of duty. Jesus Christ, after working out a perfect righteousness for us, submitted to the penalty of the law as though he were a transgressor; thus bequeathing to the believer his pure and spotless robe of righteousness, for which he had no need himself.

Having thus gone over the ground covered by one subject, let us examine its practical bearing. And, first, we see that faith is founded on the perceptive reason of God, and that it has its source in his revelation of himself. We see that this revelation harmonizes with our knowledge and experience, and that the fruit of it is eternal life; and, secondly, we see why it is that there is so wide a difference between real and nominal Christianity.

How is it that thousands of persons, who admit the truth of Christianity, are still unconverted and unsaved? It is because they are without this evidence of experience—without faith. They admit that Christ died to save sinners; but they refuse to come to Him to be saved. They know that unless a man be born again he cannot enter into the kingdom of God; but they have no desire for a new heart. They accept the testimony of others, but decline to make trial of the gospel for themselves, and the only result of their greater knowledge is to plunge into a deeper perdition; and what can I say to my Christian friends who read the gospel, and yet are still unconverted? Is it not written, "He that knew not his Maker's will and did it not, shall be beaten with few stripes; but he that knew his Master's will and did it not, shall be beaten with many stripes."

But you say, how shall I escape? What way is open to me? How can I make this saving evidence of experience which you have described, my own? I answer, by consi. deration of the truths that bear upon yourself. By thinking of *your* guilt, of *your* ruin, of the love of Christ for *you;* of his bearing *your* sins upon the cross; of *your* pardon, *your* hope, *your* reconciliation to God.

Perhaps I am addressing some who, while disposed to admit the general truths of Christianity, are yet unwilling to accept its direct and practical bearing upon themselves, have not yet concluded to receive revelation as a final and absolute authority.

They ask for stronger and more convincing proof than the existence of a written and reasonable record. They require some signs and wonders ; they demand a demonstration which shall be irresistible. We say that such a demonstration is open to them, and that it lies in this evidence by experience which we have described. The person who accepts the truth in the love of it, receives the highest of all possible demonstrations, viz., that of his own senses ; he sees, he feels, he tastes, he handles the word of life.

There may be a few who would say,—"Show me a good proof that you are right ; give me a sufficient evidence, and I will believe !" Well, my friends, this evidence of experience is the evidence I offer you again ; and indeed it is the only evidence which is of any real value to you, because signs and wonders and human wisdom will never convert you. Even if you received and admitted all the facts and truths of Christianity, it would do you no good without this experimental evidence. Thousands, yea, tens of thousands, call themselves Christians, who of course admit the truth of Christianity, and who know nothing of its power ; and you,

too, who are unconverted, might do the same, and be as god-
less and hopeless as you are now, and will remain so, unless
you give your hearts to the Lord altogether, and receive this
experimental evidence.   But the truth is, there is not the
want of evidence.   It is not the intellect which rebels against
Christ and his gospel, but it is the heart.   If our hearts
were humbled and changed, it would be easy for us to believe
all the rest.   Every difficulty would vanish like the mist off
the waters before the rising of the sun.

I appeal to your consciences.   There is a stern witness
there in my favour.   Even now you cannot entirely suppress its voice.   It troubles and alarms you ; and the day
will come when all the blendings of time and sense will be
swept away, and the call of your consciences will witness
against you in a terrible remorse.   Oh! I entreat you to
think of these things.   Accept the testimony of one who
has himself, by consideration, arrived at the truth.   Accept
the testimony of one who has found a remedy for his sins
and wants—a cure and satisfaction for his soul !   For me it
has brought life and immortality to light.

Try it, my dear friends, for yourselves, and surely it will
do the same for you ; and you, too, will ask no other evidence or signs, for you will then have the greatest evidence
—that of your own experience—which is the power of God
and the wisdom of God.   Amen.

And now I can fancy I hear the fastidious critic, who has
taken the trouble to wade through this production, exclaim,
as he throws himself back in his chair and adjusts the mark
in his book, "What a stupid thing it was of him to publish
that sermon !"   "Why, my dear friend?"   "Because it is
full of blunders and mistakes."   "Well, I am not surprised

at that ; it is my greatest surprise that there are not more
of them. I do not consider a few orthographical mistakes a
fault at all, for your English language does not pretend to
write its words as it pronounces them ; and, I must confess,
there would have been a great many more of these if I had
not constantly referred to the dictionary while preparing it."
" Well, but the composition is faulty." Answer: " I had
not at that time studied either *Quackenbos* or *Whately's
Rhetoric.*" " Well then, your logic is not always clear, nor
your arguments conclusive." " Perhaps not ; but at that
time I had not sufficient command of the language to put in
just the right word in the right place, and perhaps some of
the words I made use of I did not know all the meanings
of." " But, worse than all, your theology is very muddy in
places, especially in regard to the imputed righteousness of
Christ." To this I reply, " My object in inserting this sermon was not to exhibit how much I knew, but how much I
did not know. And now, Mr. Critic, you may turn over
the page, and commence another chapter ; for the sermon is
there, and there it must remain."

CHAPTER VIII.

THE preceding sermon I preached for the first time in the
Wesleyan Methodist Church in Quebec. The church was
crowded to excess. Most of the Protestant religious denominations were represented in the congregation, and even
some of my old Jewish friends. I was particularly interested in these, as I was desirous to know whether it was
a principle of curiosity which had brought them there, or a
sincere desire to arrive at truth. This I was not long in
discovering, for while they listened attentively to all I said,
I could see the exhibition of a feeling of uneasiness, whenever I mentioned the name of Jesus, or spoke of my own
experience. It was not, however, the uneasiness of conviction, but rather that of disgust or impatience, and I fully
expected before the close of the service they would originate
some disturbance. This supposition proved unfounded, for

all passed off quietly, and I was permitted to return home undisturbed.

The next morning I met one of them, a Mr. G——n, who was a very intelligent and respectable man, and one for whom I had always cherished a most particular regard. He accosted me as follows :—" Well, Mr. Freshman, you know I am not one of those who could spit in your presence, or pronounce the common curse over you, for I always respected you, and still have feelings of kind regard for you ; but I must confess I was surprised to hear you repeat such nonsense as I listened to yesterday from you. Of course, I do not believe the report that you have received several thousand dollars for becoming a Christian, for I know your family are in very straitened circumstances, and I believe I am correctly informed, that your children ate nothing yesterday but rice, and even that was sent you as a present by Mr. C——." " Come," said he, " you need not suffer any more. You know I can help you, and all your old friends are similarly disposed. If you will only come back and be our Rabbi, and confess that you renounced your religion in ignorance, we will welcome you cordially, and all will again be well." Thus he continued to urge for about an hour, I all the while listening very attentively. When he had stopped to take breath and collect his thoughts for a fresh attempt, I invited him home to my house, where we could finish the conversation and come to a mutual understanding. This he decidedly refused to do ; and as I had no disposition to let him have everything his own way, we walked together out on the common, and spent about another hour ; but this time I had my *say*, and I occupied the whole of the time in reasoning with him about the Messiah. It was of no avail. Prejudice was stronger than reason. However, he could appreciate the reasonableness of my arguments, and began to be afraid, if he remained any longer in my company, he would be convinced outright; so he turned suddenly to leave me, saying, as he did so :—"One thing I am sure of, and that is, that you are not mad, for I see that you can still talk sensibly; but I am very much afraid a *ruach hotama*—(an unclean spirit)—has taken possession of you. You have done a great injury to my soul already. I bid you good-bye," he continued; "but I know I have committed a great sin in listening so long to a *meshumed*," the name by which every converted Jew is designated. "Good-bye," said I; "I hope the Lord may soon convince you of the errors of your belief." "Shame! Shame!" said he, and ran off. I fear the poor man who, I believe, was "almost persuaded to be a Christian," is still in the "gall of bitterness and the bonds of iniquity."

When I came home, I was surprised to find my eldest son there, for I had engaged him some time before to a Jewish wholesale merchant, to learn the business. "What is the matter?" said I, on meeting him. "Why," said he, "my employer has sent me home, saying he does not require my services any more, since I now am a Christian, and have been baptized." "Never mind, my son," said I, "the Lord will provide something else for you to do yet." And, blessed be His name, He had other and better work in store for him, for he is now a preacher of the gospel, and many precious souls have already been converted to the Saviour through his instrumentality. Just now, as I write, he is engaged in a most glorious revival in the village of Poole, county of Perth. Little did I think, when I thus strove to console him for the loss of his place, that he would one day become the second German Missionary in the Wesleyan Methodist connection. I believe it was in answer to my strong faith in God in those days, that he has since opened up my pathway, and brought me and my family by such a way as we knew not of. Here I may state that my son Jacob, now an ordained minister, never was at a school in his life, except the Sunday-school. All his education has been received at home, under the supervision of his parents ; and perhaps I may say, without parental partiality, that he stands at least as high in the estimation of those to whom it is his privilege to minister, as any of his brethren in the English work, even although they may have the laurels of a University on their brow, and the piety of a Nathaniel in their heart. From his earliest years he was a pious child, and from that time to the present, his moral and religious character has been all that a fond parent could desire. May God keep him faithful unto the end !

When I look back upon those times, I almost wonder that my faith failed not. I had trials to endure which none but God and my own soul know anything about. My family was a sharer with me in many of my difficulties, but my mind was often racked with anxiety which I would not breathe even to the wife of my bosom. However, these were among the "*all things*" that we are assured work for good to those who love God. They taught me patience and endurance. They inspired confidence in God, and many special providences can I recall when relief would come in some time of need, although no human being knew about that need. Bro. Elliott was always very kind to me, and encouraged me to hope that the Lord would open up my way. His own calm and consistent Christian career did more than anything else to "stablish, strengthen, settle me." He wrote a letter to Dr. Nast, of Cincinnati, explaining the circumstances of my conversion and my present position, and asked him if any door of usefulness could be opened for me there.   I saw several openings in other churches, if I had chosen to accept them ; but my heart clung to the Wesleyans, as the heart of Jonathan to David.   I felt it my duty to preach, and yet I could see no prospect of usefulness in this capacity among the Wesleyans, for I well knew I was not competent for the English work.   But I reasoned, if the Lord converted me by means of this church, and has given me such a love for it, He will find something for me to do in it ; and I was not disappointed.

Brother Elliott advised me to travel through the country, deliver lectures, &c., as by that means I could support my family until the Lord would direct me to something more permanent and reliable.   With a view to this, he gave me about a dozen letters of introduction to ministers in different parts of the country.• Ministers of other denominations in Quebec did the same ; and thus, with about thirty letters in my valise, I was about to start from home.   But how was my family to be supported in my absence ?   At that time they had no provision in the house whatever.   In this time of need, also, the Lord was my helper.   It was suggested by some friends that I should deliver a few lectures on Judaism before leaving, from which I might realize enough to meet present necessities.   I immediately fell in with this idea, and by this means, with the help of a few kind friends, I was able to leave them about eighty dollars before I took my leave.

My first visit was to Montreal, where my letters of introduction facilitated me in becoming acquainted, in a short time, with all the Protestant ministers in that place.   Here, for the first time, I met the Rev. J. Gemley, well known in our connection as a small man with a large mind. I experienced the utmost kindness from himself and his interesting family. He proved himself a brother beloved, and I pray the Lord may long spare his life of great usefulness to the church of his adoption. Friends, clerical and lay, vied with one another in kind expressions of regard, and more tangible proofs, also, of their unselfish Christianity. Among the lay friends who are worthy of especial mention, I must not omit that of James A. Mathewson, Esq., a gentleman in every sense of the word, with a large heart and generous disposition. From him I received many tokens of esteem and regard on which my mind to this day delights to reflect as on the bright spots which illumined the dark cloud which hung over that part of my history. May the Lord abundantly reward him in that day when He comes to number up His jewels! I remained in Montreal about two weeks, preaching and lecturing, and was everywhere so well received that I soon forgot all my troubles, and began to enjoy fellowship and communion with my brethren in Christ very much.

But one day, as I was passing the door of an old Jewish friend of mine, I stopped and thought, "I must go in and see how he is getting along, and talk to him about Jesus." With this intention I knocked at his door, but the moment his eye rested upon me his countenance assumed such a fiendish expression as is seldom capable of being put on by the inhabitants of this world. I however offered him my hand, but he indignantly refused to accept it. "What!" said he, "shake hands with a *meshumed?* Never!" and he stamped his feet, and spit out before me several times. "What is the matter?" said I; "is it because I believe that Jesus is the Messiah?" But scarcely had I mentioned the name of Jesus when he lost all control of himself, and worked himself up into such a perfect rage that he actually foamed at the mouth, and 'his flaming eyeballs kindled with such a demoniac glare as I had never witnessed before, and have no desire to witness again. At the same time he made use of such blasphemous language as would make the hair of the inhabitants of Billingsgate stand on end. In short,—

> " Take him for all in all,
> I hope I ne'er shall see his like again. "

" Go," said he at last, "go; and may the curse of God pursue you until your name and memory is blotted out!" Still, my heart yearned for him, and I lingered, thinking, after all, he might become calm, and give me an opportunity to reason with him. But he seemed determined; and I believe if I had not prudently taken my leave, blood would have been shed. " Well," said I, "if I must leave, remember the day will come when you will need a Saviour to save you from eternal condemnation. Good bye." And off I went, all the while reflecting on the blessedness of that religion of Jesus which alone made me to differ from him; and glad, moreover, that I was not afraid to speak of my Saviour, even to one who despised His very name. After remaining about two weeks in Montreal, my ministerial friends made an appointment for me to come again in the month of September, and give them a few more lectures. They did not, however, permit me to return to my family empty-handed.

On my return I could not repress feelings of the liveliest gratitude to God, for having raised up so many kind friends for me in Montreal, many of whom, in various denominations, continue my friends to this day. My confidence in the providence of God was stronger than ever. The more

I experienced of the power of Christianity in my heart, tho better I liked it; and the more frequent exhibitions I witnessed of the enmity of the Jews, the more thankful I felt for having escaped the trammels of a religion which permitted its worshippers to cherish such feelings of bitter animosity; and the more light I received, the stronger was the contrast between my present and my former position.

But now I thought I must write to my friends in Hungary, and tell them what the Lord had done for my soul. I felt an anxiety for the welfare of all mankind, but especially for those of my own flesh and blood, whose minds I still knew were dark and ignorant, still waiting for the coming of a Messiah who had already so gloriously accomplished his mission. I wrote several letters to my own relatives and those of my wife, but in no case did I receive a single answer except once, from my own brother; and from the tenor of his letter, I gathered that they neither wished to know any more about me nor the Saviour whom I had found, and so I was reluctantly compelled to bring my one-sided correspondence to a close. I hope, however, before this time light may have penetrated even the dark places where they still reside.

I now commenced a vigorous attack upon the English language. No one who has learnt it upon his mother's lap can appreciate the difficulty which a foreigner experiences in acquiring a fluent use of its copious, though many times intricate, forms of expression. These have not only been alluded to, but elaborately dwelt upon, by others, and my experience would only be a repetition of that which has been better told by more competent persons, so I shall not here dwell upon it. I wished especially to master the whole field of Wesleyan theology, and compare it with that of other

Christian churches, which differed in any important respects. In this very laudable undertaking I was materially assisted by my best of friends, the Rev. J. Elliott, whose library was always at my service, and of whose time I also engrossed a larger share than I am sure he could very well spare. I felt my deficiency in theology beyond those doctrines, the truth of which I had myself experienced. In my preaching also, when I would have occasion to quote a passage of scripture, I was just as likely to be incorrect as not; for although I read the English Bible a great deal, it was the text of the German which would come up in my memory, and it was a translation from this I used to give in my quotations. This will be seen by a reference to my sermon published in the preceding chapter. But in obviating both these difficulties I was much assisted by Bro. Elliott.

Just about this time I was visited by a Mr. Meyer, a converted Jew, of New York, who happened to be in Quebec. I had the pleasure of returning this visit about four years afterwards, in his own home, in New York. He came in company with Dr. Helmuth, and brought me a Commentary on the Epistles, written in the Hebrew and Chaldaic languages, and sent to me by the author, Dr. Büsenthal, a converted Jew, of Berlin, Prussia. This Commentary did me a great deal of good, and enlightened my mind on many passages. Its gifted author, himself a converted Jew, knew exactly those passages which would be perplexing to the mind of a Jew, and he employed his rare abilities in satisfactorily explaining them. I shall ever be sensible of my indebtedness to him for this valuable present. I afterwards received a very encouraging letter from Dr. Büthensal himself, in which he exhorted me to continue faithful to the end, and hold myself prepared to endure persecutions, not only from the Jews, but from the Christians also. "For, dear brother," said he, "the Gentiles, and even some who are converted, always look with suspicion upon a converted Jew, and no matter how great the sacrifices you make, or how exalted your piety ; no matter how far you exceed them in ability or outshine them in usefulness, still they will always look upon you as a Jew, even though a converted one. Look to Christ, my dear brother, and pay no attention to what they say about you. I know it will be hard for you to find a suitable position in the church ; but wait only on the Lord, and let us thank God, while we reflect, that Paul and Peter were once in the same position." He requested me to write him a detailed account of all the circumstances connected with my conversion, which I accordingly did, and sent the manuscript by the hands of Mr. Meyer, who goes to Europe about once a year.

When the month of September arrived, I was again just about to start for Montreal to meet my engagement there, when I received a very insulting letter from a man who belonged, as he said, to the Church of England, but who, I learned, had originally been a Roman Catholic. He must have been a stupid person, at any rate ; and perhaps, if " Darwin's Theory of the Origin of Species" be correct, we should find one of his forefather's to have had longer ears than usually falls to the lot of a human being,—even a Roman Catholic. In this letter, he said I was bound to give a public reason as a converted Jew why I had not been baptized in and joined the Church of England, as that was the only church which I should have chosen. He further told me I must publish all my credentials from the different Rabbies in Europe, else he would look upon me as an impostor, and treat me as such. Much more such stuff did that precious document contain to the same effect, which I will not burden these pages by transcribing; but I must say I never received more amusement from any letter I ever had sent to me. I, however, took no notice either of the man or his letter; but casually learned soon after that the would-be Church of England man belonged to no church at all; or if he did, it was to that one which existed in the time of the Apostles, and who were called "Busy-bodies-in-other-men's-matters." I suppose they retain the "Apostolic succession," for I have met a few of them in every place where I have gone.

After this little episode, I proceeded to Montreal, in order to meet my engagement there. I was again most cordially welcomed, and my lectures were very well attended; but I must confess I still experienced a great deal of difficulty in using the English language extempore. I could think in it straight along when by myself in my study; but when I was on my feet addressing an audience, the right word for a particular place would come up in four or five other languages, and the poor English word perhaps not be among them at all. I made some amusing mistakes in the selection of some of the words I did use, such as "extinguish" for "distinguish," "distract" for "extract," and such like.* But the good people displayed remarkable forbearance, and even encouraged me to go on, with the hope that I would some day become an Englishman, as far, at least, as the use of the

---

* One of these occurred when I announced for Dr. Nast to preach in Hamilton, and called him one of the most "*extinguished*" men in the German work in the United States. I never discovered my mistake till Joseph Lister, Esq., playfully pointed it out to me after the service.

language was concerned. In this manner I again was enabled to provide food to eat and raiment to put on, for myself and those over whom God had constituted me the guardian and protector. This time I remained a couple of weeks, when I again returned to my home in Quebec.

One morning, shortly after my return, a knock came to my door, and what was my surprise when, in responding to it, the very man who had written me the insulting letter before alluded to, was ushered into my presence. I invited him to be seated, and let me know his business.

"Well," said he, "I would like to know why you did not answer my letter?"

My face immediately relaxed into a broad grin, as I replied, good humouredly,—"I never knew that I was obliged to bark at every dog that barks at me, and so you have my answer; and if you have any more questions of that nature, I am at your service."

He seemed a little disconcerted at my good humour, but seemed determined to insult me if possible.

"Well then," said he, "I would like to know whether you are really a converted Jew, for the Jews around here predict that you will prove to be an impostor before a year is over; and I, as a Christian man, wish to know the real cause you had for resigning your position among the Jews!"

"What do you mean by a converted Jew?" said I. "Do you want to know whether I am a Jew, or whether I have been converted? If you mean the first, I answer,—My father and mother were Jews, and they taught me a great many useful things, which I hope I will never forget. Among others, that it was very impertinent to meddle with things that did not concern me; and as I see that your Christianity did not teach you that, I am that much of a

Jew to this day. If you want to know whether I have been converted or not, I am going to preach to-night, and I shall be very happy to tell you all about it in my sermon."

But this would not do for him. I saw he was about to put to me another of his weighty and unanswerable questions, and in order to be beforehand with him, I said:

"Pray, sir, let me ask you,—Have you been converted yourself?"

"That is none of your business," said he.

"Well, then," said I, "have I not as good a right to ask you why you left the Roman Catholic Church, as you have to ask me why I renounced the Jewish faith?"

Here my man discovered that I was prepared to meet him on his own ground, and make use of his own weapons, so very little more was said by either, and he was not long in taking his leave.

I never could discover what his intentions were. Very evidently there was "a screw loose" in the upper story somewhere. Certainly he was the strangest specimen of a Christian I have ever met with.

Previous to this, and also during this time, I had received and was constantly receiving letters from my ministerial friends in Upper Canada to visit them, and preach or lecture for them. I had contemplated this visit for a length of time, and had devoted a good deal of my leisure towards preparing for it. I was now ready to start, but Mrs. Freshman did not like the idea of parting with me for such a length of time as I intended remaining away, and raised all kinds of objections. She looked upon Upper Canada as a foreign country, and but partially civilized at that :—full of wolves, and bears, and Indians, and rattlesnakes, and all the dreadful things she had ever read about. After, however, disabusing her mind of all fears of danger from these sources, and promising to come back and see her every three weeks, she finally consented to let me go.

Before leaving Lower Canada, I may be allowed to mention the kindness which I experienced from a pious Christian lady named Mrs. Dickson, then residing at Three Rivers. Her elegant home was not only open to receive me, when I visited her, and to accommodate me while I remained, but her Christian conversation and kind encouragement to myself, as well as her many acts of disinterested generosity to my family, endeared her to me beyond measure. I shall never forget a letter which this lady wrote to Mrs. Freshman, while yet unacquainted with her, which is so worthy of being preserved, that, with her kind permission, I take the liberty of here inserting it :—

"THREE RIVERS, July 11, 1859.

"MRS. FRESHMAN,

"My dear sister in Jesus Christ, although I have not the pleasure of being personally acquainted with you, yet I feel a deep interest in your welfare, both spiritual and temporal. I hope that God will raise up for you in the Christian church better friends than you have given up in renouncing Judaism. Though I speak or write of this first, do not think it is first in my mind. No, my dear friend; the salvation of your soul, through the merits of the Crucified, must ever stand foremost. I thank God that the veil has been taken from your heart, and that you not only feel convinced that Jesus of Nazareth is the true Messiah, but that you enjoy His converting grace ; that you can, through Christ, 'read your title clear to mansions in the skies. Glory ! glory to God for his unspeakable gift, and the gift

of the Holy Spirit, which witnesses with our spirits that
we are the children of God!

"Your dear husband's heart is filled with gratitude to
God for your conversion. Next to his own soul, your's was
the most precious to Mr. Freshman. I have not had as
much conversation with him as perhaps I ought. I am
not so free to talk on the all-important subject as perhaps I
should be. That is one of my many faults. But I am much
pleased with Mr. Freshman's spirit. I feel convinced that
he is a sincere follower of the meek and lowly Jesus. Do
not be discouraged because of the difficulties of the way;
you will meet many. Satan will make many assaults on
your faith. He is an enemy that is never discouraged;
when baffled in one way he will attack you in another.
But he is the father of lies—do not believe him; always fly
to Jesus when a doubt or fear crosses you. Mind, Jesus has
said to his disciples, 'Lo, I am with you always, even unto
the end of the world.' We are not left comfortless; the
Holy Spirit is given to be with us forever. May you enjoy
His presence every moment; it is your rich privilege!

"And do not feel disappointed, my dear sister, if you find
many who are called Christians who have not the mind of
Christ, out of the church and in the church. As it was in
olden times, there were many who called themselves Jews
who were not the people of God, because they did not obey
God; so it is in the Christian world. But the religion of
Jesus is true for all that. Jesus has said, 'Let the wheat
and the tares grow together until the harvest,' then it will
be known who has served God and who has served him
not.

"Let your eye of faith be continually fixed on the Saviour,
and he will lead you in the narrowest part of the narrow

way. I hope that you will have the sympathy of the Christian church, and that the Lord will open up a way whereby your dear husband may be able to provide for the wants of his family. The Lord will provide; He has said it. Do not doubt His promise. When Martin Luther found his way hedged up and could see no light, he always read the 46th Psalm, and always found light and comfort there· Try it, my dear sister. I send you a small present, which you may find useful for your little ones. I hope you will soon have your worldly affairs settled to your satisfaction.

"I remain,

"Yours affectionately in Christ,

"HARRIET DICKSON."

This letter, being written at Three Rivers, recalls to my mind a reminiscence of that place. While still a Rabbi, I was called upon to attend the funeral of a Jew who resided there. On this particular occasion, I became acquainted with a relative of the deceased, a Mr. H——, a lawyer, of considerable reputation, himself also a Jew. I conversed with Mr. H—— on the errors of Christianity, at which time I found him very weak in the faith. This only led me the more earnestly to endeavor to persuade him, according to my own belief, that Jesus Christ had no claims whatever to be considered as the Messiah.

The first time I visited Three Rivers again, after my conversion, I sought out this man, thinking he would be a suitable subject to receive the doctrines of the Cross. Imagine my surprise on being told that if I even entered his house he would throw me out of doors! "That cannot be," said I, "I will not believe it." So I went to see for myself. I was told when I went to the door that the master of the house could not be seen. I, of course, did not press the matter, and came away. as I thought it was as civil in him to leave me outside as to let me in and then throw me out. There is plenty of room "out of doors" for every body to live in, even if some houses are too small to contain two individuals. So, with these sage reflections, I came away, thinking I should perhaps never see him again. When I was leaving Three Rivers, however, I was surprised enough to see him on the steamer on which I was travelling. I thought this meeting a providential opportunity afforded me to do him good. With this intention I went forward and offered him my hand. This he not only refused to take, but stared at me, with a look of hatred and utter contempt gleaming from his eyes, and overspreading his countenance. He continued all the while spitting out before me, and using such blasphemous, and even indecent language, that no Jew even could make use of without blushing. I could not restrain the tears from coming into my eyes, as I saw the depth to which the poor fellow had sunk, for I now knew that he was neither a Jew nor anything else that was good and respectable. Poor man! I never gave him any occasion for such an exhibition of passion. On the contrary, I had always endeavoured to do him good, as far as my ability and light would allow. I hope the Lord may convert his poor soul!

But this is a digression; I trust, however, a pardonable one. I was now prepared to start for Upper Canada, but, I must confess, not without fear and trembling. My fears were not of wolves or bears, Indians or rattle-snakes;

but were fears lest my blundering use of the English language should militate against the success of my mission.
I had a great many things to say, if I had only known how
to say them. The Lord was, however, better to me than
my fears and misgivings. What I said and did, heard and
saw, felt and experienced there, must be reserved for
another chapter.

6*

CHAPTER IX.

My first visit to Upper Canada, in the capacity of a lecturer, although looked forward to for a considerable time, and prepared for with some care and much anxiety, was comparatively short. The only place I visited was Brockville, which, though one of the smaller towns, contains very many large-hearted and liberal-minded people. The Wesleyan minister stationed there at that time was the Rev. Mr. Brock, who, from the similarity of his name with that of the town, might be supposed its founder, were it not that the itinerating habits of our ministers preclude the possibility of their founding a city or town during the brief period of their sojourn in any particular place. However, if he was not the founder of the town, he was the finder of most exquisite accommodation for myself; and I was the finder in him of much large-hearted generosity and disinterested benevolence. He opened his church for me and

procured me a congregation, and his pious and devoted help-
mate ministered to my temporal wants; both of them exhibiting such kindness as I shall never forget, and, probably,
never be able to repay. Here, also, I found Dr. Edmonson,
an Elder in the Presbyterian Church, and a good Hebrew
scholar. He at once became my firm friend, and, I am
happy to say, remains so to this day. I was very kindly entertained at his house also, and was much benefitted by his
godly conversation and consistent Christian deportment.
But where all were so kind, time would fail me to specify
each individual. Suffice it to say, that most of the Protestant clergy of the town opened their churches to me, and
permitted me either to preach or lecture to their congregations. I used to think, in those days, I must be a very witty
or humourous speaker, as whenever I would look at my
congregations I could witness the broadest expanse of countenance dilated into the pleasantest of smiles during the progress of my lectures, and sometimes even in my sermons.
I have since either learned more wisdom or have less conceit
in myself, for I now believe it was my foreign accent and
mispronunciation of your "plain English" that excited
most of the smiles aforesaid. However, if I made them
smile, they made me smile too, when I came to witness the
proceeds of the various meetings which I held amongst them;
and if they were as well satisfied as I was, I am sure there
is no occasion for complaint on either side.

But, after all the kindness of the Brockville people, I
began to consider that man a very profound philosopher, and
gifted with a large amount of the knowlege of human
nature, who wrote, "There's no place like home!" Mrs.
Freshman extracted a promise from me before I left my
family, that I would visit her at least every three weeks.

Before the three weeks had expired I was glad enough to return, which I accordingly did, bringing home with me pleasant reminiscences of Upper Canada and its interesting people.

On my return home, I found several letters awaiting my arrival; among the rest, one from the Rev. John Carroll, the Wesleyan minister then stationed at Ottawa, and who is now likely to leave behind him a reputation, as an author, which will not soon be forgotten. His letter invited me to visit him, and preach an anniversary sermon in his church. I hesitated before accepting this invitation, as I knew I would meet with some celebrities in the Wesleyan connexion, before whom I felt a great reluctance to preach, as I had in some of my lectures painfully experienced my deficiency in command of the language. However, after carefully preparing and writing out a sermon, I thought it would answer; and wrote him a reply accepting his invitation, and in a few days I again took leave of my family and started for Ottawa.

I suppose no one can write a book about preachers and preaching, without having some amusing things to tell about them; and, I dare say, no one makes a practice of preaching written sermons without experiencing some mishap, sooner or later. I was not to be an exception, as the sequel will show.

I arrived in Ottawa on the Saturday before I was to preach, with my sermon in my pocket instead of in my head, where it ought to have been. On the Saturday evening a severe storm arose, which continued during the night, and with somewhat moderated violence during the following Sabbath-day. A great deal of damage was done by the gale, and among other things the roof was entirely blown off the Methodist Church in which I was to preach, so that it was impossible to make use of it when the time came. In this emergency, the Town Hall was procured, and the congregation was notified to assemble in it, which they did at the proper hour. Now came the time for my sermon. During the period of preparation for this service, such thoughts as the following had been running through my mind,—" Large church,"—" Great men to hear you,"—" Fashionable congregation,"—" Must give them a great sermon." When I ascended the pulpit, I saw the Rev. Dr. R—— and the Rev. J. Carroll, seated on the platform in front of me ; and I proceeded to insert my " great sermon"—which was written on separate sheets of paper— between the leaves of the Bible. All being ready, the service was commenced as usual, and all proceeded smoothly enough until I had got nicely into my sermon, when a sudden gust of wind, coming through some broken panes of glass in one of the windows of the hall, scattered my manuscript sheets in all directions, and left me standing in shame and confusion before my congregation, and especially before the two distinguished brethren on the platform, before whom I was especially anxious to preach with acceptability! Quick as thought, Bro. Carroll snatched up the scattered leaves, and with that remarkable agility which always characterizes him, jumped into the pulpit and handed them to me. But what was I to do with them ? I had not time to arrange them in order, as they were not even numbered. If ever I called to God for help, it was then. My manuscript was now useless, so I just did the best I could without it ; and in short and peculiar metre, finished that luckless sermon. I could see I had the sympathy of the congregation ; but, after all, not for a great price would I place myself in such a position again. I, however, learned some useful lessons from the circumstance, which, after all, perhaps, were worth the humiliation I experienced. Among these were,—"Never try to preach great sermons; preach Christ." "Never preach to great men, as such, in your congregation; to the poor the gospel is preached." "Never depend so much on notes as on the assistance of the Spirit of God." These lessons, I trust, I shall never forget, and I insert this circumstance for the benefit of others as well as myself.

I lingered in the pulpit after the service was over, hoping the congregation would disperse, as I was ashamed to be seen by them. But in spite of my wishes, and as if to punish me, a good many remained, desirous to speak with me, so I had to come down. None of them embarrassed me, however, by any allusion to my mishap; and Brother Carroll spoke very kindly to me, saying I had done very well under the circumstances, and was sure I would do better the next time. This encouragement, from so good and experienced a brother, determined me to begin to preach extempore, or at least with but very few notes— having a bare outline before me. This, as I acquired additional facility in the use of the language, I was also enabled to do away with, and have had many of my happiest times when I had not even the scratch of a pen before me in the pulpit.

As I had now adopted a somewhat nomadic mode of life, Ottawa was not attractive enough to detain me any very great length of time, nor had I any desire to linger in the scene of my humiliation, so I bent my steps in the direction of Kingston, or rather in the direction of the cars which were starting for Kingston. It will thus be seen that I had an easier method of transfer than that which characterized my early life ; but I do not know that I was any happier. I was still unsettled, and had no notion of settling down as a professional lecturer, with only a run home to my family every three weeks ; and as yet I saw no other prospect. However, I never had reason to complain, as I always experienced the utmost kindness.

When I arrived in Kingston, I went to the home of the Rev. Mr. Grey, the Presbyterian minister of that place. He took me round to see the sights, and kindly entertained me during my stay there. I spent a very happy week in the city, during which I became acquainted with the Rev. Mr. Ebstein, a converted Jew, whom the Presbyterians (the Old Kirk) were about to send as a missionary to the Jews in Palestine. Before doing so, however, they were going to send him to New York to learn the medical profession. This appeared very strange to me. I could not understand why a man, whose business it was to preach the gospel, should spend three years of the most valuable period of his life, at an expense of more than three thousand dollars, in studying a profession which had not the most remote connection—as far as I could see—with preaching the tidings of salvation to fallen man.

"Why," said I, to Dr. Macher, with whom I had some conversation about him, "why not give him a thorough theological training, and teach him the languages spoken by the people among whom he is to labour, so that he may be able to cure all mental and spiritual maladies, instead of teaching him, in New York, to cure diseases which he will likely never meet with in the Holy Land?"

"A knowledge of the medical profession," replied Dr. Macher, "will be more likely to procure him a favourable

reception among them, and inspire them with confidence in
him ; then, when he has gained their confidence as a physi-
cian, it will be all the easier for him to break to them the
bread of life."

"I do not believe a word of it," said I; "no Jew will
ever place any more confidence in him on account of his
profession ; and, for my part, I have no faith in the success
of his mission.   I would rather send him to the heathen,
for it is my belief that the heathen are first to be converted,
and then, with the fulness of the Gentiles, the Jews will
be brought in."

During another conversation with Dr. Macher, after I
became better acquainted with Mr. Ebstein, the Doctor
asked me what I thought of him (Mr. Ebstein).

"Well," said I, "I found him a very intelligent and
clever man.   I believe he is a pious man, too; and he has
a pretty good knowledge of the Hebrew language."

"Yes," said the doctor, "and that is the reason we send
him as a missionary to the Jews."

I still had my doubts, however, as to his success, and told
the doctor,—"Before two years are over, your mission will
prove a failure."   .

I am sorry to say that I possessed the gift of prophecy
once, at least, in my life; for after that church had expended
thousands of dollars on their missionary, and kept him there
over two years, he did not succeed.   He is there still, it is
true, but not as a missionary.   He is only a "doctor," trying to heal the poor bodies of the benighted Jews, while
their minds are still beclouded with worse than Egyptian
darkness.

About three years afterwards, I met Dr. Macher, who
said to me, "After all, you were right about Mr. Ebstein

and our mission to the Jews, for we have already had to abandon it."

While in Kingston, I preached in the different churches on Sabbaths, and gave a few lectures during the week; after which I took the cars for Toronto, where I became acquainted with, and was the guest of, that well-known and deservedly esteemed Christian gentleman, John McDonald, Esq., whose Christian benevolence and princely liberality place him on a higher pedestal than that accorded to blood-stained warriors or triumphant conquerors, and give him a more lasting title to the remembrance of posterity than polished brass or costly marble can furnish. Although since that time he has been elected member of parliament for Toronto, and greatly prospered in his worldly business, he still continues the same humble, generous, devoted, self-sacrificing Christian gentleman—still answering the description of that couplet :—

"A man was thought by all the country mad ;
The more he cast away, the more he had."

The Revs. George Douglas and John Borland were the superintendents of the two circuits into which Toronto was at that time divided. Both of them received me very cordially, and afforded me every facility to preach or lecture, as the case might be. I became acquainted, also, with several of the ministers belonging to other churches, preached for some of them, and delivered a few lectures on "Judaism." The cordiality with which I was everywhere received, and the cheerfulness and elevated Christian piety of my noble host, contributed greatly to my temporal happiness, and, I trust, also to my spiritual welfare and growth in grace.

The kindness of the Rev. W. Pollard, and his good and amiable lady, I shall never forget.

During the delivery of my lectures I used to be favoured
with the presence of a number of Jews.   One night I mentioned, among other things, a Jewish ceremony which is
practised by each of the orthodox among the Jews, and consists in taking a living fowl, on the day before the atonement, and striking it three times against his head, and
saying, "Be thou my sacrifice : this fowl is now to be killed,
and I shall go to eternal life."   During the recital, I had
noticed a Jew in the congregation who was evidently ill at
ease.   He appeared as if about to interrupt me, and hardly
had I finished when up he jumped, appearing very much
excited, and said :—

"If the audience will allow me, I would like to say that
this is not so ; there never was such a thing done among the
Jews."

I simply requested the chairman, Rev. Mr. Borland, to
allow me to convince him that he was wrong—to do which
I had only to take his own prayer-book, and read to him
first in the Hebrew, and then to the audience in English,
the very portion of the ceremony to which I alluded, and
with which every little Jewish boy ought to be well acquainted.   This was an argument which he could not answer,
and he had to sit down in great confusion, amid the plaudits
of the congregation.   It turned out that the poor would-be
Jew knew very little about his own religion.   I am sorry
to say there are a great many Jews of that class, whom I
shall notice more fully in my lectures on "Judaism," which
I intend to publish.   Another instance, however, just here,
may not be out of place.

The next Saturday, after delivering the lecture above mentioned, I was walking leisurely through the market, when I
observed a man carrying a side of pork on his shoulder.

I immediately recognized him as a son of Abraham, and was surprised enough to see the double desecration both of the moral and ceremonial laws. I accosted him with the question :—

"Are you not a *Yehuda?*" (Jew).

"Yes," he replied, "I am;" and seemed to glory in his statement.

"But," said I, "is not this your Sabbath?"

"Why, yes," said he; "but what of that?"

"How in the world," said I, "can you thus publicly violate your law, and desecrate your Sabbath?"

"Violate the law!" said he, "what law? The whole world goes to market to-day."

"It is the law of Moses I mean," said I; "do you not know you are doubly violating his law?"

"The law of Moses! Pshaw!" said he. "What has Moses to do with me here in America? This is a free country."

"But, then," said I, "how can you buy such unclean '*chassir?*'" (pork).

"Ha! ha!" laughed he; "unclean stuff, do you call it? It is the best stuff in the world! I guess if Moses himself were here, he would eat it with me. I tell you, my dear friend," he continued, (thinking me to be a Gentile), "you Christians and we Jews are both humbugged. Moses and Jesus were very smart fellows, but I guess they could not do much now-a-days; we are too wide-awake for them. We know more than to believe in such nonsense!"

"But," said I, "you are a Jew."

"Yes," said he, "and will die one."

"Well," said I, "I was one too, but I am now a Christian."

"Ha! then you are the man who lectured last night!"

"I am," said I. "Were you there?"

"No," said he. "What is the use for me to go and hear a *meshumed?* I was born a Jew, and will die a Jew. I believe on *Torath Masche,* (the law of Moses), and do not want anything to do with your Christianity."

"Why," my dear friend," said I, "you just now said that we were all humbugs; that Moses himself was a humbug, and you did not care what he had written; and now you believe in the *Torath Masche,* do you?"

"My load of pork gets very heavy," said he. "I must hurry home," and off he went.

This is but one of numerous instances which might be adduced, how evil men and seducers wax worse and worse, deceiving and being deceived. I observed also in Toronto that many of the Jews keep their business places open during the whole of Saturday, (their Sabbath).

On Sabbath, I preached in Richmond Street Church; and on coming home in the evening with my kind host, I overheard the following conversation between two ladies who were behind us, and very evidently unaware of our close proximity :—

"Well, have you seen the Jew now?" said one.

"Yes," replied the other, "but I was greatly disappointed."

"How! in his preaching?"

"No, not at all, for I don't care a great deal for any one's preaching; but I certainly was disappointed in his appearance. Why, he looks just like any other man. I always thought a Jewish Rabbi must have a peculiar appearance—fossilized, or musty, or antiquated, or something of that kind. We read about them in old books of antiquity, and the New Testament, and such old-fashioned books. If I had known as much before, I would rather have joined Mr. and Mrs. ———, who called on me after tea to take a walk."

" Why," said the other, " I enjoyed the service very much, especially the prayer. (It was the Rev. Mr. Douglas who prayed). Of course the poor man who preached could not speak English very well, but I liked what the Methodists call his experience."

And thus they went on until we came to a lamp-post, when I intentionally turned abruptly round to let them see me. This little manœuvre brought their conversation to a close, and if there was not silence, it was at least only in whispers, loud enough, however, for me to hear them for a short time, and understand that they felt guilty ; for after a whispered, " Why, that is the very man we have been talking about," they became quite silent.

However, I had the consolation of knowing that I was not the only preacher whose sermon is criticised in these walks home from church.

Before leaving Toronto, I had the pleasure of being introduced to the late Rev. Dr. Stinson, who was then President of the Conference. I also became acquainted with several of our distinguished fathers and brethren in the ministry. Among the rest, the Rev. R. Jones introduced me to the Rev. Enoch Wood, D.D., our worthy and distinguished Superintendent of Missions, who has perhaps for a longer time than any other man enjoyed the fullest confidence of his brethren, and occupied the highest positions in their power to bestow. Bro. Jones invited me to accompany him to Dundas, where he was stationed. I gladly accepted his invitation, and soon became greatly attached to him.   He has always proved himself a zealous Christian, and a devoted brother in the Lord.

I again met with the Rev. J. Carroll on my return from Dundas to Toronto, who was there on business.   He proposed that I should join the church at the coming Conference, as in all probability they would open a mission among the Germans, and employ me as their missionary.   I gladly assented to the proposal, as I always had a warm heart for the Methodists; and after completing my visit to Toronto, I went home rejoicing that the Lord had thus opened up a way for me, in which my whole time might be employed in the great work of saving souls.

When I arrived again in Quebec, I found Bro. Elliott very glad that the authorities in Conference had taken an interest in the German work, and told me to hold myself in readiness to be examined at the May District Meeting, as it was only through that I could be recommended to the Conference.   The late Rev. Dr. Stinson also spoke kindly to me, and encouraged me; and, in fact, all the principal ministers with whom I conversed were well-disposed towards me, with one single exception.   I thought his opposition very strange at the time; but with a thankful heart I can now say that even he has become one of my best friends; yes, more than a friend—a brother beloved!

Before the District Meeting, I visited London, where the Rev. G. R. Sanderson and Dr. Cooney were stationed.   I immediately liked Bro. Sanderson, and still esteem him highly as a sincere and upright brother in the ministry.   Dr. and Mrs. Cooney were also very kind to me; but time would fail me either to tell the number of places I visited, or mention the names of all from whom I experienced kindness. Wherever I went, however, I always found our ministerial brethren prepared to receive me kindly and welcome me heartily, both in their churches and in their houses. Never, while memory holds her seat, shall I forget the many acts of kindness which I experienced, and the many happy hours I have enjoyed with our brethren while travelling before my reception into the ministry. Old as well as young seemed to vie with one another in making me happy, and helping me on. During this period I formed acquaintances with our ministers, which soon ripened into the warmest friendship—friendships formed on earth which I trust shall endure till time shall be no more, and then only become more firmly cemented in heaven.

During these visits, and this intercourse with our brethren, I learned a great many things; and inspired by their holy conversation and godly deportment, I was enabled to grow in grace day by day. I sincerely pray that those devoted men, to whom I am so much indebted, may long live to teach others, by precept and example, the straight and narrow way, not only to obtain the forgiveness of sins, but that full salvation; that perfect love, which casteth out fear; that holiness of heart without which no man shall see the Lord! May they continue in labours more abundant, until the Divine Master shall say, "It is enough, come up higher."

"There we shall meet again,
  When all our toils are o'er,
And death, and grief, and pain,
  And parting are no more :
We shall with all our brethren rise,
And grasp thee in the flaming skies."

When it became known that it was likely I should join the Wesleyan Church and become a German Missionary, the

Jews in Quebec again made a vigorous effort, and offered powerful inducements to dissuade me from it, but I am happy to say without effect. My family were now effectually separated from all their attachments to Judaism, and firmly grounded in the principles of Christianity; and instead of now opposing my progress, entered heartily into it. It was with their full consent and concurrence I began to prepare myself for the District Meeting. I felt, while being there examined, more like a school-boy again than at any period during the past twenty years, and I daresay I had some difficulty in fully expressing my answers to all the questions then put to me; but the brethren bore with me, and expressed themselves satisfied with my views on theological doctrines, my experience and abilities, and cordially recommended me to be received at the approaching Conference, to be held in Kingston. Between District Meeting and Conference various inducements were again held out to me to join other churches; but, as I have before stated, my attachment to the Methodist Church, its doctrines, and many of its ministers, rendered all such efforts powerless to change my purpose, and although I have done a great many things in my life that I am sorry for, I trust I shall never be sorry that God thus directed me into this providential pathway.

As I was now interested in the sayings and doings of Conference, I visited it at the commencement of its session, and was introduced to most of the brethren present, with whom I was unacquainted, and renewed my acquaintance with such as I had previously met. I had great pleasure during Conference of being with the Rev. Dr. Jeffers, at the home of Mr. and Mrs. Cowan, whom I pray the Lord may abundantly reward for all their kindness to me! I found the society of Dr. Jeffers very agreeable, and soon discovered that he had a mind of a very superior order. Since then I have become greatly attached to him ; and his efficient services as editor of the *Christian Guardian*, now for several years, fully justifies the opinion I first formed of his mental qualifications and ability.

I shall never forget my impressions on witnessing the first session of Conference which I attended. How different from the assemblies of the Rabbies ! Here were about three hundred assembled from all parts of the country, all engaged in the service of that Saviour whom I had despised. The grave and dignified deportment of the elder brethren, the precision with which they despatched all kinds of business when it came up ; the cheerfulness which beamed from the countenances, and sparkled in the eyes of the younger ones ; the love and Christian harmony which pervaded the whole, and their devotion to a common cause, which bound old and young together ;—all were calculated to form an impression on my mind not easily to be forgotten. During the session, a debate arose in regard to myself, whether I should be received into full connexion, or only taken on trial. A great many were in favour of my reception immediately. A few, however, were more cautious, and spoke in favour of giving me one year of trial at least. I have no reason to think that these brethren were even then actuated by a spirit of antagonism to myself, but merely from prudential motives. However, be that as it may, I am happy to be able now to say that those who then opposed my reception into full connexion, have now become my friends, all of whom I highly esteem ; but among them is one whom I more than esteem—I love as a dear and affectionate brother in the Lord.

7

The result of the debate, however, which did not last long, nor become very warm, was the decision that I should at once be received into full connexion and ordained. Accordingly, on Sabbath, June 10th, 1860, I was ordained by the late Rev. Dr. Stinson, assisted by the principal officers and members of the Conference; and Hamilton and its vicinity, embracing the whole of Canada, was appointed as my future sphere of labour among the Germans, under the supervision of the talented and venerable Rev. E. Wood, D.D., General Superintendent of Wesleyan Missions.

After my ordination, I preached in Kingston from the text, "This is the day which the Lord hath made : we will rejoice and be glad in it."—Ps. cxviii. 24. I then visited Hamilton, to make preparations for moving my family thither. In Hamilton I was the guest of the Rev. S. D. Rice, D.D., and the first day at dinner he very pleasantly introduced me to a large piece of pork, thinking I had not yet met with that commodity as an article of diet. I give him all due credit for his good intentions, but must award the merit of such introduction to the Rev. Mr. Warner. However, if Dr. Rice did not afford me this pleasure, which he anticipated, I must acknowledge his services in another capacity, which were more grateful and acceptable to myself. He very kindly assisted me in procuring a suitable residence, and was always ready to give me a helping hand and assist me with his valuable counsel in every time of need. While in Hamilton, Dr. Rice was to be my superintendent ; and I am truly thankful to God for bringing me, at the outset of my career, into contact with a man so well qualified in every way—by piety, by education, by experience, and by a profound acquaintance with human nature—to become my instructor in those very points in which my own education and experience had been defective. After procuring a residence, and making other preliminary preparations, I set off to Quebec, to pack up my goods and chattels, and move my family to Hamilton. But before doing so, I must not forget to mention the extreme kindness of Joseph Lister, Esq., and his amiable lady, to myself and my family. I trust they may be rewarded in the day of the Lord with good measure, pressed down, shaken together, and running over! As my removal to Hamilton was an epoch in my life, the recital of its labours, its trials, and its successes, may well be reserved for consideration in another chapter.

CHAPTER X.

THE first Sabbath after we arrived in Hamilton, I went to
hear a brother of the "Allbright" denomination preach.
He preached in the Presbyterian Church to a congregation
of about twenty people ; and although they had kept up
their mission in the above city for about seven years, they
appeared to have but slight success. His was the first
sermon I had ever heard in the German language. The
text was,—"Is there no balm in Gilead?" The sermon
contained some good things, but was very simple in its style,
and devoid of all arrangement. There was none of the fire,
or zeal, or energy, which I had seen exhibited among the
English Methodists. I must however say, in behalf of the
"Allbrights," that they have got converted people amongst
them.

There were, besides these "Allbrights," a good many
Lutherans—but no pastor. Also some Roman Catholics ;

and many who cared for no religion, and were " living without God, and having no hope in the world."

The trustees of the John Street Wesleyan Methodist Church very kindly offered me the use of that building in which to hold service on Sabbath afternoons. I also commenced, during the week, to visit from house to house ;— talking to the people about their souls, and inviting them out to hear me preach. The first Sabbath my congregation numbered about a dozen. After preaching to these, I announced that I would again hold service on the Wednesday evening, in the large vestry of the same church. ·

This I continued to do ; visiting, in the meantime, from house to house, and was gratified to see my congregation steadily increase, until at the end of about six months it numbered about fifty persons. These were of opinion, that, if they had a church of their own they would be better satisfied, and also that we should have more success. I had but very liitle experience in such matters, but I immediately went to work with a will, and we very soon had a neat little church erected on Rebecca Street, which, I trust, will never prove any discredit to the connexion ; but, with the blessing of God, may result in the conversion of many poor souls from nature's darkness into the marvellous light of the gospel of Christ !

While the building of this church was being talked about, a strange circumstance happened, which it may not be out of place here to relate :—

Before we advertised for tenders, a German carpenter came to me, wishing to borrow four dollars. I was anxious to oblige him ; but, not having the money myself, I sent my son to borrow it from the Rev. George Douglas. I did this without any misgivings, as the man promised to return the money the next week, as he then said he would have plenty of work. Bro. Douglas gave the money readily, and I handed it over to Mr. K——, the carpenter. He received it with thankfulness, and promised to come to church next Sabbath. I have found some of the Germans very ready to promise, and would therefore recommend these,—as well as many others afflicted with a similar propensity,—to study the common-sense problem, given in an old book :—

> " They who are always promising,
>   The weakness of their minds betray ;
> How can they ever keep a thing
>   Which they so often give away ?"

However, according to promise, Mr. K—— was at church the next Sabbath, and appeared very attentive. He came regularly to church for a few weeks, and even gave me his name, as wishing to join—but the four dollars came not ! I soon discovered his motive in coming to church, for when I reminded him of his failure to return what I had lent him, he said he would pay it in work on the church.

" Besides," said he, " if you are a good man, and feel as much interest in the German people as you pretend to do, you will get me the job for the whole of the carpenter's work on the church."

" That," said I, " I cannot do, as the work is to be given to the man who will agree to do it for the lowest figure, and is, in other respects, satisfactory ; but if you send in your tender you will stand as good a chance in getting the work as any one else."

This he said he would do ; and on the evening appointed to receive the tenders, he and some of his friends were present. His tender was found to be two hundred dollars higher than any one of the others—so, of course, we could not employ him. His sordid and base motives, in joining the church, then began to exhibit themselves, as he indig-nantly exclaimed, — "I shall never again have anything more to do with either you or your church!" He became very angry, but gave no violent outburst of his passion, in the expression of his feelings, whilst in our presence. He and his friends then left the room, and he never entered our church again.

I would have been very glad if he had kept his promise, and never had any anything to do with us again; but alas! it was not so. His doings, however, were all in the way of opposition. On Sundays he used to watch for our people as they were returning from church,—molesting, insulting, and cursing them and their preacher.

This practice he continued for some time; when, on a cer-tain Sabbath, as he stood as usual, reviling our people on their way from church, and with uplifted arm threatening them, his wickedness seemed to have culminated. The sen-tence was pronounced,—"Thou fool, this night thy soul shall be required of thee!" On that very night he was struck with apoplexy, and before morning he was a lifeless corpse!

Strange to relate, the hand which had been uplifted in a threatening attitude towards the people of God, was found after death in that uplifted position, stiff and cold, so that it was found impossible to bring it to its proper position without breaking the bone; and rather than do that, a coffin was made to fit the position of the arm. Did any one ever harden himself against the Lord and prosper?

Our church, when completed, if it had no other merit,

had at least that of being the first German Wesleyan Church in Canada.

As our minds go back over one hundred years, and contemplate the infancy of Methodism on this continent; as we see it cradled in that first church in John Street, New York;* and look forward during the next hundred years, —who can tell what may be the position of our German work in Canada at the end of that time! One thing is very certain,—we have the same God to smile upon us as Embury and Webb, Pilmoor and Boardman, and the host of other heroic and devoted men, their co-laborers, had to smile upon them. We have scarcely more difficulties to contend against. than they had to encounter; and so far we have no reason to complain of our want of success. May the Lord make every German Missionary "in labours more abundant!"

When our church was completed, we secured the efficient services of the Rev. Dr. Nast, of Cincinatti, and the Rev. Dr. Wood, of Toronto, to dedicate it to the worship of God. Thus, it will be seen, if we were small we were ambitious; for nothing less than the services of two of the most eminent men—the one, in Canada, noted for his connection with the work of Wesleyan Missions; and the other, for his connection with the German work in the United States—would satisfy us; and we were abundanly repaid in the rich showers of blessings which attended the ministrations of those devoted servants of God.

---

* Strange coincidences often happen. The German work was commenced in John Street, Hamilton, and the German Church was built on the street bearing the same name as my old grandmother, who first called me her *Tana Gaddell.*

Dr. Nast remained with me a few days, and assisted me in a protracted meeting which I started, and which, I am happy to say, resulted in the conversion of about twenty souls. This was very encouraging to me, but it was not without its drawback, as is true of most sublunary things. Previous to the commencement of the revival, I had about seventy names of regular attendants on my ministry; but alas! not one of them converted.

As soon as I began to enforce the discipline among these, and urge the necessity of being converted, in addition to lives of morality, a great many of them left me, and came back no more. I am thankful, however, that the Lord did not forsake me, as the gracious out-pouring of his spirit a short time after may attest; and from that time I determined to acknowledge no members but those who were truly converted to God. Many, I am happy to say, are now witnessing a good confession on earth, and some have already been gathered into the garner of the Lord. To His name be all the glory!

During the week I used to visit places outside of Hamilton, searching out Germans, and preaching to them. On one occasion I went as far as Pembroke, where we have now an established mission. I also visited Preston, and other places in the county of Waterloo, where I found a great many Germans perishing for lack of knowledge; but where, I am now thankful to say, we have several efficient labourers employed, and which has become the centre of the whole German work in the Dominion. During these excursions I got an insight into the extent of the field which was to be worked, but had to lament that I was alone in it; and as I could not be in more than one place at one time, I was very anxious to obtain an assistant.

7*

The Lord was, however, raising me up one from a source which I little expected. My eldest son, who had always been a pattern for piety, even in the Jewish Church, when he became converted, threw himself into the service of Christ with all his heart. At this time he was scarcely eighteen years of age, and yet had already begun to supply for me in my absence, and soon began regularly to travel as a local preacher; so that in cases of emergency, I found him of great service as an assistant, and used to hear very good accounts of him from those places which he visited. This induced me to hope and believe that the Lord was preparing him also to work a work among the Germans— "a work which they would not believe, even though a man should declare it unto them."

My first year's experience in Hamilton taught me that the Lutherans and other German denominations cherished anything but a friendly feeling towards me; and very soon I and my family had to suffer reproach and persecution at their hands. Still, I did not waver in my duty, but determined to go straight on in the name of my Lord and Master.

But external trials were not the only ones I had to surmount. I had internal difficulties to master. In the first place, I had no religious German books out of which to study, except the Bible. I found this a great deprivation, for unless a person will study, he cannot improve his mind. I tried to obviate this difficulty by translating some of Wesley's sermons into the German language. This was a most unsatisfactory process, and very little to my taste; and I was glad to discover, some little time after, that the Rev. Dr. Nast had translated the whole of them into German, and had already published the book. I immediately wrote for it, and derived great benefit and blessing from reading it. I used to carry the volume sometimes to the Lutherans, and tell them to examine for themselves, whether there was any difference between Wesley and Luther.

"Wesley, you see," I would say, "preaches 'ye must be born again,' and so does Luther."

One Lutheran said to me, "It is true that Luther believed in the new birth; but what he meant by being born again refers to a process which takes place after death."

"Ah!" said I, "I am afraid you never read your Bible, or you could not talk in that manner."

"Read my Bible!" said he. "Certainly I do! I have read it so much that I have become tired of it."

"If that is the case," said I, "your Bible must be pretty well used up by this time; will you let me see it, and I will prove to you that the new birth does not take place after death?"

He searched up and down, high and low, but no Bible was to be found in his house.

He appeared greatly confused, but at last stammered out, "I do not want to have anything to do with you Methodists." And, opening the door, "I am a Lutheran," said he, "and mean to live and die in the faith of my fathers."

Seeing the door open I took the hint, thinking to myself, "You are not even a good Lutheran, for if you were you would not speak a falsehood."

Another difficulty I now experienced was the want of German hymn-books. This I tried to obviate by translating some of the English hymns into the German language. These I would write out on slips of paper and distribute among the people; but this was a slow process, and only furnished a scanty supply. But even with this scanty supply, who was to sing! I could not raise a tune myself, nor could I find one in my congregation who was able to do so. In this emergency the Lord provided for me, and that again in my own family. My second daughter, who was then only nine years of age, but had a clear and musical voice, and withal had even then made great progress in musical acquirements, came to our rescue and led the singing; and by-and-by we formed a choir, with my little daughter at the instrument. A choir could not long be contented with a few hymns on slips of paper, so I introduced the German hymn-book used by our brethren in the United States; but so bigoted were some of the Lutherans that they strongly objected to sing from a Methodist hymn-book, or even to take one in their hands.

I was a close observer of our English brethren, and whatever I saw beneficial in their great churches, I strove to adopt as far as possible in our little one. One thing thus adopted was the Sabbath-school. I had always appreciated it ever since my introduction to it in Quebec, before my conversion. I however had no one to commence with but my own children; but thanks to a kind Providence, they were already numerous enough to fill up a corner even in a large church. Four of them I placed in a class; a fifth, I appointed a teacher; a sixth, was librarian; and last, but not least, was the seventh—the singer. From this small commencement it increased by degrees until it numbered about forty.

This seems to be the place to mention with thankfulness the kindly assistance and efficient services rendered to me in this department by Miss Davis, now Mrs. Chisholm, extending over a period of more than two years. Her memory is still in that Sabbath-school, and in my family especially, as ointment poured forth.

About this time a very learned German gentleman, by the name of B——, came to the city of Hamilton. He was by profession a lithographer. As soon as I became acquainted with him, I invited him to come to church.

"Well," said he, "although I do not believe in Christianity, still I will come and hear you preach."

Sure enough, according to his promise, he came the next Sabbath, which made me think he was at least an honest man; for often when I would ask the Germans to come, they would promise me a dozen times for once that they would come. Mr. B—— not only came, but remained after service, and said to me:—

"Sir, I thank you for your discourse, and, if possible I shall regularly attend your church."

After this it was an unusual thing to see his place vacant. He used to pay great attention to the preaching; and I often thought, if only the Lord would convert his soul, what a fine missionary he would make to extend our labours among the Germans! I paid him marked attention; visited him frequently, lent him books, and assisted him in his temporal affairs; but above all, urged him constantly to give his heart to God. This he promised me he would endeavour to do, and soon after he joined the church, and helped us in the Sabbath-school, although not yet clearly converted. But on a certain Sabbath, as I was preaching from the following words, "Though I speak with the tongues of men and of angels, and have not charity, I am become as sounding brass or a tinkling cymbal," he professed to have found peace with God; and, coming to me next morning, said, he was now prepared to go and preach the gospel to the ends of the earth. I, having little experience in such matters at that time, asked the authorities for permission to employ him immediately as a travelling assistant in our work. But they were gifted with a more prudent foresight, and advised me first to try him for a few months. This, they told me, I could do by taking him with me on a missionary tour, letting him preach and conduct the services; during which time I could form an opinion of him, and, if favorable, he could then be regularly employed.

In accordance with this advice, I took Brother B—— with me to Preston, and told him that we should preach every night in a different place, among the Germans of Waterloo county. "Above all," said I, "be sure you tell the people everywhere how the Lord converted your own soul, as it will do them more good to hear it from you, who were yourself an infidel, than if I should tell it to them; and such preaching is more efficacious with them than any other."

"Very well," said he; "I will try."

We first came to Preston, where he preached in the evening, but not one word about his conversion. This I thought very strange, but thought in the embarrassment of his first sermon he might have forgotten it. After service, we remained all night under the hospitable roof of Robert Hunt, Esq., sen., whose kind hospitality I have often shared. Mr. B—— and I occupied one room, and I observed he went to bed without even saying his prayers. I was shocked—almost horrified—at the thought of a Christian going to sleep without first commending himself to God, and asking Him for protection! I almost feared to sleep with him, still I had to do it, mentally resolving to admonish him for his conduct in the morning.

When morning came, we had to start for Waterloo village, travelling by the stage, which started from the North

American Hotel at eleven in the morning. While waiting for the stage, he said :—

"I would like something to eat."

"Well," said I, "we will soon be in Berlin, where we can get our dinner; but, if you are hungry, I suppose the hotel-keeper here can give you a bite."

So I ordered some bread and cheese, and a cup of tea for him, which he devoured with an appetite; after which he called for a glass of beer. I felt mortified beyond measure, and on our way to Berlin I began to reason with him on his conduct. First, as to his conduct on the preceding evening, and then in regard to the beer.

"What," said I, "will the Missionary Board say to me when I present them my bill for travelling expenses, among which will be found an item for beer! And further," said I, "you must know that the money which we receive, comes from the poor as well as the rich, and the five cents which you spent for beer, may have been the last mite of some poor woman, which might have been better employed in procuring food for her children. Besides," said I, ' if you must drink at all, never drink in a hotel; for while all things may be lawful for us, all things are not expedient."

He appeared to be very sorry, and promised to be more careful in the future; but alas! scarcely had we returned home ere I ascertained that he had spent a whole night in Mr. G——'s hotel, drinking freely all the time. I was very sorry to hear this, as he had unquestionable abilities, and went to see him the next morning; but he frankly told me that he did not feel fit to be a Methodist Missionary.

"Well," said I, "take care that you do not lose your soul."

"Oh! as to that," said he, "I guess I am all right."

Right or wrong, I was surprised to hear that he preached to a Lutheran congregation the very next Sabbath, and shortly afterwards their Synod took him in, and ordained him as one of their preachers. So ended my first attempt to secure the services of a regular assistant in the work.

A short time after this, I was sent down to the neighborhood of Ottawa, to open up a mission among the Germans there. I was still, I might say, alone on the field of labor, which was a very large one; and one or two additional missionaries might easily have found employment. I was authorized to write to Dr. Nast, and ask for assistance from the other side; but they had none to spare. Nothing daunted, however, I proceeded to the Ottawa, and stopped awhile at Portage du Fort, where the Rev. Mr. Morton resided, who was that time Chairman of the Pembroke District. This good brother was very kind to me—took an interest at once in the object which had brought me there; went around with me to the different places where Germans and Poles were to be found, and to whom I preached in their respective languages. I found these poor people famishing for the bread of life, and I was the first person to break it to them; so the Wesleyan Methodist Church has the credit of being the first to introduce the gospel among the poor people of that destitute neighborhood. Here I found many poor souls scattered up and down in the woods, like sheep without a shepherd, having no man to care for their souls. Even the Lutheran Church, which claims all the Germans as the children of her inheritance, did not think it worth its while to provide these poor forsaken ones with the gospel of Christ; the reason, I suppose, being that the people were too poor to support a teacher. But strangely enough, scarcely had we sent a missionary amongst them, when their temporal circumstances began to improve; so much so, that almost simultaneously three other denominations—the Lutheran, Allbright, and Church of England—thought it now their duty not to let these people perish for lack of the gospel. Bro. Schmidt was our first missionary to them, procured for us by the united efforts of Rev. J. Carroll and James A. Mathewson, Esq., of Montreal ; but his constitution was fragile. His health soon failed him, and, before a year had elapsed, he was called to his reward.

Mr. L——— was sent to supply his place, and in the commencement of his career gave great promise of usefulness ; but, unfortunately, it was not of long continuance. He was found to be unfit for the work after a period of trial, and his name was dropped. Still the Lord was not unmindful of us, and his place was supplied by a young brother— although married—named Charles Allum, who lived in Peterborough, while Bro. Carroll was there. He willingly offered himself for the German work, in fact seemed very desirous of being employed. Bro. Carroll also gave him a good recommendation ; but when I came to examine him, I found he had almost forgotten his mother tongue. Still, I encouraged him to come to Hamilton, where I could assist him in preparing for his work. This he did. and was then sent down to the Ottawa to supply the place of Bro. L———.

I have several times hinted at the despite in which we were held by the Lutherans, and in fact by most of the German sects ; but I despair of ever being able to give an adequate idea of the extent to which this feeling prevailed among the Lutherans, and its depth and virulence with certain individuals.

A Methodist! Why, the very name was enough to drive a German as far away from me as he would run from a rattlesnake, and a great deal farther than I could persuade them to run from the devil; although I sometimes gave his Satanic Majesty a black enough coat, and a far blacker character! I was for a long time at a loss fully to account for this deep enmity; but a letter, which fell into my hands on one occasion, partially opened my eyes, a translation of a part of which I subjoin. The letter is dated "Manheim, 1860;" and is addressed to Pastor Stalsehmidt, a Lutheran minister, and is written by another minister of the same church. The following is the extract :—

"There is a certain converted Jewish Rabbi, named Dr. Freshman, who is connected with the Wesleyan Methodist Church, and is travelling around the country preaching to our Germans; but beware of him! for as the Methodists only do harm to our cause, I would strongly advise you to raise your voice against him, and not allow him to enter any of our pulpits."

By this it will be seen that the adverse feeling was owing to the influence of their pastors, and was easily effected ; as many of the poorer Germans hold their pastors in as much veneration, and follow their instructions as implicitly, as the poor Roman Catholic that of his priest.

I used to visit Preston once a month for the purpose of preaching, but soon ascertained that the Lutheran minister there had no friendly feeling towards me. He was reported to have said that there was no need for me to preach while he was already there. I, however, thought differently ; for although he was there, he used to preach to a congregation numbering scarcely more than twelve persons, in a place where hundreds might have been gathered, most of whom spent the Sabbath-day in the taverns. But although aware of his unfriendly feeling, I went to him on the occasion of my next monthly visit, and asked him for the use of his church to preach in.

"Well," said Rev. Mr. W——, "the trustees I am sure will refuse you; but, since you are here, I have no objection if you obtain their consent."

I went to the trustees, and found them quite willing to let me have it; so I returned to Mr. W——, and told him how I had succeeded.

"Indeed!" said he; "and what text are you going to preach from to-night?"

"Never mind my text," said I, "I have not chosen it yet. I generally chose my text when I see my congregation."

"That is very strange," said he; "but I should like to know your text beforehand, as I could then choose the hymns to correspond, and also read a suitable portion of scripture."

"Oh, as to that," said I, "I never care for such ceremonies; but read wherever you please, and with the help of God I shall endeavour to preach from that portion of scripture which you read."

This seemed astonishing to him, but with that understanding we went to church. The chapter which he read was the ninth of Acts, and I took my text from the fourth verse,—"Saul! Saul! why persecutest thou me?" I had a good time, and felt that the Lord was with me. I suppose I said some things which were not relished by Mr. W——, for after this he used his influence to prevent me from having the church any more. On my next visit, I had to

preach in the Town Hall ; but, notwithstanding the opposition, a goodly number came out, so much so, that I felt
justified in again writing to Dr. Nast for an assistant, and
to my great satisfaction he mentioned the name of Bro.
Kappelle, who had already preached two years in the
United States, but had been discontinued on trial.   I sent
for him immediately to come to Hamilton ; and obtaining
permission from the authorities to employ him, he was sent
to Preston, and so this place was at last provided for.

CHAPTER XI.

I HAVE previously adverted to the fact that I used to derive
occasional assistance from my son Jacob. The manner in
which he was almost thrust into the work, may not be uninteresting to those who have subsequently become acquainted
with him and his labours, and I may say, to the glory of
God! with his successes. It was in this wise :—I received a
telegram from Montreal, inviting me to a missionary breakfast in that city. I felt a strong desire to go ; but as the
meeting was fixed for Friday, I saw I should not have time
to get back for my Sabbath work in Hamilton, and I did
not like to leave my little flock and Sabbath-school without
a pastor. I wrote to the Rev. Dr. Wood for advice, stating
my difficulty. He advised me to make every exertion in
order to be present. This advice was very much in accordance with my own inclination, and it is not to be wondered
at that where there was a will there was found a way.
After thinking and praying over the matter, the thought at

last struck me that, perhaps, my son might be able to do something for me. It is true, he was only eighteen years of age, and very boyish in appearance even at that; but as I had superintended his education myself, I knew he had a mind quite equal to the emergency, notwithstanding his youth. When I mentioned the subject to him he thought I must be beside myself. He knew he never could do such a thing in the world. Even if he should attempt it, he was afraid the people would laugh at him. He was sure somebody in the congregation was much more suitable than himself. These and a thousand similar excuses he had to offer immediately. When, however, I had answered them one by one, and still continued to press the matter, he almost commenced to cry, for the boy was as destitute of confidence in himself as he was of a beard. Still, I continued to urge him.

"Since the Lord has converted your soul," said I, "surely you can tell them how it was done, in your own simple language of the heart. God never intended that you should hide your light under a bushel; and how do you know but if you refuse to enter this open door, God may remove the candlestick out of its place. Think of Moses, who was, according to his own estimate, slow of speech and of a slow tongue, and yet God made use of him for the accomplishment of a glorious deliverance to his own people. Think of Jeremiah, who pleaded his youth, to whom the Lord did answer, 'Say not that I am a child, for thou shalt go to all that I will send thee, and whatsoever I command thee thou shalt speak.'"

Thus I continued to urge him until near midnight, and in a few hours I was to start on my journey. He was still undecided when I parted with him to seek my couch; but on going to him again, before I started for the station, he very reluctantly consented to do as well as he was able; but I believe in five minutes afterwards, he was sorry for having yielded. I was far enough away, however, in those five minutes, to be out of his reach; and so, "*will he, nill he,*" he had bargained to supply for me, and felt bound to comply. I believe he is never likely to forget the mental struggles with which he was engaged, from the time of my departure until the Sabbath arrived; he could read nothing, study nothing; his mind constantly went forth to the point of time in which he must appear before the public congregation; and anxiety so filled that mind, that when Sabbath came he was quite as unprepared to say anything as when I left him.

I, however, went on my way rejoicing. I knew the same "Lord over all" who had so often put words in my mouth would assist my son; and I already began to see in his studious disposition and deep piety, the evidences that God was preparing him for a great work. The greatest work in which a man could be engaged, I considered, was in preaching the gospel of Christ, and reclaiming lost sinners from the error of their ways; and I have not since had occasion to alter my opinion. Although I have found it a discouraging work, a thankless work, an uphill work, a work which men can never appreciate as it deserves, still, I believe the record is on high. It was for this great, difficult, discouraging, thankless work, that I believed the Lord was preparing my son, and with a full view of its arduous nature, my heart was filled with gratitude to God at the prospect. No earthly position which he could have occupied would have given me so great satisfaction as that of an ambassador for Christ; and as I journeyed to Montreal, I devoutly prayed that God would make him a useful instrument in his hands in turning many to righteousness, and a faithful co-labourer with me in the German work.

I arrived safely in Montreal, very happy to meet and greet many old friends, and form the acquaintance of new ones. Not the least attractive part of the meeting was the breakfast provided for the occasion, although it hardly accorded with the usual time at which such a meal is supposed to be eaten. But this was only another of the many wonderful things I have observed since I became an Englishman. Dinner, for instance, is sometimes celebrated in a public manner at ten, eleven, and twelve o'clock at night, with the usual accompaniments of toasting, speechifying, and singing such nonsense as "For he's a jolly good fellow," and many other childish things which men of sense could never be guilty of indulging in, if it were not that they are so toasted as to have their usual sensibilities very much blunted. This mistake of putting dinner off till midnight could never occur in Germany, for in our language we call dinner "*mittags-mahl*," that is, the "mid-day meal;" and to partake of the mid-day meal at midnight would be too paradoxical for the matter-of-fact Germans. Our breakfast, however, was not so far out of place, after all; and although we sung not about any "jolly good fellows," we had as many of them there as could sit around the table. Methodist ministers have usually been characterized for their cheerfulness and humour in the social circle; and those who were there assembled were no exception. Their humour and cheerfulness, however, took a benevolent turn. The coffee made their hearts warmer than the wine-cup had ever done; and by the time the inner and mental man were satisfied with "the feast of reason and the flow of soul," the purse-strings of those present were so far relaxed, that twelve hundred dollars were subscribed then and there towards the funds of the Missionary Society, before we separated, as will be found by a reference to the report of that year.

I fear I shall be thought a very discursive writer, but, even at the risk of meriting that appellation, I must relate an incident which occurred at this place some six months before. It was on the occasion of one of my visits to Montreal, to collect funds in behalf of our German Church in Hamilton. The Rev. E. B. Harper, M.A., who was then stationed in Montreal Centre, very kindly accompanied me to some of the most generous among his wealthy, kind-hearted congregation, and, in his bland and winsome manner, enlisted their sympathies in our behalf, so that in less than two days we had over three hundred dollars subscribed. Among others, we visited the office of David Torrance, Esq. Before entering, however, Brother Harper said :—

"I am afraid, doctor, we shall not get much here ; for Mr. Torrance, although a very liberal man, has experienced some very heavy losses of late ; but I am sure he will give you something, and perhaps would not like to be passed by."

So in we went, I expecting at most to get about five dollars. Mr. Torrance received us very kindly ; and after a short conversation about our German work, in which he seemed very much interested, he asked to see my subscription book. This I handed to him, and great was my surprise when he returned it to me with the remark, "I am only sorry I can do no more for you at present," to find his name down for fifty dollars, and a cheque for that amount in the book. I was overwhelmed, and thanked him heartily for his generous donation. When I left his office, I said to

Bro. Harper,—"I hope the Lord may return to him for every dollar a thousand!"

Strange to say, a few days afterwards I received informmation that Mr. Torrance had cleared a large amount of money on one single transaction—a cargo of tea. These are the men—noble, disinterested, generous—whose names ought to live as patterns to future generations, an effective comment on the text,—"There is that scattereth, and yet increaseth, and there is that withholdeth more than is meet, and it tendeth to poverty."*

After this digression, I come back to my visit to the Missionary breakfast. The good people of Montreal not only gave me my breakfast, but I enjoyed their hospitality until after Sabbath, when I again returned to my charge in Hamilton. Great was my joy and gratitude to God, when, on coming home, my wife and several members of my congregation told me how much they had been pleased with the ministrations of my son on the Sabbath. Although he had been unable to make any preparation, he realized the truthfulness of the promise—" Open thy mouth widely, and I will fill it;" and the hearts of many of his hearers burned within them while he talked with them about the great work of conversion, and described, with tears of joy, and voice choked with emotion, the great things God had done for his own soul.

From this time I encouraged him to devote his time more fully to the study of theology, as a preparation for the work of the ministry; but this he strongly objected to do, on account of his youthfulness and incapacity. I did

---

* Many thanks are here also due to the Rev. W. R. Parker, B.A., who was stationed on the East Circuit.

not press the matter, believing if God had work for him to do, He would himself make those impressions on his mind, which would induce him to fall in with the divine appointment. Great was my satisfaction at the next quarterly meeting, to find him willing to offer himself as an exhorter; and afterwards, at a regular local preachers' meeting, at which the Rev. S. D. Rice, D.D., presided, he submitted to the usual examination, and was duly accepted as a local preacher. From this time he used to preach regularly, taking my place in Hamilton during my absence, as well as travelling to my other appointments, in all of which he was uniformly well received. After a year's probation in this capacity, he was duly recommended by the May District Meeting, to be received on trial as a preacher into our Conference. During the years of his probation, the Lord continued to smile upon him, and bless his labour; all of which time he was appointed to labour with myself. At the Conference of 1867, held in the city of Hamilton, he was received into full connexion, and ordained by the Rev. J. Elliott, President of the Conference. I shall have occasion to enlarge on this point in its proper place.

Bro. Kappelle continued to labour in Preston with some degree of success. After a time he thought it desirable to hold a quarterly meeting, and so I was called upon to administer the Lord's Supper. We had a very good time, and after the service, ten persons gave their names, whom I received on trial. These ten formed the first society there, and I am thankful to say that eight of them continue faithful to this day. Still, we had no church, and Bro. Kappelle was afraid to commence one without funds.

"Never mind the funds," said I, "the work is the Lord's, and He will provide the funds."

Although I am neither a prophet, nor, as far as I know, the son of a prophet, yet I have often had occasion to wonder at some almost prophetic utterances, which, with full confidence in God, I was then enabled to make. Sure enough, the Lord in this case also opened up our way. It was in this wise :—

In my travels through Waterloo county, I had become acquainted with a Mr. Hespeler, a very wealthy German gentleman, residing in the village of New Hope, now called Hespeler, after his name. When paying him my first visit, I told him my object was to preach to the Germans of his village (for it is nearly all his own), and tried to enlist his sympathies in my behalf. I did not expect a very favourable reception. Contrary to my expectation, however, he became at once interested in the object of my visit, and gave me every encouragement to proceed. He even promised that if we would gather together a congregation in Preston, which was sadly neglected at that time, he would give us the best building-lot he owned in that village for a church. I cordially thanked him for his liberal offer, and took a note of it. Now was the time to avail myself of it. When Bro. Kappele was going round, first trying to buy an old out-of-the-way building, and next thinking seriously of the desirability of a new church in some central location, I bethought myself of Mr. Hespeler's offer, and we went up to Hespeler village to see him. When we had stated the object of our visit, he immediately took down a map of the village of Preston, and said—

"Here, gentlemen, these are my lots ; choose which ever you please."

We selected a very eligible corner-lot, close to the public school, and worth, at least, one hundred dollars, of which he gave us a free deed; an example of generosity which proves that he has, at any rate, a generous disposition, and, I would fain hope, a heart not altogether unsusceptible of receiving saving impressions from that gospel whose progress he, in this case, so materially aided. Mr. Hespeler has ever since evinced a very friendly feeling towards us, and I hope the Lord may bless him with salvation, for with this world's goods he is already sufficiently endowed. As we had now the lot, we required funds to commence building. In this, our friends in Hamilton assisted us very materially; but our friends in Montreal did nobly; so that we soon had the satisfaction of seeing the building commenced, which is now an ornament to the village. And not an ornament merely; for three times on each Sabbath its bell is heard summoning congregations of devout and attentive worshippers within its walls; and, I trust, good seed has already been sown throughout its sacred precincts, which will bring forth fruit unto everlasting life.

Although I had now several appointments in charge, the Macedonian cry, "Come over and help us," was again repeated in another direction. The Rev. Mr. Fawcett, who was then in charge of the St. George Circuit, informed me of a number of Germans in and around that village. I visited them, and gave out for an appointment the next Sabbath evening. My appointments for the Sabbath now were: Hamilton in the morning; Dundas at half-past one; Sheffield at half-past four; and St. George at half-past seven. To preach four times on a Sabbath was nothing unusual for me in those days. I scarcely know whether the work was harder for myself or my horse. Many of the brethren, and especially Brother Fawcett, inclined to sympathize more with my horse than myself, and often would predict for it an early grave. I thought at that time with Henry Ward Beecher, that " horses were made to go ;" and certainly I allowed mine the full benefit of my opinion. But, after all their sage predictions, it still lives, after accompanying me over more thousands of miles than I am able to count. It is to-day munching its hay with as much satisfaction as if nothing had happened ; and it is my opinion that it will never die while it sees anything before it to sustain its life. I feel an amount of affection for the faithful companion of my travels, which must be my excuse for introducing it in this place, and I hope it may long live to share in my trials and successes ; and, when finally it is no more, that some liberal-minded Christian, such as some I have named, may find it in his heart to furnish me with a better one to supply its place !

I was now, with the assistance of my son, able to attend these new appointments regularly. I soon discovered that God was preparing some of the people of St. George to give their hearts to him. In order to follow the indications of the Spirit of God, I announced for a series of protracted meetings, to commence immediately. To be present at this meeting, I set out from Hamilton on the 2nd of January, 1862, a day which is remembered by many on account of its extreme coldness. My wife and family urged me not to go, for it was piercing cold ; but I felt it was my duty ; and when they saw I was resolved they commenced to weep bitterly, for they were sure I would be frozen to death on the way. But there was the appointment announced for me, and I always considered it would be a sin to disappoint an expectant congregation ; and I am thankful to say that, whatever other crimes I may be guilty of, that is not one of them, and on this occasion I could not be recreant to a principle. So breaking through the influence of their tears and entreaties, I left my family, and, trusting in God, faced the storm.

It was good sleighing, and my pony started off briskly as usual ; but the stock of heat I had laid in before I left home soon became exhausted, and before I reached Dundas I was so stiff that I could hardly get out of the cutter, and was fain to stop at Brother Whiting's to warm myself. Mrs. Whiting kindly got me something hot to drink, not whiskey or brandy, but something a vast deal better,—" a cup which cheers but not inebriates." She also warmed my clothes, and soon restored me to my normal condition, but was greatly surprised when I told her I was going on to St. George.

Mrs. Whiting expostulated with me, but in vain. I was soon again in my cutter ; and from that time till I reached St. George, I never met a human being, nor beheld a living thing : all I saw was a poor dog, laid by the road-side —frozen to death. I began to be almost insensible myself and my hands were so benumbed with cold that I was utterly unable to hold the reins. I thought my eyes must be frozen, for they became very painful ; but my horse, which had been often over the ground before, went merrily on, independent of my guidance ; and when at last I arrived in St. George, I was so stiff and insensible that I could not move a limb, and had to be assisted out of the cutter. The good people of the house where I stopped were very kind to me, and soon got me warm and comfortable again.

I never had occasion to regret this exposure, for the Lord abundantly rewarded me for my venturing to trust Him. As soon as the good people heard that I had come such a distance on such a day, they said to one another :—

"Now we believe that he loves us, and is indeed interested in our welfare."

The whole neighbourhood rallied to the meeting; and that very Sabbath the Lord poured out his Holy Spirit upon them, and many were convinced of sin. I remained with them a few days, preaching every evening; and on the third night God was graciously pleased to convert every soul in the congregation, except one family, and they were very bigoted Lutherans. All those who were then converted continued to witness a good confession; some of them have now fallen asleep; and I hope to greet every one of them on the "banks of deliverance." Brother Fawcett rejoiced with me in the presence of the people, and magnified the Lord for his great mercy towards them. A class was immediately formed, with Brother Shupe as the leader. His piety and devotion to God eminently qualified him for this position, and under his guidance they grew strong in the Lord and established in the faith. One poor sinner, who had been a great drunkard, and very degraded, found peace at that meeting, and became so happy that he used to kneel down even in the street, and shout the praises of God; and, about a year after, died triumphant in the faith once delivered to the saints.

Although this was a fine, rich old country, with good roads in all directions intersecting it, yet even here no one seemed to care for the souls of these poor Germans until our church opened the way. Others then became interested immediately. The Rev. Dr. D——, a Baptist minister, came along and congratulated the people on having found the Messiah; and, from pure kindness of heart, no doubt, further advised them in reference to their duty, and of course had to ride his hobby, "dipping under water." The good people, however, felt no inclination to be dipped under the ice, and told him that their preacher recommended the baptism of the Holy Spirit, which they believed they had experienced; but he persisted in his efforts to draw them to his view of the matter, until some of them became wearied enough.

The Lutheran minister from Preston, also, now began to prick up his ears. He never would come to preach to them except they gave him four dollars for every sermon; but he now reduced the fare to three; and finding that even this was not likely to be forthcoming, he still further reduced his charge to the very moderate fee of one York-shilling a-piece from those who came to hear him. This, I think, brought him about three York-shillings for his sermon, which, after all, was, I believe, more than it was worth; except, indeed, it was intended to be used to supersede "Mrs. Winslow's Soothing Syrup."

Our members continued steadfast, and were not to be moved either by the dipping of the one or the scolding of the other. We had now two classes—one in Hamilton, the other in St. George—the members in both of which places gave satisfactory evidence, by their godly life and conversation, that they had been with Jesus. These blessed results encouraged me to go on, surmounting opposition and obstacles of various kinds; for well I knew who it was who had promised, "in due season ye shall reap, if ye faint not."

Two very remarkable conversions occurred in Hamilton, which I deem worthy of special mention in this narrative. The first was a Mr. S——, a very intelligent German gentleman; but, like too many others, his intelligence had only made him more familiar with objections against the religion of the Bible, than attentive to its sacred truths. I never

8*

could induce him to come to church until after the death of his eldest son. During his illness, I visited him, and was even allowed to pray at his bedside. As there was no hope of his recovery, the parents were very much stricken on account of his illness, and in anticipation of his death, but still did not know where to look for consolation in their affliction. The youth gradually sunk under the disease, until death put a period to his sufferings.

I was away from home at the time, preaching in Waterloo county. As soon as I returned I visited the bereaved parents, but found only the mother at home. I tried to console her for her great loss, and pointed her to the loving Saviour, who does not afflict willingly, nor grieve the children of men. She seemed much affected, and desired that I should converse with her husband, whom, she informed me, I should probably find at Mr. Palm's, (a hotel keeper). I went there to see him, and sympathize with him. I again invited him to come to church; but knowing how difficult it is to get men of his stamp to come for the first time, I promised I would preach a funeral sermon on the occasion of his son's death, the next Sabbath, if he would come. This was a nail in a sure place. He seemed much pleased, and promised he would come. According to promise, both he and his wife were present when Sabbath came. The Lord gave me liberty in preaching, and I tried to impress, especially on the minds of the bereaved parents, the necessity of experiencing a change of heart, which I was fully persuaded they as yet knew nothing about. All the time I was preaching, I believed God would convert their souls; and, to the glory of His Name be it spoken! I was not disappointed. During the sermon, I saw them frequently moved to tears.

After this, they came regularly to church, but were not yet converted.

We then started a protracted meeting, and soon had the shout of a king in our camp, and several rejoicing in the knowledge of sins forgiven. But Mr. S——, although awakened and struggling hard for pardon, still found no peace to his troubled soul. On a certain evening, however, after the congregation had been dismissed, and it was now far on in the night, Mr. S—— remained; and so great was his mental anguish, that he declared he would not leave the place.

"For," said he "I am an unpardoned, lost sinner! If mercy is for me, I must have it to-night!"

"Then," said I, "we will remain here with you, and pray for you. In the meantime, pray mightily for yourself; and look up to God with unwavering faith for a present pardon."

My son, and several of the brethren, remained with me, in earnest supplication, till about midnight, when the Lord was pleased to reveal himself, and set his soul at liberty. He never afterwards doubted; and no one who had intercourse with him had reason to doubt the reality of the change that then took place. His wife, also, has since given her heart to God; and they now travel hand in hand together towards that bright land, where, I trust, by-and-by, when their labour is accomplished, they will meet their dear son, who has gone before, and that Saviour who—

> "Reaches out the glorious crown,
> And bids them take the prize."

But the conversion of the other was still more remarkable, and more satisfactory also; for he has since gone to his reward, and so forever beyond the possibility of falling, and beyond the reach of the wiles of the devil and the seductions of wicked men.

He was a Mr. D——, a tailor by trade, but a perfect slave to drink. I visited him frequently; and whether drunk or sober when I called, he would always promise to do better, and come to church. But the poor man seemed to have lost all control over his own will, for I verily believe he many times despised himself on account of his degradation; but as often as a new temptation would arise, however slight, he was away again—forgetful of his fair promises and good resolutions, and wallowing in the mire as deep as ever. I often prayed for him, and I believe the Spirit of God followed him.

On a certain Monday morning I went to visit him, and enquire the reason of his absence from church on the previous Sabbath. I found him at home, but a most pitiable spectacle. His head bound up with bandages; his face covered over with wounds and bruises, which he appeared to have received in a recent brawl.

I enquired how all this had happened, but received no reply.

"I am very sorry to see you thus," said I; "but surely this would never have happened, if, as you promised me, you had been to church yesterday."

In this I was quite correct; for I ascertained that it was on that very Sabbath, while neglecting its sacred duties, with some drunken companions, in a neighbouring tavern, he had received those wounds and bruises.

"Oh! Mr. D——," said I, "come, be a man! Look at your poor wife, clad in rags, and your starving children. You have a good trade, and could, if you chose, keep them respectably. Why not take the money which you spend in the taverns, and buy bread and clothing for your poor wife and children? What ever will become of you and them? Besides, think of your poor soul, for which Christ died; what will become of it if you continue in your present course of dissipation?"

Scarcely had I mentioned the Saviour, and alluded to his sufferings and death, when his eyes suffused with tears. I asked him to allow me to pray with and for him; but he exclaimed, more like despair than anything I had before witnessed:—

"O, I am such a lost, undone sinner; God will never listen to your prayers for such a miserable wretch as I."

I however knelt down and fervently implored the grace of God, which bringeth salvation, to appear unto him. He seemed most wretched, scarcely daring again to promise to do better, so often had he broken that pledge; but I discovered in him a settled purpose to seek the blessing of God, and lead a different life. From that time he gave up drinking altogether, and his place was rarely vacant in the sanctuary of God, on Sabbath or week evening. After a time it pleased the Lord to pardon his sins, and he became a most devoted and active member of the church. He lived very close to God, and every one who saw him after his conversion, was constrained to acknowledge that no power but that of God was capable of effecting such a change as was exemplified in his life. He became one of the most pious and exemplary men I ever knew among the Germans. A class was entrusted to his care, many of whose members can attest how near he lived to God, and how he stimulated them, by precept and example, to entire consecration to His service. But his warfare was soon to be accomplished.

For over a year he let his light shine, and so bright was
the halo cast around his path, that it was feared he would
soon be removed to illumine the courts above. This fear
was too soon verified; he was prostrated on a bed of sickness, from which he never rose again. When the physicians had given up all hopes of his recovery, the good
brother was heard to say :—

"Thanks be to God, that, in his righteous judgment, He
did not cut me down in my sins, when a poor, rebellious
profligate! I do not fear to die! My Saviour, I long to
be with thee! Glory to God, I'm going home!"

A short time after this, he said to me, taking my hand
in his :—

"Bro. Freshman, sing 'I'm going home!'"

We did so, and also prayed with him; and it was about
midnight when we left him to return to our abode. Truly
it was the house of God; and I think I never was nearer
the gate of heaven, than when in that poor man's dying
chamber.

The next day was Friday. In the afternoon I was sent
for, to come to him, as he was thought to be dying. I
found him exulting in his Saviour; perfectly conscious that
he was passing away As soon as he saw me, he said, without the least tinge of sadness in his tone :—

"Brother, I will not be with you on Sunday any more;
you will lead my class, for I shall spend my next Sabbath
in heaven."

He then called his wife and children around his dying
bed, and in their presence, said to me:—

"Oh! Bro. Freshman, try to watch over my children,
and see that they all grow up in our faith."

He then embraced them, one by one, and gave them his blessing, charging them to meet him in heaven. Just then the clock struck five. He enquired what time it was. When told the hour, he replied—

"In another hour I shall be with my Saviour, in glory for evermore."

He lifted up his hands, and seemed to pray. I said :—

"Bro. Dapp, you are on your journey home; is your Saviour still precious?"

"Yes," he replied; "precious, precious! Blessed be His holy Name for ever! Glory! glory! glory!" he continued. And with the language of heaven still on his lips, and a sweet and placid smile lighting up his countenance, his spirit burst its fettered bonds, and returned unto God who gave it.

Never before had I witnessed so triumphant a death-bed, and if the whole of my ministry had resulted in nothing else than the triumphant salvation of that soul, I would consider my life well spent. My own soul was greatly encouraged; and, all who were present and witnessed the last hours of this saintly man, were built up in their most holy faith, and encouraged to proceed with more unwearied zeal in the divine life. All praise and glory be ascribed to God for the marvellous power of his blessed gospel!

We all mourned his death, and felt his loss very keenly. Especially did his class miss his pious counsels and his godly example, and it seemed as if they never could have his loss repaired. But the Lord's ways are not our ways, and while he buries His workman, He carries on His work. However humbling it may be to our minds, I believe the world could do without any one of us, and God could raise up men to fill our places, who would do our work, perhaps,

better than we can do it.   At any rate, another class-leader
was provided for us, in the following manner :—

When I was returning from the Quebec Conference, by
steamboat, we stopped at Prescott, where a number of
German emigrants had just arrived by train, and were
awaiting the arrival of our boat, in order to take passage
for the United States.   They were soon crowded on board
when I went down among them, and commenced to converse with some of them in their own language.   The poor
people crowded around me on all sides, and asked me all
sorts of questions about the country ; its climate, soil, population, &c.   Among them, I particulary observed one man,
whose manners and conversation were of a different stamp
from that of the others.   I immediately became interested
in him ; and in conversing with him, soon discovered that
he was a truly converted person, and had long enjoyed
religion in the old country.   I found him anxious to settle
somewhere where he could enjoy religious privileges among
other blessings ; but he did not know where they were to
be found.

After some further conversation with them, I asked permission of the captain to preach to them.   To this he had
no objection ; so, taking my New Testament, and inviting
some of my ministerial brethren* to accompany me, I went
down again, and calling them together, told them I was
going to hold a religious service for their benefit.

"O," said Mr. Andrew (for this was the name of the person whom I have mentioned as being converted), "that will
be quite refreshing to us, for we have not heard the gospel
preached since we left Germany."

* Ministers returning from Conference also.

I commenced the service by prayer; and after reading a chapter, told them how the Lord had converted my own soul, reminding them that He had the same great blessing in store for them. He had shown his love for them by preserving them from the dangers of the ocean, and bringing them safely to land. But He had yet a higher method of testifying this love, even by the gift of his Son to die for them, and they might all be brought, after the tempestuous voyage of life, to land in the Eden above.

After the service, a great many of them came to me, and asked me where I lived, expressing, at the same time, a great desire to settle in the same place. The result was, that about twelve persons, among whom were Bro. Andrew and his son, who was then about seventeen years old, came with me, and settled in Hamilton, where most of them were soon after converted to God, through the instrumentality of His preached word. Bro. Andrew was appointed a class-leader, in the place of the late Mr. Dapp, and by his piety and devotion, soon won the affections of the people, and was as much beloved as his predecessor had been. His son, also, became truly converted, and a very exemplary young man. When his father had removed from Hamilton, he took his class, and is now, in the providence of God, preaching the gospel as a co-labourer with my son, on the Waterloo Mission.

But it must not be inferred from these examples, that all the people with whom I had dealings were converted, and became exemplary characters. Every picture has two sides, and my experience has not always been to view the brightest. By way of contrast with the above, let me here give an example of another class of men with whom I have had to do.

A certain Mr. S—d lived at this time in Hamilton. He was an intelligent man, and very well educated. I had sometimes conversed with him, but could never induce him to come to church. At last I had the pleasure of seeing both him and his wife at our church. After service he expressed himself greatly delighted with, and profited by the sermon. After that he came regularly to church, not only on the Sabbath, but on week-evenings to the prayer-meeting.

This encouraged both Dr. Nast (who was then with us) and myself, to entertain great hopes of the man, and give him every encouragement. He continued to attend, and things went on very nicely for several weeks—I, meantime, finding him plenty of employment among the friends in Hamilton. This pleased him exceedingly, and the more work I procured for him, the more he praised my sermons—a faculty which is usually supposed to belong of exclusive right to the natives of a certain British island, which shall here be nameless. This is a mistaken idea. This man had as much "blarney," when I got him a job to do, as if he had licked the very stone which is invested by tradition with the power of giving the tongue full command of all those pretty nothings which are called in English—"compliments." I never like to hear a man flatter my sermons while he remains unawakened and unconverted by them; and so I began to have the faintest possible shadow of mistrust of this man. Still, I hoped for the best, and was careful to do all in my power to assist him. It happened, however, that his wife, who was a dressmaker, took it into her head to have a sewing-machine. I wish she had kept it there, and never let it come out. But "Woman" has an influence,—as Mr. Stephenson beautifully shows in his lecture on that subject; and this woman gained her point. Her liege lord came to me, and, after acquainting me with his wife's desire, solicited my assistance. I went with him without hesitation to the place where a variety of them might be procured, from among which he chose one, for which I promised the payment in four months, as Mr. S—d had said he would be sure to pay punctually. The first payment he met promptly; but as to the other three, I had to borrow the money from the late Samuel Cann, Esq., to pay two of them, as he had none on hand to meet them. At the end of the four months, I went to him, and remonstrated with him about his dereliction, but he declared he had not the money.

"Well," said I, "you surely do not expect me to meet those payments for you? I fear I shall lose the money, after all, which I have borrowed for you. If you were an honest man, you would try to meet your own obligations."

When he saw that I was in earnest about the matter, he said :—

"Well, I suppose if you cannot do it, I will have to; but you may be sure of one thing,—you will never see me in your church any more!"

Poor man, thought I, so at last you appear in your true colours, and I have been deceived so long! But he only pronounced his own doom, for in a short time afterwards he was taken ill with a mortal disease, and, after lingering about four months, died a most horrible death. Dr. Nast and I went to see him once during his illness, and prayed with him, still hoping for his recovery. But it was not to be. He passed away to meet his doom in great agony of body. It may be that the Lord, who is rich in mercy, had compassion upon him in the hour of his extremity; but I never wish to see any of my friends die as did this man; for, to say the least, he had not a "sure and certain hope of a glorious resurrection."

In connection with this I remember to have received a useful lesson from the Rev. Dr. Rice, to this effect:—Never induce a person to come to church by promises of temporal assistance, for if a man is actuated by no higher motive than that, there is no hope of his salvation; and in order to retain him even in your congregation, you must keep continually assisting him in some way.—In after times, I have proved the truth of this; for I have met with many such cases, both among Jews and Gentiles. His advice, however well intended, I am sorry to say was not acted upon at the time. I was always too confiding and trustful; but now, with Cowper, I can say—

> —— "I, too, have seen,
> Much of the evil ways of men,
> And grieved for having seen 'em!"

The remainder of this stanza* I cannot adopt, as I think my head is worth more than a jackdaw's; but I am sorry I did not profit by Dr. Rice's larger experience from the first, as it would often have saved me from many difficulties, and preserved the contents of my purse for more worthy purposes.

From the spiritual concerns of our church, as detailed above, let us now turn to its temporal interests.

---

* "Would cheerfully these limbs resign,
For such a pair of wings as thine,
And such a head between 'em!"

CHAPTER XII.

My principal business, since I became a minister, I have always considered to be, to preach the gospel and labour for the salvation of souls ; but I have often had to labour in another capacity,—on behalf of the temporal interests of churches with which I have been connected. Our church in Hamilton—although noble efforts had been made when it was built to pay for it—was still encumbered with considerable debt. This, by dint of lecturing, collecting, &c., I had the satisfaction soon of seeing entirely removed.

I had a fine opportunity, on these collecting excursions, of observing human nature, and moralising on the spiritual condition of some church members, as evinced by their donations. I believe the best way for a minister to ascertain the spiritual condition of the members of his flock, is to take a subscription paper among them. Some he would find "not at home" every day in the week—if they knew he was coming! Others would meet him with smiles; banter him, in a serio-comic sort of a way, about his begging propensities; detain him half-an-hour with some kind of gossip; read over his subscription-list from beginning to end; and then give him—TWENTY-FIVE CENTS!

Others you will find of a vinegar aspect, who look upon you as a necessary evil, which they must endure just as they would the bailiff when he comes, but seem to think it desirable to get rid of you as quickly and cheaply as possible. They dole out their pittance with the air of a man who would say,—"There! I have placed you under everlasting obligations to me, and I hope I shall never see your face again on a similar errand."

Some you will find who would give four or five dollars any day, if they thought their names and donations would be published; but if there is never to be any more heard or said about it, they become poor widows or widowers immediately, with all kinds of hard times before and behind them, and have only a mite to give you.

Then, there is the man who will enter into your business with a gusto, is deeply interested in a moment, and will promise you any amount; but when you come to collect it, you must hire a little boy to do the dunning for you.

Then, there is that generous creature, who will give to every subscription, for whatever the object, but is careful to keep the amount of his givings, in this way, out of his minister's salary at the end of the year. The Lord have mercy upon such little souls!

But I must not fail to commend that class of givers from principle, who, if they approve your object and can afford to assist you, will do it in a moment, cheerfully, disinterestedly, and just to the extent to which they feel they can afford it

—be that only five cents, or be it five hundred dollars. Not like some who uniformly give twenty-five cents to everything, neither more nor less. This they have done for twenty years, more or less prosperous or adverse, and they have no idea of either rising or falling.

All these kinds of people, and others too numerous to mention, I used to meet on my collecting expeditions in behalf of our Church in Hamilton. But diverse as were their dispositions, their manner of receiving me, and their donations, I never was refused but by two persons, and one of these a respectable and wealthy man.

I happened one day to be in his company, with my subscription book in my pocket. Two other persons were present, and he, in conversation, made a statement to this effect :—

"Several years ago, when I came to this country, I was very poor, and what is worse, without a knowledge of true religion. But now I have a fine farm, with good outbuildings; owe no man anything, and best of all, I bless God that I enjoy religion."

This, thought I, is the very man to assist me, and this the very nick of time to present my book, when his heart is warm with gratitude to God. But imagine my surprise when, on handing him my book, he all at once became as poor as he had been twenty years before. He had met with short crops and losses, and his stock had depreciated in value, prices of farm produce low, had barely enough to do to live, and in fine, handed me back the book, with the polite refusal —"I am sorry I can do nothing for you."

There is another story, which one of our leading ministers is very fond of telling at missionary meetings, and which, I believe, he professes to have come under his own experience when a young man; and as it illustrates another phase of character, I am tempted here to insert it. It is that of a rich farmer, who professed the enjoyment of sanctification for a number of years. So full was he of his theme, that when any pious person visited him, he would talk of nothing else but sanctification. But especially when any person came to visit him with a subscription paper, he would talk so constantly on this subject while they were present, and often prevent them from stating the object of their visit at all. So many of our zealous missionary collectors had been treated in this manner, that at last they refused to visit him any more, and the minister had to take him in hands. Calling upon him on day, in company with another person, the minister began to approach the subject which had brought him to see him, and he began, as usual, to talk about sanctification. The minister listened courteously for a while, and at last said :—

"My time is limited and I must be off. Shall I have the pleasure of getting your subscription."

"Well," said he, "the fact is, these are hard times. We farmers are always subject to such heavy losses and misfortunes, that we find it difficult to give when we would." "Only think," continued he, "I had a fine calf, which was very valuable; its mother I brought out from England, at great expense, and bestowed a great deal of care in rearing it. It gave a great deal of promise until it was a year and a half old, when it suddenly sickened and died. And when a person is liable to such losses as that, he cannot always give what he would wish."

"But," said the minister, "How long ago is it since your calf died?"

This was a poser, as he intended it should be, for he had heard that the man was accustomed to evade every subscription which was presented, for the last eight or ten years, by the calf story. So, covered with blushes, instead of answering the pointed question, he asked for the subscription-book, with the remark, "I suppose I shall have to give you a little, after all."

The greater part of what I collected for the church was contributed by our own people.* The ministers of our own denomination were always very free to assist me, and used their influence with their own congregations in my behalf; and in this manner the burden of the debt was removed, and I was, as I then thought, done with the disagreeable business of collecting; for, after all—when one meets with every encouragement—it is not the most desirable occupation, and I hope none of my children will ever adopt it as a profession. But I was not yet done with it, as I soon realized. After I had been removed to Preston, I had to begin the old business afresh; but I must not anticipate.

The work of the Lord continued to spread, and, as a consequence, violent opposition was the result. The Lutherans everywhere spoke against us. Their preachers publicly denounced me as an imposter—hypocrite—Pharisee; said I was serving the church for the sake of my salary; and, in short, did all in their power to hinder the people even from coming to hear me preach.

---

* The subscription-list was headed by Edward Jackson, Esq., of Hamilton, with the liberal sum of one hundred dollars. His good lady, besides giving a liberal donation, laid the foundation-stone of our church.

9

On a certain occasion I met one of the Lutheran preachers, and, in conversing with him, he said to me :—

" I think that as we were already here, there was no need for you Methodists."

" Well," said I, " if you were here so long, will you tell me what good you have done ? Why, the most of your members are Sabbath-breakers ! In the morning, perhaps, you will find them at church, and some of them even dare to take the holy sacrament; and in the afternoon you will find them in the taverns, drinking and playing cards, and in the evening dancing. Are these your specimens of converted members ? Is this the religion of Jesus Christ ? or even of Martin Luther ? Far from it !" said I. " ' Ye must be born again !'" And so I left him to his own reflections.

Wishing, if possible, to make some capital out of this interview, he told his congregation next Sabbath, with a great flourish of trumpets, how he had used up the Jew—meaning myself.

Poor man ! thought I, he little knows what he is talking about ; for while he may now affect to hold the Jews in contempt, he surely is not ignorant that the first originators of Christianity were Jews ; that Jesus Christ himself was a Jew, and if it had not been for the Jews he might have been a heathen. I, however, bear no malice against any of them. The worst I wish them is, that they may all speedily become more like Luther, whose footsteps they profess to follow.

About this time I received a letter from a young man, by the name of Anselm Schuster, a school-teacher at the time, in which, after stating that the Lord had converted his soul, he affirmed his belief that the Lord had called him to preach the gospel, and he felt a strong desire to labour among the Germans. I wrote to him in answer, that I could see no immediate opening in which to employ him, but if the Lord had called him to work in His vineyard, He would open up his way. Soon after, he gave up his school and came to reside in Hamilton, earning his bread by the labour of his hands, and proving, by his daily life and deportment, that he was a pious and truly converted Jew. He was then baptized by Dr. Rice, and as soon as an opening presented, he was received on trial as a preacher. He now labours with Bro. Kappelle among the Germans on the Ottawa mission, and thus far the Lord has been pleased to own his labours in the conversion of souls. May he grow in grace day by day, and in the knowledge and love of our Lord and Saviour Jesus Christ!

Among others converted at the last protracted meeting in the German church, Hamilton, was a fine young lady— a Miss P——, daughter of the before-mentioned Mr. P——. She continued faithful for more than a year, and shone as a luminary in our church; but after a time her love began to wax cold. She became acquainted with an unconverted, worldly man, and was married to him. After this, she never came to our church again; but I never lost sight of her, and often yearned for her return to the fold. This I was not to see, for an accident which she met with a short time after terminated fatally. As she and her husband were returning one day from a pic-nic, a short distance out of the city, as they were crossing the railway track their carriage was overturned by the train, and she was instantly killed. I was glad to learn that her mother, and some of her friends, had hope in her death. It would have given my own mind a great deal more satisfaction if she had continued in the enjoyment of her first love. But I know that God, who is rich in mercy, has a mansion in glory for every one who repents of their sins, and continues to maintain their confidence steadfast unto the end. I like to exercise the largest amount of charity in the case of all; and I hope she also is safe home in heaven; but I know that "godliness is profitable unto all things, having promise of the life that now is, and of that which is to come." I have not the least doubt that, had she continued faithful to her God, she might have been alive at this day, and perhaps instrumental, by her godly walk and example, in "turning many from darkness to light, and from the power of Satan unto God."

But while the piety of some was thus shown to be as the morning cloud and the early dew which passeth away, that of others,—and, thanks be to God! many others,—seemed grounded firmly on the Rock of Ages. I took encouragement from this fact, and also from the fact that we had some English friends who took a deep interest in our work, and encouraged us by their presence and counsels. Among these, Mr. Sandford, of Hamilton, deserves especial mention. He evinced a great deal of interest in the German work in general, and in the Sabbath-school in particular, which he frequently visited, and encouragingly assisted us on various occasions, by his counsels, his gifts to the children, and his donations generally to the funds of the school. I mention him in particular, because of his interest in that department which is too much neglected by our church members. Some day I believe it will be ascertained that he who labours in the Sabbath-school—especially a German Sabbath-school—or does anything to promote its interests, has contributed more to the interests of the church, than he who, by his faithful admonitions from the sacred desk, is successful in converting sinners; for I hold him to be a wise man who first gave utterance to the proverb, "Prevention is better than cure." And if, as political economists inform us, "he is to be counted a wise man who causes two blades of grass to grow where only one grew before," that wisdom belongs in a pre-eminent degree to the man or woman who promotes the work of God by assisting the Sabbath-school. I have said especially a German Sabbath-school, and I now give my reasons :—because, in a German Sabbath-school, we get the children of parents whom we never could reach by our preaching—the children of parents who are deeply tinctured with some of the double-refined essences of infidelity, which prevails to an alarming extent among the Germans. The parents are glad enough to send them off to Sabbath-school, or anywhere else, where they may be out of the way. We get them, and accomplish a triple purpose : *First*, We keep them away from home during that part of the Sabbath when they would be most likely to drink in the poison of their parents' conversation with those visitors who may drop in to have a talk ; *Secondly*, We keep them away from the streets, where they would be found desecrating the Sab-bath, and acquiring bad habits ; and, *Thirdly*, We teach them the purest doctrines of the Bible, which are able to save their souls. A child educated in the Sabbath-school can never become an infidel, no matter how rank the creed of its parents may be ; and how often are those children the means of the conversion of their parents! All this, it is true, is applicable to English Sabbath-schools, but in a much less degree ; for there is not one-fiftieth of the infidelity among the English, in proportion to their numbers, that we find among the Germans, nor is there the same carelessness in regard to the education of their children. The children of English parents will usually get some kind of religious instruction, whether they go to Sabbath-school or not; but German children, or most of them, may grow like "Topsy" in "Uncle Tom's Cabin"—in ignorance of what they are, or whither they are destined.

Wesleyan Methodist Sabbath-schools are yet in their infancy, but it is my opinion that when those children who are now being educated in them, become men and women, they will exert a mighty moral force on society around them, which will make the strongholds of error of all kinds quiver to their very foundations. The Lutheran Sabbath-schools rock them to sleep with a doctrine more soothing than their mothers' lullaby; and when they are thus asleep, the first monster of error that comes along gobbles them up into his capacious maw. It is because I feel the importance of this subject I have thus dwelt upon it, and mention the name of Mr. Sandford—not only out of gratitude to him, but with a view to stimulate others to follow his noble and useful example. And just in proportion to my admiration for the men who are thus found devoting themselves to its service, is my impatience with,—my almost contempt for,—those, some of whom I have found in Preston, who seem willing to compass heaven and earth in order to destroy it. To their own master let them stand or fall!

Everything went on very nicely in Hamilton, with the exception of a little reproach which I had to suffer for righteousness' sake, but which I did not mind at all while the Church of God prospered. There was no fear of me, however, incurring that woe which is threatened against us, when all speak well of us. I was yet, however, to pass through a more bitter experience than ever before. A certain Jesuit came into our midst with recommendations from a good brother, and desired to connect himself with our church. He gave me to understand that he had experienced religion; that one of his chief inducements in coming to Hamilton was to enjoy religious privileges among truly converted people, as he believed we were.

> "Oh, that deceit should steal such gentle shapes,
> And with a virtuous visage hide deep vice!"

I foolishly listened to his fair speeches, and, with my usual confidence, believed him a good man; but I often afterwards wished I had gone to Dr. Rice for his advice in the first place. I, however, received him at once as a member; and, after being with us about four weeks, so high an opinion did I form of him, that I thought, as he was an educated German, he might some day become one of our missionaries. But, alas! how far was I wide of the mark! I soon discovered him to be not only a drunkard, but in other respects an immoral man. I admonished him several times of his conduct, when he would as often express his sorrow, and promise to do better. But finding he did not keep his promises, I had to threaten him, and at last expelled him from our church. But no sooner had I done this than he became a very devil; like his old namesake, he went around like a roaring lion, threatening to shoot me down like a dog, and burn the house I lived in; but as either of these courses would have entailed trouble on himself, he wisely forebore. However, he got a number of placards of the most damaging character printed and posted up in different parts of the city, and swore a fearful oath that he would never rest until he had ruined me. I had to suffer from the slanders of this adversary for several weeks; but I trusted in the Lord, and he interfered for me. One of this man's companions in persecuting me, suddenly took ill, and died, when he himself immediately left the city, and was never afterwards heard of. I hope, if he is still alive, that he has obtained mercy from the Lord, for I am sure I forgive him with all my heart.

But not from Gentiles alone had I to suffer. Jew and Gentile combined to persecute me, which proves, to "both Jew and Gentile, that they are all under sin."

A Jew, named H——, who had heard me preach in Montreal, came to see me at Mr. Sinclair's, where I was stopping. I asked him his business, when he replied:—

"My dear sir, I was delighted to see and hear you preach yesterday. My mind has long been troubled in regard to the Messiah, but under your sermon all my doubts seemed to be removed. Still, I would like to ask you a few questions."

I had not the slightest objection that he should do so, and so he continued asking me various questions, the answers to all of which he received with evident satisfaction.

"And now," said he at last, "could you not come and see my wife! I should like very much to be baptized immediately, but would much rather have my wife do so too at the same time."

I consented to go with him, but found his wife a very stiff, bigoted Jewess. I am sure if Mrs. Freshman had been half as inexorable, I never could have prevailed on her to say "Yes," on one very important occasion when that monosyllable made me happy. I have many a time been thankful that I did not get some men's wives: but this only makes me prize my own the more. This good lady, however, was not at all insulting. She even told me that if her husband wished to become a Christian, she had no objection; but as for her, she would remain a Jewess as long as she lived.

He seemed very anxious to be baptized, notwithstanding his wife's reluctance; but Brother Harper advised me not to have too much confidence in the Jew until I knew more about him. But he gave such strong evidence of sincere repentance and faith in Christ, that, after a public examination in the basement of the Great St. James' Street Church, we came to the conclusion publicly to baptize him, which we accordingly did then and there.

But scarcely had I returned to Hamilton, when I received a letter from Mr. H——, in which he complained of the persecutions to which he was subjected on account of renouncing his faith and becoming a Christian. He pleaded earnestly for assistance to enable him to come up to Hamilton. This I procured for him; and he, his wife, and family, came direct to my home, where we kept the whole of them for several weeks, in the hope that his wife, by intercourse with Christian people, might be brought to renounce the errors of her belief—I, in the meantime, endeavouring to find employment for him, but without success. I advised him to go into business, but he said he had no money with which to commence. Here again I made a sad mistake, never for a moment thinking that he might possibly turn out as his predecessors had done. With full confidence in his integrity, Dr. Rice and I went to one of the wholesale establishments in Hamilton, and there gave security for him to the amount of seventy dollars. His wife was shortly after this baptized, but was, I believe, a great stumbling-block to him, and perhaps the cause of all the mischief that followed.

Soon after, while I was absent from home, they left the city without informing any one of their intentions, and, of course, left their debts all unpaid.

9*

This was, no doubt, the purpose for which they had turned Christians. I would not give a kreutzer for a hogshead of such! I had now seventy dollars' worth of knowledge of human nature to dispose of, and I would have let it go at a discount. Such incidents as these were calculated to create a distrust in my fellow-men, especially in strangers, which it would have been to my advantage to have learned long before.

But it must not be imagined that all Jews who pretend to be converted are hypocrites; in fact, in all ages of the world there have been some good, no matter how greatly the evil might predominate. When the old world was to be drowned, on account of its wickedness, we find a pious Noah, who is deemed worthy to survive, and become the second father of his race. In Sodom, we find a Lot; and among the corruptions of the Church in Sardis, we find a few names of those who had not defiled their garments. So in Hamilton we had a Jew, by the name of T——y, who, when he came to Hamilton, was still unconverted. He, however, came to hear me preach, after which he asked me for a Bible, which I gave him. He also attended our prayer-meetings, and showed a great desire to be instructed in the way of salvation. He continued to attend the services until he became convinced of the truth of Christianity, and I believe truly converted to God. He was then baptized; and while he remained in Hamilton, his Christian character and conduct were unexceptionable. After remaining a short time with us, he removed to Toronto, and there joined himself to the society under Mr. Elliott's care. By the way, he was a bachelor when he left Hamilton, but in a short time afterwards he informed me, by letter, that he had found a wife.

I saw him soon after that, and enquired how he had succeeded in getting one so quickly!

"Why," said he, "just this way:—I went to a prayer-meeting one evening, but had no hymn-book. A young lady* who stood behind me very kindly offered me hers, and in doing so she smiled at me. After the prayer-meeting, I returned her the book, when she smiled again. When I came out of church, I had to pass her near the door, when I noticed she looked at me and smiled again. This made me think it was a good omen from the Lord. Next morning I plucked up courage to enquire where she lived, found her out, and—married her." The happy couple now reside in Montreal.

Moral to the above :—Young ladies can sometimes find a husband as easily by attending a prayer-meeting as by promenading the streets ; and the chances are that one found in such a way will prove infinitely better than the street-corner beau. Kindness and courtesy to a stranger cost us nothing, and are often abundantly rewarded. It is quite as cheap to smile and be cheerful, as to cherish a cross and surly disposition.

During my residence in Hamilton, I was blessed with most excellent health, so that, I think, during the whole four years I was there, I never missed one appointment owing to indisposition. I was much benefited while there by the ministrations of the Revs. Dr. Rice, R. Jones, G. Douglas, and R. Whiting—the ministers stationed there at that time. Their different talents and abilities furnished me with a pleasing variety ; and I learned many useful lessons from each of them, by which I have since profited greatly. I was also stimulated by their examples, and en-

---

* Between thirty and forty.

couraged by their counsels, to persevere and give myself
more fully to the Lord, and keep "an eye single to His
glory."

It was also my privilege to attend all the Conferences
held during my residence in Hamilton. These occasions
have always been "seasons of grace and sweet delight" to
my soul. I felt very much refreshed at the Quebec Conference—the place where my poor blind eyes were opened;
the place where my wandering footsteps were reclaimed;
the place where I first beheld the reconciled countenance of
my Redeemer; the place which must ever be endeared to
me as the city of my second birth. There, also, I enjoyed
very much the re-union with many old friends, known and
loved in days before, and could look forward from that Conference, with a bright and encouraging prospect, to that
time of a more imposing and pleasant re-union when, I trust,
we shall safely meet in our Father's house above. The
Toronto Conference was also a season of signal blessing to
my soul. I thought the late, and now sainted, Mr. Thorn-
ton, who presided on that occasion, more of an angel than a
man. I received while there such a baptism from on high,
as I had never experienced—

> " Since first by faith I saw the stream
> Christ's flowing wounds supplied."

And what, perhaps, enhanced my delight in the Lord was,
that here it was where my own son was received on trial,
and appointed to labour in our regular work. Truly, the
Lord has dealt graciously and bountifully with me!

Brother Kappelle was still labouring in Preston; and, as
our work was now pretty extensive, it was thought expedient
to ordain him. For this purpose, the Rev. Dr. Green, then

President, invited me to meet him in Guelph on a given Sabbath, which he named. I went at the time appointed, and, with the assistance of the Rev. James Brock, then stationed in Guelph, and Chairman of the District, Bro. Kappelle was ordained for special purposes—but he was not yet received into full connection.

During my last year's residence in Hamilton, I was requested by several of our brethren in the ministry to write a reply to Bishop Colenso's attack on the Pentateuch. I never had much opinion of my ability to write well in English, but the persuasion of my friends finally overcame my scruples. I felt well enough disposed to give Colenso a drubbing; for I was grieved in my soul that a Bishop, eating the bread of the church, and wearing her garments, should attempt to undermine her constitution in such a vital part; and if I had had him in German, I would have handled him without gloves. As it was, I did write a pamphlet in answer to his book, which, after submitting it to the examination of Dr. Jeffers and the late Rev. James Spencer, I had published—not for the sake of getting my name up, as it was slanderously reported, and as some affirmed that I did, but purely from philanthropic motives. This was my first attempt at authorship in English, and, whatever people may say about it, no one can truthfully say that I made a fortune by it. My expenses in connection with it were about eight dollars, and my remuneration a vote of thanks from the next Conference! Certainly, I had the pleasure of sending a copy of it to Her Majesty Queen Victoria, and the honour to receive a letter acknowledging its receipt from her private secretary, Sir Charles Phipps, under seal of the privy purse. But if an author does get a little honour for his toil, what is the use of growling about it, for in most cases he gets nothing else; and honour costs no one anything.

During this year, I would often find my thoughts wandering away to the sacred spots and hallowed associations connected with my childhood's home. I was much concerned for the salvation of my relatives and friends, who were, I well knew, still living without a knowledge of the Lord that bought them. I wrote several letters to my friends, and especially to my brother, in which I dwelt upon the proofs of Christ's Messiahship, and urged them to search the Scriptures and prove whether these things were not even so.

My wife also wrote several times to her family and friends, before either of us received a word in reply. At last my brother became so angry with me that he sent me a very unbrotherly letter, from which I inferred that I could do no more good by any future correspondence, as they did not wish even to recognize me as a member of the family any longer. But, although cast off by our earthly friends, we have a kind and loving heavenly Father, and an affectionate elder Brother in heaven, who has promised never to leave—never to forsake us.

I have said a good many things about the Lutherans, and I never grow weary speaking about my friends. I used to visit the Lutheran families occasionally, and could sometimes prevail on them to come to church. One Saturday morning, as I passed by the door of one of these families, I thought I would step in and invite them to church. I knocked at the door, but received no reply. Still, I lingered, for I was sure I heard some one stirring within. At last I went up to a window, which was partly raised, and saw the woman of the house rocking herself to and fro in a chair. As soon

as she saw that I noticed her, she called out, without getting
up from her seat :—

"Nobody to house ; dere's nobody in !"

"What !" said I, "nobody at home ? Then you are nobody !"

"No," said she ; "but I guess you are, or you would not
come bothering us so much to come to church. Our *Pfarrer*
(preacher) never troubles us about it ; we may come when
we please, and stay away when we please."

But I thought I knew better, for her *Pfarrer* had no
doubt been there a short time before, giving her a lecture
on the evils of Methodism. This woman came the nearest
to the manners of fashionable life of any that I had seen—
the only difference being that she told her lies herself ;
whereas, some people of fashion employ their servants to do
that business for them.

Before I was removed from Hamilton, another Jew came
to see me, who, I suppose, thought he was fully competent
to converse in the English language, when the following
colloquy ensued :—

"Am you von converted Jewish Rabbi ?" said he.

"Yes, sir," said I.

"Den you haff find de Messiah ?" said he.

"Yes, sir, I have," I again made answer.

"Vell, den, vill you so gute be, und dell me some gwes-
dyuns about de Messiah ?"

"I shall be most happy to do so," said I.

We then entered upon the discussion of the question, I
answering all his questions, and expounding various passages, both from the Old and New Testament, apparently to
his satisfaction ; after which, I read and prayed with him.
He then came to me and said :—

"I zee you pe one learned man ; I like you ver mooch. [vash to zee ein Roman Catholic priest, und he dell me I moost pe paptized, vitch me, poor Jew, tink no do my poor zoul ver mooch goot, zo I comes to zee you. You haff done me mooch goot ; und now, how mooch you sharge ?"

I was very much surprised at his question, but simply said :—

"Nothing to me, sir ; but give your heart to God."

And so he left me. I know nothing more about him than that he was a rich German Jew from Berlin ; and in process of time I almost forgot the circumstance. About three years afterwards, however, my attention was directed to an article in the *Christian Times*, published in London, England.* This article asserted that the Rev. Wm. Taylor — the California street-preacher — had related the above-mentioned facts at a love-feast, and the conversion of the same Jew through my humble instrumentality. The facts he had from the Jew himself, whom he had met somewhere subsequent to his conversion. All praise and glory to the Lamb !

During the remainder of my residence in Hamilton, nothing of particular interest occurred. I had, at times, great satisfaction in labouring at my ordinary work. At other times, unpleasant circumstances would occur, owing to the persistence with which persons, like some I have already described, would endeavour to injure me. But, amid it all, I believe the Lord was with me, and blessed

---

* This article I might never have seen had my attention not been called to it by Mr. Miller, a prominent barrister in Galt, and an active member of the Church of England.

my labours. After I left Hamilton, I heard rumours unfavorable to my jurisdiction while there. These I have never attempted publicly to refute, as I was persuaded that if left to themselves they would die a natural death, if, indeed they be not already dead. Many sacred recollections still cluster in my memory, connected with my Hamilton charge; and it is almost with reluctance I turn away to contemplate another field of labour.

CHAPTER XIII.

IT was decided at the Toronto Conference that I should remove to Preston, with my son as a colleague. Brother
Kappelle was to take my place in Hamilton. It was with
fear and trembling I contemplated the prospect of removing
my family into the midst of a people who hated the very
name of Methodist; but I had put my hand already to the
plough, and if I looked back, I felt I should not be fit for
the kingdom of heaven. It was, however, a great trial to
leave the many kind and tried friends—lay and ministerial—
whom I had in Hamilton, and the little flock whose infant
cry had first greeted my ears, and over whose tottering
footsteps I had watched with so much solicitude, and go
into a strange place, where I had few friends and no
sympathy, not knowing what would befall me there. But I
knew who had said, " He shall choose our inheritance for

us;" and I accepted the appointment as from the Lord, and
in His name moved my large family to Preston.

I found a few families of English Methodists living in
and around the village, who used to attend Zion Chapel,
about three miles distant, on the Berlin Circuit, as they had
no English preaching nearer.   It is true, the Berlin minister
used to come once in a great while and preach to a handful
of people in "Hunt and Elliott's Factory," and afterwards
in an old building in a remote part of the village ; but there
was no regular appointment, and very little encouragement
to open one.   Besides these, the New Connexion minister
preached to about a dozen people in the old Town Hall.   A
Roman Catholic priest used to come once a month, warning
his small flock to beware of the Methodists; but these have
since died a natural death, with no hope whatever of a
resurrection.   Their neat and handsome church stands as a
refuge for the moles and bats, with the exception of a
meeting held occasionally among themselves.

The Lutheran sect was predominant.   In fact they had
the place almost to themselves, although their minister often
had to preach to more empty benches than full ones ; but
his people were all right as long as they would keep away
from the Methodists.   Our German cause in Preston was
also very weak.   We had barely ten members, and some of
these were about to leave for the United States, so that our
influence was very small ; in fact, we could hardly yet be
said to have a foothold.

The Lutheran minister was the only one who resided in
Preston ; and his sympathies, so far from being with me,
were all the other way.   He and I have since, however, become very good friends.   But at that time everything looked
dark enough.   No society for my family, none for myself,

opposition on all hands; and, worst of all, my old friend, Robert Hunt, Esq., who had always received me hospitably, was on the point of removing with his family from Preston to reside in Blenheim.

However, work was to be done, and my son and I commenced in the name of the Lord, and we soon, in the pressure of our engagements, forgot, in a measure, our trials and privations. In addition to Preston, we also attended several other appointments in the adjacent country, within a circuit of fifteen or twenty miles. Some of these Brother Kappelle had preached in, others we opened up ourselves.

The children in Preston seemed to be sadly neglected on the Sabbath-day. I found them flying their kites, rolling their hoops, playing ball, marbles, &c., in the streets and on the public common, with no one to reprove them or teach them any better. Brother Kappelle had collected a few German children, and commenced a Sunday-school, but there was none for the English children. I believe an English Sunday-school had formerly existed, which met in Mr. Hunt's factory; but when that building was burned down, the Sunday-school was dispersed, and for nearly a year they had no one to look after them or care for their souls. These English children I gathered in, and with the Germans, soon had a united school of great promise.

Our few German members were so small in number, compared with the hosts against whom we had to contend, that I sometimes feared their hearts would fail them in the unequal contest, but they were converted people,—and only give me truly converted people, and I am not afraid of the devil and all his emissaries. However, it is hard work to advocate an unpopular cause against so much odds, and it was very difficult to persuade people to come to religious service in an

obscure place, with only a handful of people, past the very
door of the large and commodious Lutheran church. I,
however, trusted in the Lord, and awaited His time. I expected better things when we should have a church for ourselves, in the middle of the town, where I might preach as
often as I pleased, without let or hindrance. In the meantime, however, we had to live by faith.

In passing through the streets I was very often insulted ;
even my children used to be called after publicly in the
streets, and molested in different ways ; so that they became
afraid to venture out of doors, except in my company.
Even the Lutheran minister, instead of preaching Christ to
his congregation, made use of his pulpit as a rostrum from
which to declaim against us, and incite his congregation to
persecute us. All these things kept my congregation very
small, and most of these were converted people, so that I
longed for an opportunity to preach Christ, and him
crucified, to sinners, and I had not long to wait.

It happened that a young lad, belonging to a very respectable family, and a member of our Sunday-school, became ill
and died, when his parents invited me to officiate at his
burial, and preach a funeral sermon. I knew that on such
an occasion the people would attend in crowds, and I took
advantage of this opportunity to inculcate upon my large
congregation the necessity of a true change of heart before
they could become entitled to eternal felicity, as I believed
this young boy was, for I am persuaded he was truly converted to God. This was a new and strange doctrine to
most who were present, and as I had entirely ignored
morality and good works without faith in Christ, much opposition ensued. The people were now acquainted with my
doctrines, many of which they misrepresented, and others

they ridiculed,—but none would they adopt. I felt thankful, however, that the Lord had enabled me to deal faithfully with them, which I am determined always to do—whether they will hear, or whether they will forbear.

Even the few friends whom I had in Preston had very little encouragement to give me. These would say to me,— "I fear you will never accomplish anything here. So many have already made the attempt without success, that the chances are you will fare no better than they."

I knew, however, that if the work was of the Lord, men could not overthrow it, and I awaited the completion of our church, which was then in progress, with some solicitude, hoping for better things. At last it was completed and dedicated to the worship of Almighty God, in the month of September. Dr. Rice, of Hamilton, preached in English, and I in German.

Meanwhile we had opened an appointment in the town of Paris, where we soon had a handsome church erected, the ground for which was generously bestowed by Hiram Caperon, Esq., a gentleman belonging to the Congregational Church. This appointment being so far distant, we could only supply once every two weeks. My appointments would then be,—St. George in the morning, Paris in the afternoon, and sometimes return to Preston in time for the evening service. I also occasionally preached in Princeton. Our other regular appointments were Strasbourg, Roseville, Conestoga, New Dundee, Doon, and several other places which we could only attend at irregular intervals. In Strasbourg we also built a church, and a few souls were converted to God, who remain faithful to the present day. May the Lord increase their number!

Our Sabbath-school in Preston increased in interest and

in numbers. The German and English children united in harmony and love. I now began to hold service in the English language in the evening, for the benefit of those who had no other means of grace convenient. Crowds came to hear me, and it was soon found necessary to increase the number of pews in our church for their accommodation. Thus in spite of the enemy, the Lord worked gloriously; but the greater the amount of our success, the more the enemy raged. It was now impossible for any of us to go into the street without being publicly annoyed, if not insulted. People would shout after us " *Yute! Yute! Nix-come-a-rouse;*" and other silly and foolish epithets. They called our church a " *Yuden Kirche;*" and even attacked and insulted those who would come to hear me preach. The principal topic of conversation in the taverns and at the street-corners now, was—" Freshman!" In•short, so violent did the opposition become, that I was repeatedly admonished not to venture out into the street at night alone. But long ago I had learned not to fear them who have power to kill the body, and after that have no more that they can do. Before our first Quarterly Meeting my soul was made happy in witnessing the conversion of several precious souls, among whom was one very amiable lady, the wife of Jacob K. Erb, Esq. But we were not permitted to enjoy her society a great while, for the Lord took her to himself soon after; but while she did live, she witnessed a good confession, and died shouting the praises of Him who loved her, and washed her from her sins in his own precious blood.

> " O may I triumph so,
>   When all my warfare's past ;
>   And dying, find my latest foe
>   Under my feet at last. "

As a considerable debt still remained on the church, I again resorted to my friends in Montreal, whose generosity I have already had occasion to mention on more than one occasion. While there I had occasion to address a public meeting, in which I gave them some account of our German work in Upper Canada, dwelling particularly on Preston and its vicinity. I simply stated facts as they really existed, and, among other things said, that the Germans all through that section of country are broken up into a number of sects, such as Lutherans, United Brethren, Old Mennonites, New Mennonites, Dunkers, Baptists, Allbrights, Swedenborgians, Roman Catholics, Rationalists, and even open Infidels. That notwithstanding this array of religious persuasions, much Sabbath-breaking was publicly practiced, and that even by some who claimed to be members of a certain church, which I claimed .was a sufficient justification for me, or any one who was interested in the prosperity of Zion, to introduce a pure gospel amongst them, calculated, at least, to reform their morals, if not to save their souls. What was my surprise, the next morning, to see an article in the Montreal *Witness*, in which my speech was altogether misrepresented, and even some reflections cast upon the whole of the Germans of Waterloo county, and statements made regarding them which I had never uttered. The same evening I met the editor of the paper at the house of Jas. A. Mathewson, Esq., and pointed out to him the inaccuracy of the report of my address, desiring him to publish my vindication next morning, as I expressed a fear lest the Germans, when they got to hear it, would take great offence at what I was reported to have said.

"Oh," said he, "do not trouble yourself about the article ; you know our reporters seldom give a strictly correct account of what is said at such meetings; and, after all, the Germans concerned will never see the paper, so that it is not worth while taking any further notice of it."

Those editors have an easy way of overcoming one's scruples, and so I did not press the matter any farther.

But my worst fears were very soon realized. Scarcely had I returned home when a "hue and cry" was raised immediately, and spread in all directions. The report of what I had been supposed to say got here as soon as I did. It travelled faster than I could do, even if I had had the "wings of the morning" to assist my progress. One German, claiming some influence in this place, undertook to publish a vindication of the Germans, in doing which, of course, he had to abuse me. For this purpose he collected all those epithets expressive of contempt, abhorrence, scorn, and hatred, which the dictionary could furnish him with. These, when thus collected, he put into his composition, without stint or measure. As this worthy gentleman (?) was a tavern-keeper, he had a fine opportunity to supplement his composition by abusing me in the presence of his customers as they sipped their beer over his counter. But *"magna est veritas et prevalebit"*—the truth is mighty and shall prevail. Although they kept up a ferment for a time, I waited in patience until the troubled waters became calm.

Another worthy—an infidel, and editor of a German newspaper—called upon the people, in an article in his journal, to "tar and feather" me, or stone me, or hang me up.

Another tavern-keeper also took up cudgels against me, and offered a reward to any one who would catch me out at night—the object, no doubt, being to carry out the suggestions of the infidel newspaper;—so that, among them all,

I had a pretty warm time of it for a while. I, however
went on as usual; going out or in, by night or day, as I had
occasion, fearing the face of no man, for I had a clear conscience.

When the storm was at its height, however, I went to
one of the principal men of the town, and gave him my
explanation. I also sent an article to the editor of the Galt
Reformer, who had allowed the notorious article to appear
in his columns, giving him an explanation of how matters
stood, and desiring him to insert my reply. This he accordingly did, but to small purpose, for the people were
only too glad to get something against me; and when, at
last, they nervously clutched at a straw, they would not
easily let go their hold. Seeing I could not stop this out-
break by local means, I now wrote to the editor of the
Montreal *Witness*, telling him what I had to suffer in consequence of the blunders of his reporters, and asking him
again to do me the justice of repairing the evil.

This request he now granted, but it was too late to be of
any service to me. The people were determined—especially
the tavern-keepers—to cling to their very small hold upon
the man who they imagined was doing so much injury to
their business—so that I could do no more. Three gentlemen,—two German and one English,—then undertook to
publish answers to the many attacks which were made
against me through the medium of the papers. In these
answers, the characters of my enemies were fairly ran-
sacked, and it was clearly shown that, even if I had said
everything that the report charged me with saying, still a
thousand times more could have been said to their detri-
ment—and all within the bounds of truthfulness.

Matters were in this state, when a procession of some kind passed my house, and we could distinctly hear the crowd, in passing, crying out,—"Hang up the Jew!"— "Away with him!"—"Tar and feather him!" and such like epithets—all expressive of their "*goodwill*" towards myself.

My family commenced to weep and tremble violently, imagining the procession was formed for the purpose of laying violent hands upon me. But I feared them not; and with a prayer,—"Father, forgive them, for they know not what they do,"—I took no further note of it, except "a note" in my journal.

Taking no further notice of these men or their doings, I soon had the satisfaction of seeing the better-minded Germans convinced of my innocence; and, strange enough, the very men who were my first and greatest opponents, have since become some of my best and firmest friends in Preston! The German newspaper, also, which thought— with one tremendous thunderbolt—to annihilate me, has itself now ceased to exist.

Before this happy state of things ensued, however, I was made the subject of a most gross attack or outrage, which, only for the mercy of God, might have resulted in serious bodily injury—if not loss of life—to myself or my family.

On a certain Saturday night, a large stone, of about eleven pounds in weight, was hurled violently through my bedroom window, smashing the whole of the upper portion of the sash, and making a deep indention in the floor where it alighted. This was followed a short time after by two smaller stones, beside other missiles. The larger stone, I supposed, was intended to bring me to the window to see what was the matter, when the smaller ones could then, when so exposed, have been aimed at me with sure effect. Providentially, the very night previous to this diabolical outrage taking place, I had changed my sleeping apartment from a downstairs room to one upstairs, where I continued to slumber throughout all the tumult, unconscious of all danger.

My two daughters, however, who occupied the room thus violently attacked, were so terrified as to be unable to make any outcry whatever, and it was not until about four o'clock next morning that they could muster up sufficient courage to acquaint the family with what had transpired. I then for the first time became aware of the great danger which had menaced us, and the great mercy of God which had defeated the machinations of our enemies and preserved our lives.

We afterwards discovered the perpetrators of the outrage, but took no steps to prosecute them—leaving them in the hands of One who hath said, "Vengeance is mine; I will repay." The Reeve of the town, Jacob K. Erb, Esq., very kindly offered a reward of twenty-five dollars to any one who would bring the perpetators of the outrage to punishment, and posted up placards to that effect—signing them, "By order of the Council."

The next day, a certain tavern-keeper, in conjunction with a former enemy of mine, issued other bills, offering a reward of fifty dollars(!) in order to discover "whether Dr. Freshman had not done the atrocious deed himself!" These posters were signed, "By order of the Nobody," in opposition to those signed, "By order of the Council." But no one ever earned the fifty dollars; and if they had, they would have had "Nobody" to pay it to them.

Thus was the purpose of our enemies defeated; and the

very same Sabbath morning the Lord enabled me to preach to my sympathising congregation, from Romans xii. 19,— " Dearly beloved, avenge not yourselves, but rather give place unto wrath, for it is written, Vengeance is mine, I will repay, saith the Lord." I also preached to my attentive English congregation in the evening.

Since that time, affairs have undergone a great change for the better. Even that tavern-keeper who had been so bitter against us, is now friendly disposed ; and although he never comes to hear me preach, yet he contributes to our Missionary fund, when the Sabbath-school collectors visit him with their collecting-cards ; and on a recent occasion, when we occupied a public hall of his for a concert in behalf of our Sabbath-school, he generously refused to make any charge for its occupancy. May the Lord in His mercy reward him with salvation !

But the Lutheran preacher, seeing that none of these things could either kill me, or frighten me to death ; and seeing, moreover, that many of his own congregation, having a desire to hear me preach, were beginning to forsake him, now began to rub open his eyes, and feel whether he had been asleep or not. He tried all sorts of persuasions, endeavouring to retain the straggling members of his flock, and even told some of them that if they desired to be converted, they could do as well in his church as any where else. To this they would reply :—

" Why did you not tell us so before ? You have been here all these years, and what have you yet accomplished ? We are no better nor wiser now, than we were before you came. Look now at the Methodists, who have only been here such a little while, and yet see how much good they have done ! Look at some who were wicked and profligate, who are now reformed and virtuous. How is it that we never see anything of this in our church?"

These were questions which he could not find answers to, either in his catechism or prayer-book; and as these were the principal books which he had read, he could not answer them at all. On another occasion, a very intelligent and respectable German gentleman, the postmaster of the place, said to him, in a conversation on the respective merits of the two churches :—

"Why," said he, "even their Sabbath-school children are altogether different from yours. While theirs are regular in their attendance both at Sunday-school and at church, yours are found as often playing in the streets and breaking the Sabbath, as attending to its duties. I tell you, we shall have to place the Wesleyan Sunday-school before us as a model; and if you do not intend to be altogether swallowed up by them, you must begin to do as they do, and preach as they preach. I visited the Dr.'s Sunday-school, and heard him preach, and I felt quite different while there from what I have ever done under your ministrations."

These views, honestly expressed, were being constantly brought before him on all hands, so that he was driven almost to his wits end to know what to do. At last he concluded to follow Mr. N——'s advice, and begin to do as we did. His first move in that direction was to commence a prayer-meeting; but alas! he had no one who could pray. How is it likely that a minister, who cannot himself pray without a book, should have members superior in ability to himself? And so, after an unsuccessful effort in this direction, it was abandoned. He then arranged his Sabbath-school on a different principle, and tried to infuse new life

into its teachers and officers, and awaken a fresh interest
in it in his congregation. But his chief effort at reform
was in regard to pastoral visitation. Before I came, I had
been told his members never used to see him at all at their
homes, except when they would send for him ; but now
he seemed to his wondering flock to be almost omnipresent,
at least as much so as it is possible to conceive a Lutheran
minister to be. If these visits had been for the purpose of
instructing his flock more fully in the things of God, I
s'iould have rejoiced ; but I was assured by some whom he
visited on those occasions, that his principal business was
to warn them to beware of the Methodists, as some had
already been deluded by them. By this means he succeeded in retaining the larger portion of his congregation ;
who, while they were free enough to confess that they derived
no benefit from him, still hesitated or feared to come to us ;
acting, I suppose, on that very old adage, " Do not throw
away dirty water, until you are sure you have clean where-
with to replace it."

But the Lord blessed our labours everywhere. Although
our appointments were now becoming pretty numerous,
still, we had not a single appointment at which the Lord
had not converted some soul or souls. Our Sabbath-school
in Preston, composed of English and German children, who
were taught in both languages, was now in a very flourish-
ing condition. We met every Sabbath morning, and I was
the superintendent myself. When about to celebrate an
anniversary of the school, I invited the Rev. E. B. Harper,
M.A., then in Hamilton, to give us his assistance by preaching a sermon for us, and being present at our tea-meeting
on the following night. This he very kindly consented to
do, and on that occasion was pleased to express a very com-

plimentary opinion in regard to our school, so much so, that he said he had never seen a better in his life. This opinion, coming from a man who had occupied stations in our largest cities in Canada, and had travelled in the neighbouring Republic, was very flattering ; however, we did the best in our power to merit it.

Bro. Harper preached an excellent sermon, in the course of which he said some very pointed things, and some peculiarly appropriate and fitting to the infirmities of some in his congregation. So numerous and pointed were these hits, that I feared lest the people should imagine I had been exposing their foibles, and instructing him what to say. After the sermon, I expressed these fears to him, when he laughingly replied :—

"O, never mind, I will set the matter right to-morrow evening."

So the next evening, at our tea-meeting, in a witty and humorous speech, he pleasantly alluded to his sermon of the previous day, telling the people they must not imagine he had been personal in his allusions, or instructed what to say, for he had found human nature the same all over the world, and his hits all applied to human nature in general ; to convince them of the truth of which, he told them it was an old sermon which he had already preached in several places, and no doubt would again.

Thus everything appeared satisfactory and prosperous. But while I had much comfort with my German people, my soul was grieved when I looked upon my large English congregation—not a soul of whom, as far as I could see, was converted. It is true, there were a few who claimed to be members of the Wesleyan Church, and they may have had religion at one time ; but long deprivation of the regular means of grace, or inattention to its private duties, had left them with "a name to live, while they were dead." I saw that my preaching hitherto had failed to wake them up; and, as I feared lest I had been speaking unto them smooth things, I began to be more pointed in my remarks,—more alarming to their consciences in my preaching. This not only created dissatisfaction with me, but a feeling against me, which soon permeated the whole congregation, as none of them had grace enough to see that I was only dealing with them as a faithful pastor who must give an account to God. They were not prepared for plain-dealing; and the consequence was, they became disaffected, and not only injured themselves, but were in a fair way to ruin our German cause also; so, "unless the Lord had left us a very small remnant, we should have been as Sodom, and we should have been like unto Gomorrah."

This disaffection resulted in a request to the Chairman of the District for a preacher for the English congregation. He sent them a school-teacher, who preached to them until the end of the year—in the meantime fanning their disaffection to a flame, which subsequently broke out into persecution against "that bad man," as he was pleased to term me. At the end of the year, the Conference appointed another English minister to take charge of the Preston congregation, giving him also two or three small congregations, detached from the Berlin Circuit for that purpose.

Since the English work was now no more connected with me, I shall confine myself to the German, with an allusion occasionally to the English department connected with our church.

But no sooner was one difficulty overcome, or one danger averted, than another would spring up in its place—like the

10*

hydra serpent with its fifty heads, one of which would no
sooner be cut off than others would spring out in its place.
It seemed as if the people could find no cause of accusation
against myself, they would try to injure my family.   A
certain Mr. W——, at that time a Lutheran, set on foot
a most scandalous report very damaging to the character of
my son Jacob, who had, I am sure, never raised a finger,
nor spoken a word, calculated to injure any one.   But he,
too, had to endure his share of the trials and crosses which
fell to his father's lot among this people.   There are many
things which I can afford to pass by without notice, and
treat as beneath contempt; but in this case the thing was
so scandalous, as well as so manifestly untrue, that I went
to Mr. W——, and told him I would make him prove the
charge thus maliciously preferred against my son.   I held
no further parley with him, but left him to his own reflections, as I was determined in this case to make short work
of it.   A person may belabour myself as much as he pleases;
but when it comes to my family, he touches the apple of my
eye, and, resolve as I please, I cannot but feel when that is
touched.   What, then, was my astonishment, when, the
following evening, a knock came to my door after nine
o'clock at night, and in came this very Mr. W——! but
not with a list of proofs, as I imagined he would try to
bring.   Falling down on his knees before me, he confessed
the utter falsity of the report, and implored my forgiveness
—stating at the same time that he had been induced to cir-
culate the story while under the influence of liquor, given
him by certain persons in order to stimulate him to it.   I
told him he already had my forgiveness, but must seek that
of One whom he had most seriously grieved—even his
Father in Heaven.   I am thankful to be able to add that

that man is now a converted and upright member of our church, and also sustains the responsible position of an officer of the same. Truly, "God's ways are not as our ways, nor His thoughts as our thoughts."

Another instance will suffice to show that, even with all my experience in regard to deceivers and wolves in sheep's clothing, I was very liable to be duped, as I had too much confidence in the integrity of those who could put on a fair exterior appearance. A certain doctor by the name of J——, came to Preston, and commenced to practice his profession. He attended our church about a year very regularly, and I used to think he was an honest and upright man. But he did not get a large practice, and was, in consequence, sometimes in great straits to make both ends meet. At times, as he needed it, I used to lend him small sums of money, which, however, he never returned. I even on one occasion presented him with a suit of clothes which I had but seldom worn. This was out of pure benevolence to him, as his own garments were becoming too shabby to consort with the dignity of his profession. He, seeing the kindness of my disposition, took courage, and begged for a still further favour, viz., that I would go with him to Hamilton, and assist him in making some purchases in one of our drug establishments there. This, with his fair speeches and seeming honesty, he also prevailed on me to do; but I was prudent enough this time not to become security for him. I also lent him several valuable books to read, which were never returned; for he and his family left the place suddenly one night, and were never afterwards heard of. They of course left their debts unpaid. The books which he had belonging to me were sold, with whatever else he had left behind, to pay his debts, or were divided among his creditors, but were quite insufficient to meet their demands. Besides the loss of my books, I also lost about thirty dollars in cash, advanced to him in small sums at different times, to meet pressing emergencies. I was sorry to hear that the drug store in Hamilton lost about twenty-five dollars by his defection.

"Oh ! what a goodly outside falsehood hath !"

I wonder whether I shall ever learn wisdom enough not to put my trust in man! After all, I felt more sorry for the poor man himself than for what I had lost by him, as I had all along great hopes of his conversion and future usefulness.

I think, however, this was the last straw* which is said to have broken the camel's back ; and I can say that from this time I became more careful, and determined not to be cheated any further. This, in fact, became necessary, for my family, who were now considerably grown up, were becoming more expensive ; and we found it necessary to begin to practice the most rigid economy, in order to which we were compelled to give up keeping servants, as we had always formerly done. But after all our efforts in this direction, by the time of the Montreal Conference I was shockingly in debt to the amount of one hundred and eighty dollars ; and had it not been for the great industry and economy commendably practised by my wife and family, as well as by myself, I would not have been able to give my children even a tolerable education. But I am happy to say that, by means of retrenchment in all directions, I was enabled to accomplish this purpose ; and one of them at least, after graduating in the Wesleyan Female College, Hamilton, will, I am sure, by Providential guidance, make her way through life.

Here I would take occasion to immortalise a certain class
of "croakers," who, like the fungus on a decaying tree, form
the excrescences of society. They will croak about paying
the minister such a large salary, as they call it, and quietly
tell you that they cannot make $600 a year off their farms.
They cannot afford to give their sons and their daughters a
collegiate education. They cannot afford to dress themselves
as gentlemen, and drive fast horses and covered buggies as
some of their ministers do. Well, in the first place, those
who croak most give least, and it is astonishing what strength
of lungs a man who gives his minister fifty cents a quarter
has got. He will rival his neighbour in the swamp, who
keeps the woods and fields vocal the livelong summer night
with his melodious music. The reverse of this is also the
case. Those who give most croak least. When I hear a
man croaking about the large salary and expensive habits
of his minister, I at once put him down as a fifty or twenty-
five cents subscriber to his salary; and am strongly inclined
to favour Darwin's view of the affinity of such,—not very
remote,—with the tadpole, which wriggles in the mud at
the edge of a pond in summer, till finally he lays aside his
tail and becomes invested with legs to jump and a voice
to croak.

In the second place, it is not true that they do not make
six hundred dollars a year off their farms. It is true, perhaps, they do not clear so much cash every year; but if they
count up every pound of butter they use, and every dozen
eggs, and every bag of flour, and every slice of ham, and
every wisp of hay, and every bushel of oats which their
family and their stock consume in a year, as well as every
article of clothing which they wear, and charge for these at

the rate which ministers have to pay for them, they will see whether it does not amount to six hundred dollars or more.

In the third place, even if they do not make so much as a minister, perhaps they have not so much invested. A minister must have education; and many of them have an education which costs more thousands of dollars than their farms did hundreds. His education is his capital, and a capital which in any market ought to yield a return in proportion to the amount invested. A minister must also present a respectable appearance before his people, and have books and periodicals to read, so as to keep posted on the state of the world and science, as it is for the benefit of his people.

All this becomes expensive; and if a minister fail in any of these respects to come up to the normal standard, these very people would despise him; and yet they would withhold from him the means necessary to come up to their own requirements. How inconsistent!

In the fourth place, even if these croaking farmers, to whom I have alluded, cannot give their sons and their daughters a college education, they can give their sons a farm, and their daughters a portion, which their minister never can do. So they have not so much to complain of after all. Clearly, I could give my children nothing but an education, and if the Lord spare me I shall endeavour that they all get one.

The Rev. Dr. Rice knew well how to appreciate the importance of this, when, on one occasion, he advised me to "give my children something which the sheriff cannot take away from them:" a memorable sentence among the many memorable sentences which I have heard him utter, and some of which I hope he may commit to the custody of the press for the benefit of the world.

After this disquisition on croakers and croaking, I turn to another chapter in which will be further detailed an account of my labours and trials.

CHAPTER XIV.

As we had now members of society at all our appointments,
and many of these were considerable distances apart, I found
it necessary, for the accommodation of the people, to administer the Lord's Supper, at intervals, at each of the
appointments.   On one of these occasions, as I was driving
home from St. George, about Easter, a serious accident befell
me, which might have cost me my life.   I had my son's
horse, which was, at times, given to shying.   At this time,
when driving faster than usual, in order to reach Preston in
time for my appointment at half-past six in the evening,
and collecting my thoughts for the service, unapprehensive
of danger,—just as I approached a high snow-bank, which
had not yet been dissipated by the vernal sunshine, and out
of which protruded some old stumps, my horse took fright,
the gig in which I was riding was upset, and I was thrown
on the frozen ground with such violence that I lay in-

sensible for a considerable time, and my horse became fastened in the snow-bank.

Shortly after this disaster, some Germans, who were passing that way, discovered me, and, extricating my horse, they assisted me into my gig, and thus enabled me to continue my journey. They did not fail to observe that I had in my possession a bottle, containing the remainder of the wine after I had administered the sacrament of the Lord's Supper. In a day or two the news was dispersed in all directions, that the Methodist minister always supplied himself with a bottle of wine, or something of that sort, when he went on a journey! This was but a little thing, and is only worth mentioning here, as showing how readily evil-disposed people are to find some cause of accusation against ministers. But I took no steps to explain it away, remembering the example of Mr. Wesley, when a similar charge was brought against him, and only sorry that I had not a "guinea" to present to the poor creatures for their disinterested trouble!

About this time, the greater part of our persecutions and troubles had ceased — at least for a considerable interval. Our work among the Germans went on and prospered. My son was still with me as my colleague, and shared in all my labours. Our care was to give no one any occasion to speak evil of us truthfully; notwithstanding which, some of the Lutheran preachers always made a great outcry, especially when souls were being converted, and when we opened up new appointments in their territories. They in this manner served to introduce us into a neighbourhood, and, no doubt, induced some to come and hear us, through curiosity, who otherwise might not have been reached—thus defeating their own object. Some few of

English extraction also delighted to say all manner of evil against us falsely ; but these things I considered of no great importance compared with what we had passed through. Our labours, also, began to be more appreciated, as an incident or two will serve to illustrate.

There was a certain German, a painter by trade, and an official member in the Lutheran Church, who, although he professed to be a converted member, always opposed us. At length Providence afflicted him ; and, after a time, the physicians pronounced the opinion that there was no hope of his recovery. He suffered great agonies during his illness, and as his end approached, his friends asked him whether he did not wish to have his minister sent for. This he refused to do. He said :—

"I am only a poor, lost sinner, and I have lived too long in his church, thinking I was a converted man ; and now that I am dying he cannot help me. O that I could now see some of those Methodists whom I have so much despised, but whom I now believe to be good men !"

Some of our German members were then, in accordance with his wishes, sent for, and remained praying with him, and pointing him to "the Lamb of God who taketh away the sins of the world." So earnest did he become in regard to his salvation, that they were obliged to remain with him day and night ; and, I am thankful to be able to say, that the result of their labours in his behalf was his saving conversion to God, and he died triumphing in the knowledge of his sins forgiven.

A short time afterwards a similar incident occurred to a young lad who used to attend our Sabbath-school, but who, owing to the influence of his friends, who were all Lutherans, was obliged to leave it. When he became sick, nigh unto death, his friends strongly urged him to have the Lutheran minister sent for, but this he stoutly refused to do, telling them he would rather die without any minister than have him present. "But" said he, "I would like you to send for young Mr. Freshman, or if he is not at home, for his father, for I believe they are good men, and did my soul much good while at their Sabbath-school." This request he continued to urge, until his parents at last, though very reluctantly, consented, and my son was summoned to his bedside late one evening. He remained with him reading, praying, and trying to comfort the young lad.

But he refused to be comforted,—"For" said he, "I am a lost backslider, and I cannot die yet. I used to love my Saviour when at your Sabbath-school, but since I left it I have lost that love, and am now most unhappy."

Thus he continued, bewailing his condition and reproaching his friends for robbing him of his birthright, and at intervals praying fervently for its restoration. At length the Lord again had mercy upon him, and he continued to praise and magnify His name until he passed away. His last utterances were,—"O thanks be to God, Mr. Freshman, He has again pardoned my sins and restored my soul, and I can now die happy!"

He made his parents promise before he departed to allow us to perform the funeral services, which we accordingly did; and from that time two families have sent their children regularly to our school, who were ill-disposed towards us before, and also come regularly to our church themselves, although they have to walk a distance of two miles. These things did us much good, and caused some change of feeling in our favour, but still we had to contend against prejudice conjoined with power.

About this time another young brother, named Schesser, presented himself as a candidate for our work, believing himself moved by the Holy Spirit to preach the gospel. I found him considerably deficient in educational ability, but I believe truly converted and pious. With the permission of the Chairman I brought him to Preston, where I superintended his instruction for some time, and prepared him for his future career, he in the meanwhile preaching in a local capacity at some of our appointments. He seemed zealous in the work, and greatly desirous of devoting his whole time to its labours; so in a short time he was sent down to the Ottawa Mission, and brought up Bro. Schuster, who was sent to Paris, where he laboured very successfully whilst he remained there.

Brother Schesser also laboured quite acceptably among the Germans on the Ottawa Mission. Thus was the Lord bringing more labourers into his vineyard, and by the time of the Montreal Conference we had six labourers in all thus employed.

One thing was a source of no small anxiety to myself connected with these young men, and that was,—what course of study during their probation would be most suited to them as a qualification for future efficiency. I already knew the importance of making a right commencement, but was somewhat at a loss to know just what to recommend in the case. As Conference was approaching I hoped to derive assistance from the collected wisdom there assembled. In this I was not disappointed, for at the Conference a course of study was adopted, which, while it is a considerable tax on their time, is yet necessary to bring them more on a par with their brethren in the English work, as well as suitably to qualify them for their own.

At this Conference our Stations were as follow :—

Brother Kappelle to the Ottawa; my son to Hamilton; Brother Allum to Strasburg ; Brother Schuster to Paris ; Brother Schesser for the Ottawa, as the colleague of Brother Kappelle ; and I was to remain in Preston. But for the ensuing year the Lord had already prepared a cup for me full of bitter ingredients, which I shall never forget, but for which I shall ever be truly thankful.

On my return from the Montreal Conference, I found everything progressing nicely, except that my son was very reluctant to go to Hamilton, where he was appointed for the ensuing year, as he thought he could be more useful where he was, since it was a much larger field of labour. Even during the sitting of Conference, before his appointment was ratified, I wrote to him about it, and found that he was not at all ambitious to go, and would much have preferred remaining with me ; but still, in reply, he wrote me :—"My dear father, I have no wish to influence my appointment ; where I am sent I will go, in the name of the Lord, and bear my cross." The appointment was not changed, and he removed to Hamilton.

And now, for the first time since I commenced my narrative, I crave permission to keep back many particulars which involve the character and conduct of others. While I am free enough to confess my own faults and failings, I do not feel the same freedom in regard to those of other people, who were, after all, the principal cause of my troubles. In order to explain the whole affair without involving others, I must go back a year or more in my history, and begin at the commencement.

After the erection of our German Church in Hamilton, I bought a Sacramental Service of silver-plate for the Lord's

Supper. These I paid for from the proceeds of some lectures which I gave for the purpose, without touching a dollar of the funds of the church. At the time when I purchased them, I distinctly stated that they were to belong to the whole German Mission, and not to any church in particular. As I had bought them and paid for them myself, I claimed the privilege of taking them with me wherever I had occasion to administer the Lord's Supper; and when I removed to Preston, I brought them along with me, but not without first obtaining the consent of my Chairman, the Rev. Dr. Rice. I had, however, two men in my congregation, against whom I had to exercise our discipline. One of them I deprived of his office, and the name of the other I dropped.

This was galling to them in the extreme, and they immediately began to use their influence against me as much as possible. Their success was but partial, while I remained to counteract their influence; but as soon as Bro. Kappelle was appointed to succeed me, these men became very good for a time, and were again admitted as members and officers of the church. No sooner had they effected their purpose, and succeeded to the additional influence which church membership gave them, than they began to rake up some cause of accusation against me, in order to satisfy their old grudge. Nothing seemed so feasible for this purpose as the fact that I had taken the silver ·service away from them. They nervously clutched at this as a drowning man would at a straw, and made the most of it. An evil-disposed man can accomplish a great deal of evil, when he tries with all his might, especially in the absence of the one whom he seeks to injure; and in a short time these two men had the greater part of the congregation worked up into a perfect ferment of indignation against me, just for that little thing. I got to hear of their doings, but simply answered :—

" The vessels do not belong to the Hamilton congregation, and they shall remain in my possession as long as I live, and at my death I will bequeath them, together with the Bible used at the dedication of the Hamilton Church, as memorials of the commencement of the German work in Canada, and they shall never become the property of any one congregation in particular."

I did not consider that I was acting capriciously in this instance, for the vessels have never yet been diverted from the original purpose for which they were purchased. I had always taken them with me wherever I was called to administer the Lord's Supper, and do so to this day. This, then, is the whole source of the trouble, and I have no doubt that many of my friends who have been misinformed in regard to it, and perhaps disposed to think unfriendly of me in consequence, will, when the true state of the case is presented, be ready to acquit me of all blame in the matter.

This being the state of feeling when my son was appointed, with a view, I suppose, of punishing the father by rejecting his son, they conspired against his appointment—thus setting the authority of the Conference at defiance. The more I reflect on their conduct, the more I am lost in amazement at their temerity. There they were, a handful of people, who, moreover, paid scarcely anything towards the support of their minister, and who ought to have been thankful to receive any person, actually rejecting the person whom the generosity of the Conference had bestowed upon them, and pledging themselves not only not to come to church themselves, but to do all in their power to prevent others (who would have been willing) from doing so until the appointment was altered! This stand they never would have taken had they not been aided and abetted by some others, whose names, I am thankful to say, I have grace enough not to mention, and who, I would fain hope, were not fully acquainted with all the facts in the case, and shall therefore pass them over in silence.

This was but poor compensation for all the labours I had undergone in behalf of that congregation, and the efforts which I had made for its welfare, and was still willing to put forth. If the fault had been altgether with me, I would gladly have borne the punishment, and done all in my power to obviate the evil; but I am sorry to say, a beloved brother, whom I still highly esteem notwithstanding, acted very capriciously in the whole matter, and I have no doubt but that one word from him would have set the whole matter right at once. But he did not speak that word; and it was no doubt very much to his satisfaction when the disaffected Germans accomplished their purpose. My son was sent back to Preston, and Brother Allum sent to his place in Hamilton.

Never since my conversion to God was my soul more sorely tempted than at this period, and my son endured agony of mind inexpressible. It seemed as though the enemy, alarmed at the inroads which were being made into his kingdom, conspired with all his force to destroy the whole German work. But, thanks be to God, he was not permitted to triumph. We were enabled to humble ourselves at the rebuke of the Lord, and from our hearts to forgive all those who rose up against us.* I received many

---

* Since writing the above, it will, perhaps, gratify my readers to know that I have preached in Hamilton several times, and am ap-

sympathising letters, full of consolation, from lay as well as our most distinguished ministerial brethren, which contributed much to still the tempest of conflicting thoughts which struggled in my breast, and restore my troubled soul to its former peace. Perhaps, after all, it was good for us that we were afflicted, as the Lord graciously rewarded us by many showers of blessings that same year—both on the Ottawa, where Brother Kappelle was labouring, and in Preston and its vicinity, on both of which missions many souls were converted to God.

It was during this year that I received a very affectionate letter from some German people, who had been converted in Preston, and united with our church there, but had removed to Louisville, in the United States. In this letter they expressed an urgent desire to have me come over and visit them, promising, if I would do so, to pay a part of my expenses. I looked upon this invitation as providential, as I had for some time desired to see Dr. Nast, whose services I wished to secure as an examiner for our German probationers at the coming Conference. I also wished to consult with him in regard to the German work, as he had a large experience and intimate connection with their extensive field on the other side of the lines. I therefore accepted their invitation with pleasure, and started on the journey as soon as possible—feasting already in the anticipation of seeing my beloved brother, Dr. Nast, and enjoying sweet inter-

---

pointed to do so now regularly once in four weeks. At one of these appointments, the man who had been the principal agent acting in this affair, went to the President of the Conference, and, in my presence, confessed his sorrow for what he had done ; stating that he had been misled by others, and was again desirous of devoting his whole soul to the church.

11

course with him for a season.   My anticipations of pleasure
were more than realized ; for his devout conversation, his
prayers, and his fatherly advice and instruction, were as
balm to my wounded spirit ; and in his presence I felt as if
old things had passed away, and all things become new.

The first night after my arrival I had the pleasure of
addressing a few words to the members of the German
Mission Church, who were assembled in class-meeting.   To
the honour of the ladies in that place be it spoken, that this
church was not only built by their efforts, but also both it
and the pastor are supported by them.   I hope Canadian
ladies may take an extract from this page for their scrap-
books, and read it, in connection with their Bibles, until
they are impelled to go and do likewise.   Dr. Nast, in addition to his numerous and various labours, was at this time
their much-beloved pastor.   We had a most blessed and
refreshing season in the meeting, and all went home rejoicing in the God of their salvation.

The next day I started for Louisville, but first had to
promise Dr. Nast to visit him on my return.   The German
brethren who had been expecting me received me on my
arrival with every demonstration of joy.   During my stay
among them I was the guest of Brother Forrell, who had
been a trustee of our church in Preston.   He and his kind
lady lavished upon me many tokens of affection and esteem,
and their kind hospitality I trust I shall never forget.   I
had much reason to be thankful when I ascertained from
this visit that all those who had removed there from our
midst were still steadfast in the faith, although all of them
had not yet connected themselves with any church there ;
but this I made them promise me they would do as soon as
possible.   Brother Klein was the minister who had charge

of the German Church in that place, and I soon had the
satisfaction to hear that they had all connected themselves
with his church. Here it might not be out of place to
remark, that while we have often to suffer from the less
of members by their removal to the other side, and who
contribute to swell the membership there, still, up to the
present time, we have not received one single accession to
our membership from that source. All we have received
we have had to reclaim from the empire of the wicked one;
but in heaven, we know, a proper adjustment will be made,
and it will then be revealed how many children the Lord
had given to the German Wesleyan Church in Canada,
whose names are not now recorded on its books.

On the ensuing Sabbath I was permitted to preach to
crowded congregations; as well as to address the week-night
service. I also had the honour of baptizing one of Brother
Klein's children before I left them. The German work in
the United States is assuming a most imposing appearance,
and accomplishing a great work in the moral elevation of
society. Although it is not yet more than thirty years
since Dr. Nast was appointed as their missionary, yet now
it had increased to an aggregate, in round numbers, of about
forty thousand members, and over three hundred ministers
and preachers. It is true a great deal of money and labour
had been expended in producing this effect, and even yet a
great many thousands of dollars are given annually, from
the English department, in extending the work; yet already
many of the circuits and stations are self-sustaining, and not
only so, but paying back every year large sums of that which
has been expended upon them, for the relief of those who
have less ability. I took encouragement from these facts to
hope that the time may yet come when we shall see similar

results in Canada, although it seems far distant at present. However, our members are already becoming educated into the workings of Methodism, and paying quarterage according to their ability, as well as sustaining the funds of our Missionary Society.   Let us thank God and take courage.

After spending some time with my friends in Louisville, and enjoying their hospitality, I took my leave of them, and began to retrace my journey homewards.   I had, however, according to promise, to call at Cincinnati, and stop awhile with Dr. Nast.   He had already, in anticipation of my coming, announced for me to preach, so that I had no choice but accede.   I must here confess, that I felt it required no small effort to preach before Dr. Nast ; but as I had passed through the ordeal before, I might do so again without losing my credit.   Yet here again, notwithstanding my experience at Ottawa, I thought I would preach a "great" sermon.   Accordingly, at the appointed time I ascended the pulpit, but asked another brother who was present to open the service with singing and prayer, after which I commenced to preach, as I thought, a great sermon. But alas ! scarcely had I commenced when I became sensible that it was going to be a miserable failure, and the longer I continued speaking, the deeper did this impression become, so that by the time I had finished I was ashamed to look any person, least of all Dr. Nast, in the face.   The good brother, however, made very light of it, and ascribed all my embarrassment to the fact that I had not opened with prayer.   Of this I had, my own opinions ; one of which was that if Dr. Nast had not been present I would have done better ; and another, that even in his presence, if I had thought less of getting glory to myself, and more of the glory of God, he would not thus have permitted me to suffer humiliation. It was, after all, a useful lesson to me, and one which, perhaps, I needed. Certain I am, I have never fallen into the same mistake since that time.

Having obtained a willing consent from Dr. Nast to be with us at the approaching Conference, I started next morning for Detroit, at which place arrangements had already been made for me to preach, both in German and English. The appointments on the Sabbath I filled as well as I could ; and knowing there were a great many Jews in that place I announced that I would address them especially,—on Monday evening in German, and on Tuesday evening in English. A great many came out to hear me, especially on the Monday evening, and I felt very grateful to God for giving me this opportunity of proclaiming, for the first time, to so many Israelites, the truth as it is in Jesus. I tried to point out to these, my benighted brethren, the folly of trusting in their many errors and fables, and exhibited the glorious light of the gospel in contrast. I felt that the Lord was with me during the discourse, and was happy in my soul, I trust also that my labour was not altogether in vain in the Lord.

After the service, a man came and thanked me for the discourse. " But," said he, " I am in the dark ; I want more light—more light." He told me, before leaving, that he had been seeking the truth for many long years, and had attended the preaching of the gospel in different churches, but still he could not see the light. I tried to point him to the Saviour, and exhorted him to pray incessantly, and read the Scriptures with a believing heart, which he promised me he would do, and I am happy to say that he is now a converted man, and a consistent member of one of our churches there.

Encouraged by this interview, which indicated that the Spirit of the Lord had applied the word, even to one soul, I

returned to my lodging rejoicing in God.   But late the same
evening a German friend came to warn me of a conspiracy
which the Jews had entered into against me,—their object
being to catch and kill me, or at least maltreat me in some
abusive manner, for having exposed the radical errors of
Judaism in such a public manner.   I thanked my kind-
hearted friend for his information ; but so little did it affect
my nerves, that, after commending myself to God in prayer,
I retired to rest as usual, and slept soundly till the next
morning, not even dreaming of an unpleasant occurrence,
although my informant's caution was calculated to suggest
dreams of cold-blooded murders, midnight submersions in
the river, tar and feathers, or some such casuality.

After breakfast I went out to visit a Mr. Ströelinger, a
Jew, and a native of my own country besides.   He and his
accomplished lady received me very kindly, and while there
I noticed some little Sabbath-school books belonging to their
children.

This I looked upon as an indication that they could not
be much opposed to Christianity themselves when they permitted their children to read such books, and emboldened
me to open a conversation with him immediately, on the
subject of Christianity.

"I do not blame you," said Mr. Ströelinger, "for changing your religion, as I believe all religion is a humbug, and
most of all the Jewish ; and if it is true, as the Jews about
here report, that the Christian Church has paid you ten thousand dollars for the change, I think you only acted the part
of a prudent man in accepting it."

"What!" said I ; "I am surprised to think that you can
believe such nonsense.   You know very well of old how I
used to despise Christ and his Church ; so much so, that ten

—no, nor fifty thousand dollars, could not have purchased my allegiance to it. Nothing of the kind is the case; and so far from bettering my position, the very reverse is the fact; for you know well, that while I remained among the Jews I had a path opened by which I might have arrived at comparative affluence, besides which, I had continual peace of mind. Now, it is true, I receive a competence, but have continual trouble and sorrow, increasing year by year. Nothing else but the salvation of my soul could have induced me to make the exchange."

In this manner I continued urging him to seek the same precious faith, but all apparently to no effect. He soon left me to finish my conversation with his wife, who, indeed, seemed more disposed to receive the truth in the love of it than he had been. Before he left, however, I invited them both to come out and hear me speak in English the next evening; but when the time came I saw neither of them were present, deterred, perhaps, by the rumours of a disturbance, which was threatened to take place that same evening. I trust that the hour I spent in conversing with them will be found, when the judgment is set, and the books are opened, to have been not altogether in vain.

When evening came I went to my appointment, trusting in that God who had sustained me amid dangers on so many former occasions. Although it was a very stormy night, a large congregation assembled to hear me, and no disturbance took place as was anticipated. But the same night I was warned to leave the city as privately and as secretly as possible, as my movements would be watched, since a certain Jew had promised five hundred dollars to the man who would apprehend me. Notwithstanding this warning I remained until the next day, and then, without the least attempt at privacy, or feeling of fear, I passed through the city to the station, in company with Brother Milizer, and received before I left, a ticket to carry me as far as London, gratuitously bestowed by a wealthy banker, a member of the Church of England; and thus after a very pleasant visit and journey I was soon in the midst of my family once more, which the good providence of God had graciously sustained during my absence.

A short time after this, the District Meeting, at which my son was recommended to be received into full connection and ordained, took place in Guelph; and as the Conference approached, I longed for its arrival, that I might at least have the privilege of meeting and welcoming Dr. Nast to the Province of Canada.

CHAPTER XV.

THE Hamilton Conference is associated in my recollections
with many pleasing reminiscences, not among the least
pleasant of which is the visit of Dr. Nast. After encoun-
tering unusual difficulties, occasioned by detentions of trains,
blunders of officials, and other casualties incident to travellers, he arrived in due course in Preston, and preached for
me on the Sabbath previous to Conference, both in Preston
and Strasburg.

As Dr. Nast is a Methodist, not many of the Germans
of Preston availed themselves of the opportunity of hearing
him, with the exception of our own congregation. It would
be just the same if the Archangel Gabriel would come to
Preston and call himself a Methodist preacher:—he would
find great difficulties in collecting a congregation.

Notwithstanding this fact, however, those who had the
pleasure of hearing him were abundantly benefited and
blessed. I was only sorry that a greater number did not

11*

avail themselves of such an opportunity to profit by his large experience and exalted piety.

After the Sabbath service I took him round among a few of the families, both of the English and the German people. This was for the purpose of giving him an opportunity to see and hear for himself, in order that he might be able to arrive at a correct judgment as to the true state of affairs in Preston, as well as its wants and requirements.

Although I took him to some of the best families and most respectable people, he did not appear to have formed any very exalted opinion of this as a field of labour; but he does not express his opinions to every one, and, perhaps, would not wish to have them published. However, he told me there was plenty of work for me to do ; and after obtaining a pretty correct idea of the nature of the field requiring cultivation by our Missionaries, he accompanied me to Conference, prepared jointly to recommend a scheme for the better prosecution of that department in which I have the honour to be a co-labourer with him. Here I may just remark that the Conference acceded to our recommendations in every particular, and the result is that a new and forcible impulse has been given to the German work.

During the present half-year which has elapsed since Conference, it has accomplished more than during any previous whole year of its existence ; and it never was in a more healthy condition than at the present time. The prayer of . my heart is, that it may go on and prosper until the last of the redeemed has been gathered from the ranks of the adversary, and takes his seat with shouting at the right hand of God !

Among the first duties devolving on Dr. Nast at Conference was the examination of the candidates on probation in the German work. This was not found in every respect so satisfactory as could have been desired; but a great deal of indulgence ought to be allowed the German preachers in comparison with their brethren in the English work. In very many respects they are pioneers. Their fields of labour are large and arduous. They require to spend a great deal of their time in pastoral visitation. Not pastoral visitation in the sense in which our English brethren understand the word,—merely going to see their members, and having a pleasant visit, and drinking a cup of tea with them : our preachers have to open up new appointments, and, in gathering congregations, have to visit people who hate them and their cause.

Instead of being invited to partake of a pleasant cup of tea, they are often in danger of having a whole kettle full of boiling water poured over them without ceremony. Still, they must persevere ; and as they do not know in a strange place who is friendly and who is not, they have to learn it by actual experience. Then, again, they are engaged in protracted meetings almost the year round, at different places ; or preaching or holding other meetings nightly. Taking all these into account, and making due allowances, it was found at their examination that they had diligently improved their time, and made considerable progress in the attainment of the studies prescribed ; so that all the candidates who were examined passed with more or less credit to themselves. Dr. Nast also assisted us in revising the course of study, which will now compare very favourably with that prescribed in the English department.

As my son had previously to the District Meeting gone to Cincinnati, to be examined there, and had brought back with him testimonials from Dr. Nast of the very highest character, as to his proficiency and attainments, he was exempted from this examination at Conference, to which the others were subjected. He presented his testimonials to the Guelph District Meeting, and was enthusiastically recommended by it to be received into full connection, and to be ordained at Conference. Notwithstanding this, he subsequently submitted to a private examination by Dr. Nast, in Preston ;—the result of which was quite as satisfactory as his previous ordeal in Cincinnati. Bro. Allum was also recommended to be ordained for special purposes, but not received into full connection.

The Conference commenced most auspiciously. The Rev. James Elliott was President; and by his affable deportment, his business habits, as well as his exalted piety, proved that the selection the Conference had made was a wise one, and during the entire session gave the greatest satisfaction. The utmost harmony prevailed throughout.

Early in the session, the young men who had been recommended to be received into full connection and ordained, were called forward, for the purpose of relating their religious experience and call to the work of the ministry. These candidates numbered twenty-three, including my son and Bro. Allum.

As time would have failed to permit such a large number to address the meeting each in turn, a few were chosen, who related their experience and call, and these were taken as representatives of the others, who had previously given ample satisfaction, in regard to these points, to their several District Meetings.

Among the number thus chosen to address the Conference was my son, and I cannot here refrain from giving the substance of an article which appeared in the *Christian*

Apologetic, — a German paper, published by Dr. Nast, in Cincinnati. He says :—

"The church was crowded to its utmost capacity when the exercises commenced. As the graduating class was large, all could not therefore speak. Six of them spoke in succession—clearly, conclusively, and with the unction of the Holy Ghost. The experience of young Bro. Freshman made the deepest impression, while he related how he, when still a little boy, had been baptized by the present President of the Conference, a short time after his father's conversion. There was not a dry eye in the church. Thank-offerings went up to heaven for the wonderful manner in which the grace of God had brought this Jewish family into the light of the gospel ; as well as fervent prayers that this young man, who had so fully convinced all who heard and saw him that he is a devoted servant of the Lord, might long be spared to the church. After he had taken his seat, a long, solemn pause involuntarily ensued. Every one wiped the tears from his eyes, and vocal and silent prayer filled every part of the house. When he was ordained, as the President laid his hands on him, he was himself so overcome by his feelings that he could scarcely utter a word. The Secretary, who also laid his hands on him, was moved in a similar manner. The Lord will certainly hear the many prayers which have gone up in behalf of our young brother !"

Although I do not think Dr. Nast is either a prophet or the son of a prophet, yet I believe his last sentence in the above extract is prophetical, for truly the Lord has been with him, and blessed his labours in an abundant manner since the last Conference !

Beside the services rendered by Dr. Nast as an examiner, his visit to Canada will never be forgotten by those who

had the privilege of hearing his experience at the Conference
love-feast ; of listening to his sermons ; to his speech before
the Conference, on the German work in the Methodist
Episcopal Church in the United States ; to his addresses
to the Conference, both in public and in private committees,
—all of which tended greatly to promote the interests of the
German work ; and I am sure no one, whether English or
German, could fail to be edified. As to myself, it was one
of the most blessed Conferences I ever attended; and I am
sure I there received a baptism of the Holy Ghost which
mitigated the severity of past trials, and prepared me to endure difficulties still in store for me in the future.

An important change was at this Conference made—in
the alteration of boundaries—by which the work was at the
same time consolidated and extended. Hitherto the German work in Western Canada had belonged to three dis-
tricts—the Hamilton, Guelph, and Brantford. It was now
determined that the Hamilton District should take charge
of the whole work as now existing, together with any ex-
tensions that might be made to it during the year. This
scheme greatly simplifies our operations, by bringing us all
together in the official meetings, where we can arrive at
mutual understandings, as well as report to each other what
we have been doing, with greatly increased facility.

The Conference appointments for the present year were :
Bro. Kappelle to the Ottawa Mission, with Bro. Schuster as
his colleague. A new mission was opened up in Waterloo
county, having for a nucleus some of the appointments
formerly belonging to Preston—but with the understanding
that new appointments were to be opened up wherever
practicable. This field was given in charge to my son, with
Bro. Schessar and Bro. Andre as his colleagues. The latter

is a young man of some promise, and is at present travelling under the direction of the Chairman. Their field is a very large one, including six townships, and involving an amount of labour almost incredible. Bro. Allum, with the assistance of a local preacher, has charge of the Hamilton and Paris appointments. I myself was sent back to Preston. By this arrangement each has a sufficiently wide field for the exercise of his talents, and there is also plenty of room for other labourers in the same vineyard.

I cannot describe my sensations in taking my seat on the floor of the Conference, in old John Street Church, Hamilton—the place in which I preached my first sermon as a German missionary, and which is associated with my most endearing reminiscences of the commencement of that work. In spite of myself, my mind would go back in contemplation of all the way in which the Lord had led me, and the work in which I was engaged ; and although it has in some places been a rough and crooked way, still I believe it is the right way, and, while I have some things to regret, I have much to be grateful for.

I must not in this connection forget to mention that, while at Conference in Hamilton, my son and I had the extreme pleasure of being billeted with D. B. Chisholm, Esq. I had the pleasure some years ago of uniting him in marriage to a pious and devoted young lady, a Miss Davis, whose efficient services I have already had occasion to mention in connection with our German Sabbath-school. They have ever been among my warmest friends, and have evinced an attachment to myself which I have always warmly reciprocated.

Although Brother Chisholm already fills very important positions in the world and the church,—being a barrister of

eminent ability, and Superintendent of the McNab Street
Sabbath-school,—still, I believe, he is not yet in the position
for which God has qualified him.   If I were the Superintendent of the Hamilton Circuit, 1 would make him a local
preacher; and I hope, before this book is issued from the
press, to hear of him occupying that position; in which
case I would do myself the honour to go all the way to
Hamilton to hear him—especially as I know I would receive a repetition of those hospitalities which were so grateful to me at Conference.

While cherishing feelings of the liveliest gratitude for the
impulse which the German work received at the Hamilton
Conference, I must not forget to mention the efficient services of Dr. Wood, and the talented, as well as zealous and
indefatigable Missionary Secretary, Dr. Taylor, in bringing
about this result.   They have been always very friendly to
us; but owing to the multiplicity of their engagements in
different parts of our work, they were unable to lend us
much of their time or influence.   However, the measure of
success with which God was pleased to crown our labours in
the past seemed to awaken in the authorities of our Conference a sense of its growing importance; and I must say
that, since that Conference, Dr. Wood has watched over our
interests with all the solicitude of a parent when studying
the welfare of his child.   All that a mortal man could do,
whether by his counsel, his assistance, or the exercise of his
influence in our behalf, has been done by him; and I trust
he may yet live many years, and see his foster-child become
a full-grown man, and a mighty power in the church and in
the world.

Dr. Taylor, besides the assistance which he has rendered
our work in an official capacity, has many claims for especial

mention in a private capacity, and on the grounds of personal friendship. He ought to be a friend to the Jew, who
has travelled so extensively through the Holy Land; and
perhaps no man in our dominion—certainly no man in our
connexion—has obtained such a reputation as a traveller,
and lecturer on his travels, as Dr. Taylor. Among many
of the interesting relics which he has collected, and some of
which I have seen, was a bottle of water from the river
Jordan, with a portion of which he baptized one of my children, who is called after him; and not only did he baptize
him, but he promised me that when he should be old enough
to go to Victoria University, he would make him a present
of a scholarship for that noble institution. My boy is growing old faster than Dr. Taylor seems to be; for although he
gets through an amount of travel and labour each year which
is well nigh incredible, he still appears as young and vigorous
as he was the first day I knew him. May his useful life long
be spared to the church!

Many events of interest occurred during this session of
Conference, the recital of which would, however, only need-
lessly extend the size of this volume. Before its close, Dr.
Nast took his departure, carrying with him, as he assured
us, many pleasing reminiscences of his visit to Canada; and
leaving behind him, among us, recollections of the most
pleasing kind. While he is not by any means indifferent to
the prosperity of the English cause, his whole soul seems to
be devoted to the accomplishment of one object—the moral
and spiritual elevation of his countrymen, the Germans; and
already he sees gratifying effects in his adopted country as
the fruit of his labours; and I trust, ere long, we shall see
the same signs follow our labours, put forth amid so much
to discourage us, in Canada.

I have hitherto refrained from mentioning the English work as much as possible. The English minister was removed, and a young brother, a stranger to me, appointed to succeed him. He did not, however, remain long a stranger. The first time I saw Brother Smiley in Preston, my heart told me we should have peace and harmony during the year. I have often observed that I have seldom occasion to change the first impression which an individual makes upon me. The utmost harmony and good feeling continue up to this time to prevail between Brother Smiley and myself. I and my whole family attend his service in the evening, and, as he understands the German language, he comes to hear me preach as often as he has opportunity. I believe we are endeavouring to bear one another's burdens, and so fulfilling the law of Christ. He is not without his burdens as well as myself. No one who comes to Preston will ever

" Be carried to the skies,
On flowery beds of ease."
[He'll have to fight to win the prize,
And sail through troubled seas !]

However, Brother Smiley's trouble was made for him, and any man who had been appointed would have experienced it. As he was a junior preacher still on probation, he was placed under the direction of the Chairman of the District, and more remotely under that of the President of the Conference and Superintendent of Missions. Receiving his instructions from these officials, it rested with him to carry them out.

But to enter upon a detail of these circumstances, with their causes and results, would be to anticipate in some degree the progress of our narrative.

Shortly after my return, I received a letter from Brother H. W. P. Allen, one of our young ministers just ordained, requesting me to officiate at his wedding with one of the fair daughters of the Elora Circuit, on which he had last laboured. "Strange!" thought I, "how willing these young ministers are, as soon as they get their necks from under one yoke to place it beneath another!" After all, it is perhaps natural, under our present economy, that this should be so.

But I believe the system which is now pursued, in regard to an ordained minister, to be a wrong one. I think that the salary of an ordained minister who chooses to remain single a few years should be placed more nearly on a par with those who are married, instead of offering a premium, as it were, to those who get married the soonest. Surely their salaries should at least come up to that of a common-school teacher, especially as many of them have been teachers, and a goodly number endowed with a thorough university training, who could, if so disposed, get their six hundred to twelve hundred dollars a year as teachers! If this matter were properly adjusted we should no longer find so much difficulty in stationing our married preachers, as we would not have so many of them; nor, again, would we find it so difficult to satisfy the claims of those places which are calling for young men, as we would then have more of them at our command. I suppose there are some who would invoke the shades of Wesley, and Coke, and Asbury, to cry shame on me for giving expression to such heterodox sentiments; but I know there are many of our young ministers who would clap their hands, and shout "Hear! hear!" to such sentiments; and I believe the time will yet come when the church must grapple with this matter, and effect an alteration in this respect,—hosts of Asburys and Cokes to the contrary notwistanding.

These were my thoughts while, in compliance with Bro. Allen's request, I slowly wended my way towards Elora, on a sultry day in July, where the expectant couple were awaiting my arrival. I very soon performed a miracle, for those whom I found existing as two separate individuals, I soon transformed into one; after which I left the happy couple, no doubt anticipating bliss in the future, which I hope they will more than realize. If grace has done as much as nature for the bride, I am sure she is in every respect qualified for her exalted position.

CHAPTER XVI.

I RETURNED from Conference more persuaded than ever
that the German work was of the Lord, and that He would
not withhold His blessing from labour faithfully put forth
in His service.

As if in direct answer to my prayer and faith for a
blessing to rest upon us at the very commencement of the
year, I received an earnest of it in our first prayer-meeting
after Conference. A young lady, at that first meeting, was
awakened to a sense of her position as a sinner, and led to
seek the Saviour of sinners just such as she was. In a short
time she realised the truth of that promise,—" In the day
ye seek him with the whole heart, he will be found of you."
I believe R. V—— was savingly converted to God. Since
that time she has continued to witness a good profession,
in the " midst of a crooked and perverse generation," among
whom she is endeavouring to shine as a light in the world.

Miss Mary A—— was also converted, and I baptized her a short time afterwards. She also continues a faithful member of our church, and, I trust, her name is written in heaven.

These things occurring so soon after my return from Conference, I took as evidences that God had not forgotten to be gracious unto us,—and I could thank God and take courage.

Another circumstance also occurred which tended greatly to increase my faith in God. A young man, about eighteen years of age, had been converted at a "watch-night" service more than a year before. So clear was his evidence of his acceptance with God, that his whole soul seemed to be on fire with love to his Saviour, and he would visit around among his friends, conversing with all whom he met, about the wonderful things God had done for his soul. He gave great promise of future usefulness; and before long I made him an exhorter, thinking he would thus have a wider sphere of usefulness, and intending, if he still maintained his integrity, to recommend him as a candidate for our regular work. But "the Lord's ways are not as our ways, nor His thoughts as our thoughts." In about six months after his becoming an exhorter he was taken sick, and it was very evident to all who beheld him that his sickness was unto death. During his illness, which was protracted for some months, he was very fond of having my son and myself to visit him. On such occasions we invariably found him rejoicing in God, content still to suffer as long as God was pleased to continue it, but fully prepared to "depart and be with Christ, which was far better." His parents, who were members of the "Allbright" church, did not care much to have us visiting him; as they, in common with some other denominations, are not so brotherly towards us as we could wish.

But the work of conversion had, in his case, been too thorough, and the Witness of the Spirit was too clear to be moved, even by the entreaties of his parents. He knew in " whom he had believed, and was firmly persuaded that He was able to keep his soul against the day of evil." He stood firm as a rock! It was truly refreshing to witness the power of the Gospel in so triumphantly saving his soul. A few hours before his death, a last attempt was made to shake his confidence in God and in the Methodists; but again he was firm.

" My dear parents," he said, " take care of your own souls. I am just about to leave you, and my body is very weak; but my soul is strong,—strong in the Lord; and I know that when my heart and flesh fail, God will be ' the strength of my heart and my portion for ever.' I know that I am going home to be with Jesus, and by the grace of God I will never cast away my confidence."

It was enough to melt any heart to see him lying there so weak, and yet so strong. Never resenting efforts to turn him aside; but suffering in meekness, as did his Master, and finally dying in triumph.

Although it would have been in accordance with the wishes of the deceased to be buried by myself or my son, the parents would not suffer such a thing to be heard of. They did not even procure their own minister, but sent for a Mennonist preacher who happened to be convenient. I did not care, however, how the body was disposed of, so long as I knew the soul had gone to be—

" Forever with the Lord."

Such death-bed scenes are encouraging to me, and it makes my heart glad when I think of the number who have already died in triumph. In this manner we labour, and the fruits of our labour pass away,—some to other localities, and some go home to heaven; but our consolation is to know that their names are recorded in the Book of Life; and the assembled universe will some day know what the German Missionaries are doing, and have done for the church and the world.

It was perhaps well that I received these encouragements at the commencement of the year, for I was yet to experience the truth of our Saviour's declaration,—" In the world ye shall have tribulation."

I have before adverted to the fact that some important changes were made at the past Conference in regard to the German work, chiefly on the recommendation of Dr. Nast, whose experience in a widely-extended field of labour well qualified him at the same time to recommend several measures, and also gave the recommendations thus made a great deal of weight with our Conference officials. Among the measures thus recommended by him was, that the German and English Sabbath-schools, which had for some time previously existed separately, should be united. He said he had invariably found this principle of union and consolidation to work well as far his observation extended. By this means a double object could be accomplished. Not only would the united school acquire additional strength and vigour, but the church which the English Sunday-school used to occupy in the afternoon, would thus be left vacant, as the united Sunday-school would meet in the morning at nine o'clock, previous to the morning service in German at half-past ten.

By this means I could hold a second service in the afternoon, and it was thought that perhaps some of the Germans who could not come to the morning service, would get out in the afternoon. I believe the scheme was a wise one; at any rate the intention was good, and I entered into it with all my heart. With the co-operation of the English minister, I anticipated no difficulty in carrying out these arrangements; especially as the authorities of the Conference had given me every assurance of their good will, and their determination to do all in their power for the interests of the German work. I conversed with Bro. Smiley shortly after his arrival in Preston in regard to these plans. He promised to lay them before his people as soon as convenient. This he did in a private manner, going from house to house and endeavouring to get their opinions, especially in regard to the union of the Sabbath-schools.

He found a feeling among his people strongly adverse to any alteration of the system under which they had existed during the previous year. He pleaded the experience and wisdom of Dr. Nast, who had recommended it, as well as the concurrence of the wisest and best men in our Conference, who had agreed with him, and urged them to give it a trial. They, on the other hand, pleaded the experience and wisdom of Bro. Miller, their former pastor, who had kept them separate; and insisted on having their "rights," as defined by the Guelph District Meeting, maintained inviolate.

These rights were defined in a document drawn up by the District Meeting before stated, and specified that the Germans should have the use of the church during the whole of the Sabbath forenoon for their Sabbath-school and service; the English were to have the afternoon and even-

12

ing for their Sabbath-school and service. For special and week evening services, a special clause was provided. These were the rights they contended for.

In this emergency the young English Brother had recourse to his Chairman. He considered it necessary during the consultation to have me also present. I accordingly went, and although we found him strongly disposed to condemn the spirit of the English people, still he advised us not to push our new regulations in too great a hurry upon them. In order to this, he thought if I would agree to hold my afternoon service for a few weeks at half-past three o'clock, and not press for a union of the Sabbath-schools, that the English Sabbath-school could meet and dismiss before my service commenced.

" And perhaps," said he, " in a few weeks, when they see you are disposed to sacrifice your convenience for their accommodation, they will fall in quite readily with the intentions of Conference."

Although I knew this arrangement was a bad one, and that half-past three was a very inconvenient hour for an afternoon service; still, I loved the English work, and would not do anything to injure it. So I fell in with the arrangement thus proposed, but I had my misgivings at the same time that it would not succeed. However, I continued it a few weeks. But no sooner did the English people see that they were left in undisturbed possession of their church and Sunday-school, than they began to triumph, and use such expressions as, " He knows better than invade our rights !" I wondered somewhat why they should thus involve me in it at all, as I had done nothing, said nothing since Conference, but simply told some of our people the measures that had been recommended,

I found an unsettled feeling beginning to enter the minds of some.

"Why," they would say, "if you have authority to unite the Sunday-schools do you not do it! If you have the power, and do not exercise it, you will be a nobody, the authorities will be nobodies, and the cause here will go to nought."

This was a serious aspect in which to view the matter, and I saw that something must be done, especially as the days were now growing short, and it would almost be dark when I could get through my afternoon service, as I was so late in commencing it. Still, I did nothing. Bro. Smiley, however, who saw the position of affairs as well as I did, saw that something must be done, and that very shortly. He communicated with some of the highest officials in the Conference to know what he must do. Their instruction to him was:—

"Carry out the original intention of the Conference, and unite the Sunday-schools with as little offence to any one as possible. The English work is subordinate to the German, as far as the occupancy of the church is concerned. The church in Preston was built, not by the English of that locality alone, but by funds collected from different parts of the Province. It is, besides, older than the English cause, and has for these reasons claims to superiority."

Bro. Smiley, after receiving his instructions to carry out the design of uniting the Sunday-schools, still lingered a few weeks, hoping to persuade them to an amicable coalition. Most of the teachers opposed the coalition government, and carried out their politics in the Sunday-school. At last he announced that on a given Sabbath morning he would be present to organize the united Sabbath-schools, and urged upon the people not to fight against God by opposing the measure, but for their souls' sake, and the sake of the children, to give it a fair trial.   All was of no avail.

On the last Sabbath in which they met as a separate school in our church, the Superintendent called upon all the children to pledge themselves to go with him on the following Sabbath, to the old Town-Hall, occupied by the New Connexion as a church.   The poor children stood up, although some of them were very unwilling to do so, but still did not wish to be conspicuous by keeping their seats.   Thus they became pledged to go with their Superintendent and teachers.   When the morning came on which the union was to have taken place, not one of them was present; but on the afternoon of the same day the teachers might have been seen ostentatiously parading the street in groups of two and three, each followed by a number of children, all wending their way towards their new Sunday-school.   Mr. K——, with a horse and light waggon filled full of children, brought up the rear of this motley procession.

The school, thus founded in opposition, increased for a few weeks with rapidity, and threatened to carry all before it.   At the present time, however, it is afflicted with a serious decline, and notwithstanding all their efforts to preserve its life, it is now a mere skeleton,—a shadow of its former self.   What has perplexed me through it all is, that I get the whole of the blame from those English people for driving them, as they say, out of their church, while at the same time they cannot lay their finger upon a single thing I have done, or a single word I have said against them. Presuming, however, that I am the cause, the Superintendent has threatened not only to establish an opposition English Sunday-school, but to bring in German teachers, and so break down our German Sunday-school, and in time destroy our whole German work.

Although our German Sunday-school received no accessions by the union, and has all this external opposition to contend against, still it is in a healthy and prosperous condition.

We had a concert in its behalf during the summer, and raised funds sufficient to replenish our library and meet our current expenses. We have not a dollar of debt, and have all our requirements satisfied, as well as a regular and full attendance of scholars and teachers.

We gave the children a festival on the Christmas-eve of 1867, and again on New Year's-day—both of which were quite successful, and very numerously attended by the children and their friends.

The efficient services of my daughter Rachel, who trains the children in music and recitation, &c., contribute more, perhaps, to the success of these occasions than anything else. Still, the attendance of such numbers in the church shows that we have yet many friends. But if it were not that the Lord is on our side, we never could have survived all the efforts that have been made to destroy us : and if we had every year to report a decrease, it would not at all be thought a strange thing by those who are fully acquainted with our position and trials.

One day, when the troubles briefly detailed in the foregoing pages were at their height, I ran down to Hamilton to see Brother Elliott, from whom I am always sure of a welcome, and a word of sympathy. While there, I had the pleasure of hearing him discourse, in his own easy and masterly manner, to his week evening congregation, in John Street Church, on the words, "Thou hast a few names even in Sardis who have not defiled their garments, and they shall walk with me in white, for they are worthy." I received a blessing during the delivery of the sermon, but I could not help thinking how much better it would apply to my little society in Preston than to this great city assembly; and so, the very next Sabbath morning, I took his text, and preached a good part of his sermon to my German congregation in Preston; for I am thankful to God that I have still a few names here whose garments are undefiled.

Athough the Minutes of the Conference only assign me Preston as a field of labour, it must not be supposed that I am entirely confined to that little town. As I have the whole work and its interests near my heart, I have several times visited the field of labour assigned to my son and his colleagues, in Waterloo county and vicinity. These visits have generally been to attend Special Meetings, Church Dedications, and assist them in Protracted Meetings. They have been doing a wonderful work, opening up new appointments, building churches, and, in general, making inroads on the enemy's territory. Already they have several classes established, and a goodly amount of success in the conversion of sinners. The greater the amount of their success, the more the enemy rages; and just in proportion as their converts increase, their enemies multiply.* In this, also, I have to endure my share of the persecution.

While assisting my son at one of these protracted meetings in Heidelberg, a certain Lutheran minister, a Mr. S——, was particularly zealous in his efforts to injure us. Failing,

---

* As a proof of this, I might say our church in Heidelberg has been attacked three several times—the windows broken, and other damage done.

however, to find any just cause of accusation against either
of us personally, he directed his attacks against Mr. Wesley,
—stating that he was such a harsh man, and so reserved in
his manners and general deportment, that even his wife could
not live with him, and little children fled in terror from his
approach.   I replied, that so far from this being the case, he
was always noted for his affection for children, and the ease
with which he secured their confidence and love.   And as
to his wife not living with him, that would prove nothing
against him ; for he must remember that the devil could not
live in heaven,—not because it was not a comfortable place,
but because his own ugly temper drove him out of it.

"But," said I, "even supposing it were all true which
you allege against him, I can show you, in a printed book,
charges against Martin Luther and his wife, ten thousand
times more criminal than anything you have yet said against
Mr. Wesley; and yet you are a follower of him.   Do you
not know that the best of men in all ages of the world's
history, have had the most serious charges brought against
them ?   Even our Saviour was accused by his enemies of
performing his miracles by the power of Beelzebub, the
prince of the devils."

One evening, when going to preach at one of their week
night services, I drove my horse and buggy under a shed,
and spent a couple of very profitable hours labouring for the
salvation of souls.   When I came out, the night was very
dark, and I went to get my buggy in order to drive away.
Something, however, seemed to impel my son and Bro.
Schesser to examine my buggy and harness, to see that all
was right before starting.   This I would never have thought
of doing, as I was not at all apprehensive of danger.   It was
well they did so, for when they came to feel around the

wheels, they found the nuts had been removed from the ends of the axles, leaving three wheels liable to drop off as soon as we would start. I had, of course, to leave my buggy there, and Mrs. Freshman and I had to walk quite a distance before reaching our place of accommodation for the night. This I again looked upon as a most providential deliverance from the power of our enemies; for most assuredly, had this not been observed before we started, the wheels must have come off when going rapidly down a steep hill near by, the buggy would have been smashed, and perhaps Mrs. Freshman or myself, or both, instantly killed.

This is but a specimen of the manner in which the old adversary works, and, at the same time, of the manner in which God defeats his projects. Notwithstanding all such opposition, the work in Heidelberg went on; and although a few months ago there was no probability of accomplishing much there, we have now a church, a class, a leader, and a Sabbath-school, as well as a nice congregation of devout worshippers.

CHAPTER XVII.

In addition to the troubles I experienced from the internal
state of affairs in Preston, my mind was often grieved when
I heard of the remarks made by some of our brethren in
the ministry occupying adjoining circuits. These remarks
had a tendency to create the impression that the German
work was a small affair.

I must say, however, that they retarded our operations
by such invidious remarks, and we could have opened appointments in other places if they had given us a little
assistance, or even if they had let us alone and minded
their own business. Yet I am glad to be able to say,
that they are now beginning to see that they have been
mistaken, and are disposed to judge of us much more
favourably at the present time than ever before.

But the light and the shade always bear some relation
the one to the other; and my lot during the present year
12*

has not been without its bright aspects. Among other things, the very friendly relations which I have sustained towards the English minister is not among the least of my causes for thankfulness. Having trials in common, we made a common cause of it, and, I believe, served mutually to sustain each other.

The Missionary Committee had expressed a desire that I should, as soon as convenient, pay a visit to the Ottawa Mission, which I had surveyed and opened up some years before, for the purpose not only of inspecting the present condition of the field already occupied, but also of penetrating beyond the limits of that field, in order to discover, if possible, whether there were others in the neighbourhood still destitute of the gospel.

In pursuance of this object I started from home on Wednesday, the 25th of September, 1867, and arrived in Pembroke at midnight on Friday, the 27th.

In the morning I went to the Chairman—the Rev. D. L. McDowell — who immediately offered to accompany me over a part of the journey,—a great portion of which was still a wilderness.

We first visited Bro. Kappelle, who, in anticipation of my coming, had already made several announcements for me to preach at various appointments.

In accordance with one of those announcements, Bro. Kappelle and I went the same afternoon to Wilberforce. The road had very greatly improved since my former visit, seven years before : but I suffered greatly from a severe attack of rheumatism.

We arrived at Wilberforce in the evening, and were very hospitably entertained at the house of Mrs. Edwards. As I entered the church on the following morning, my heart was filled with joy and gratitude to see the house of God filled with a devout assembly of German people, who were already engaged in singing songs of gratitude and praise to the Most High. I forgot all my pains and aches, and had a blessed time in preaching to them.

After the sermon we administered the Lord's Supper, and this was followed by such a love-feast as it has seldom been my privilege to witness. For two hours a continued stream of praise went up to God from the hearts of these poor people, whose sins He had pardoned. Sometimes several would be on their feet at the same time; and so anxious were the people to witness for Jesus, that it was with the utmost difficulty we could bring the meeting to a close;— and even then the people would not leave the house.

But we had to hasten to our next appointment, at Ellice; which place we reached partly by driving and partly on foot. It was only a small congregation, but we had a blessed time. After the evening service we had still an hour's walk before we reached our resting-place for the night.

The next day we continued our journey to Upper Wilberforce, where we arrived at four o'clock P.M. Bro. Kappelle had commenced to build a church in this place. In the evening I preached in the house of the German class-leader, and had great occasion to rejoice that the Lord had so richly blessed the labours of his ministering servant in this place!

On Tuesday I went to Algona. In order to reach this place we had to bring into requisition all kinds of conveyances. A part of the way we rode on horseback; from this we descended to a cart,—even this had to give place to a canoe; and finally we had to proceed on foot! I preached in the church to an attentive and crowded congregation, and I had the pleasure of seeing one soul awakened during the service.

At this place Bro. Kappelle left me well-cared for, under the hospitable roof of Bro. Mitchell, and returned to his home. I occupied the three following days in visiting from house to house—inviting people out to the services—and preaching every evening.

On Saturday, the 5th of October, it rained and snowed at intervals all day. The Sabbath evening appointment was in Sebastopol; and I was very glad when I saw that Bro. McDowell and Bro. Kappelle had come through all this unpleasant weather to accompany me. May the Lord bless the Chairman of the District for his warm-hearted, active services in the interests of the German cause!

The storm, and the miserable condition of the roads, made it impossible for us to reach our place of destination on the Saturday evening; we remained, therefore, in a tavern by the road-side over night, and continued our journey on the Sabbath morning.

When we came to the place of our appointment, we found that the greater part of the congregation had returned to their homes. Still, a few remained, and to these I preached. I found here more intelligence and refinement than in any other German settlement. They promised to give the Wesleyan Church the deed of one hundred acres of land, and contribute a portion of the salary of a missionary, if only one would be sent to them.

Mr. Holderman, a German, and the Government Land Agent, invited us to dinner, and promised to do all in his power in order to get a German Church erected in that locality.

After dinner we started for Denby, and now commenced our troubles. Bad roads, nothing to eat, rain pouring down in torrents! However we endured it all; and at last, late in the evening, we arrived at a shanty, where we passed the night.

On Monday we sought out, as we continued our travels, those families of Germans who had settled in the district, and this we continued to do throughout the whole journey. We came on Tuesday to Mr. Kenyon's, where Bro. Perry boarded, and here again we received every attention and kindness.

From this place, Brother Kappelle and Brother McDowell returned to their respective homes, and left me to continue my journey still further, to Kingston, and find out the German settlers as I progressed. Brother Perry very kindly offered to go with me, and drive me in his gig. But before we had finished a day's journey, the gig was smashed to pieces; and, while the rain poured down in torrents, we had to continue our journey on foot until late in the night. At last we found a shelter at the house of Mr. Godfrey. Seldom have I felt more thankful than I did for the kindness which we experienced from Mr. Godfrey and his excellent wife. They dried our clothes, which were completely saturated, gave us a very good supper, and offered us the only bed they had in the house.

We had still upwards of one hundred miles to travel, through a bleak, dreary wilderness, and with no kind of conveyance whatever. We saw no help for it, and philosophically determined to make light of what could not be remedied. Imagine our joy and gratitude when, just as we were about to start, Mr. Godfrey offered us a two-wheeled cart! We accepted it with thankfulness, and went on, jolting over roots and stumps; and if we had not been pretty well put together, we must have gone to pieces.

We found but very few houses on our journey during the first day, but we soon came to the German settlement we had heard of, the people of which were desirous of having a missionary sent them.*   On Friday, Brother Holmes, of Harrowsmith, offered to relieve Brother Perry, and conduct me to Kingston, where I took the morning train, and on Saturday night I arrived safely at home.   On Sabbath I preached three times—twice to my own congregation, and once to the English, whose minister was supplying for his Chairman in Galt.   On Monday I wrote an account of my journey to Dr. Wood, as I had again to start on Tuesday, to assist my son in a series of Protracted Meetings on his mission.

The prospects of our German work in the parts of Canada which I visited are good.   Brother Kappelle has seventeen appointments, four churches, and seventy members.   They have already contributed seventy dollars for the maintenance of the missionaries.   This is a great deal, when we take into consideration their circumstances as new settlers; they are poor, and struggling with difficulties.   When I came to the Ottawa Mission, seven years ago, I found neither bread to eat, nor a single converted soul.   But now, to God be all the praise and glory! they have bread enough and to spare—especially where the missionaries preach, and classes are formed.   Brother Kappelle and his colleague are much

---

* Since my return I have been empowered by the Missionary authorities to employ Brother Wasmund as a hired local-preacher for this place.   He now travels under the Chairman, and will probably be received on trial for the regular work next Conference.

esteemed and beloved, and they have accomplished a good deal ; but the field is much too large for two men.

The hardships which our missionaries have to endure are very great ; but they labour on, impelled by the love of Jesus, for the salvation of immortal souls. There was in the settlements through which I travelled, work enough for two more men, and then they could not accomplish it all. Oh ! how grateful would it be to them, if the Missionary Board would immediately extend to them a helping hand ! The work there could be separated into two circuits ; but still I would judge it for the best, to leave the whole under the oversight of Brother Kappelle. As this part of Canada has the best prospect to become settled with Germans, and as the Wesleyan Church is the first which has taken an interest especially in their spiritual welfare, so we should be the first in immediately supplying this destitute part of our land with gospel privileges commensurate with their necessities. May God, in his great mercy, not only open the door for us, but also give us grace to go up and possess the goodly land thus presented to our view !

The above is, in substance, the account which I wrote for the *Christian Guardian*, on my return. Many incidents, however, some ludicrous enough, occurred during my visit, one or two of which may not be out of place here.

During the time in which Brother McDowell accompanied me, we travelled almost a whole day without coming to a house, or having anything to eat. About four in the afternoon, we reached a small log-house, and presented ourselves as candidates for something to eat. The good woman of the house was glad to see us, but, unfortunately, had not a bite of prepared victuals in the house. She had, however, a supply of flour, and she commenced to bake—sending off a dog in the meantime, to catch a couple of chickens with which to regale us. This was altogether too slow a process for my fancy; and seizing a handful of potatoes, I threw them into the warm ashes, and before they were half roasted commenced to devour them. Brother McDowell,—who was Chairman of a District, and had a certain amount of dignity to maintain,—waited until the chickens were cooked, and the cakes baked, and then did his duty to that which was set before him.

During our repast, I ascertained from some conversation with the good woman of the house, that the Rev. R. Jones, who had travelled through that country about forty years ago, was the means of her conversion to God; and she still delights to acknowledge him as her spiritual father. At any rate, if it was not in that part he had travelled, it was somewhere where she had lived, and the fact is the same. Thus, the good seed sown in the most unpromising places is often found to take root downward, and bring forth fruit upwards,—giving encouragement to all, "in the morning to sow the seed, and in the evening to withhold not the hand, not knowing which shall prosper, either this or that, or whether both shall be alike good."

During a conversation which I had with Brother McDowell, on one of our journeys, he related an incident of the death of a Roman Catholic Priest, somewhere in that neighbourhood, which made a very deep impression on my mind.

The Priest was said to have been awakened on his deathbed to a sense of his condition as a sinner, but too late to find the Saviour of sinners, and died in great mental agony, with his last breath exclaiming:—"Oh, my God! where am I going!"

I thought of the snares which, on two occasions, had been laid to entrap me into the priesthood, and felt thankful that I had been led to become a Minister of the better Covenant, even if I did find my pathway somewhat hedged up at times.

Some time after this, in conversation with another Priest, and endeavouring to point out to him his errors, I mentioned this circumstance to him, and asked him to compare such a death-bed with the scenes recorded in connection with the last moments of evangelical Ministers of other churches ; but the poor man either had the ears of the deaf adder, which would not hearken to the voice of the charmer, or else he believed in a purgatory, where the peccadilloes of the present life could be atoned for by the fire of purification,—for he went his way seemingly caring for none of these things.

When I returned home from my tour of exploration I presented a pitiable enough appearance. My clothes were in tatters. I had to wear my overcoat buttoned close to conceal the rents in the coat beneath, and even my overcoat was in a sorry enough condition. Two large rents, extending from the top throughout, afforded free scope for ventilation ; and if I had not been inside of it, and any one had found it in the woods, they would most certainly have said of me, as the old Patriarch said of his son Joseph, "Surely an evil beast hath devoured him !" My boots were in keeping with my other garments, full of rents ; and my linen was in that condition best expressed by the word "unmentionable." However I was thankful that it was no worse, and soon after my arrival I forgot the lesser troubles of my journey in combatting the stern realities of those at home.

Soon after my return I dedicated a new church to the

worship of God in Erbsville, an appointment on my son's field of labour. I sent an account of it to the *Christian Guardian*, which account Dr. Nast was pleased to transcribe into the *Apologete*, prefacing it with a few observations of his own. As this will no doubt serve as a book of reference for information regarding the commencement of the German work in Canada, until a better óne is published, I cannot do better than translate the whole article from the *Apologete*, including the notice which originally appeared in the *Guardian*. He says :—

"We make our readers acquainted with the interesting missionary operations of Dr. Freshman, which we have translated from the *Christian Guardian*, the organ of the Wesleyan Church in Canada. Dr. Freshman is the father of German Methodism in Canada, and has imparted his pioneer spirit to the younger preachers. Our brethren in Canada labour in the present day with the same zeal and self-denial which characterized the fathers of the English Wesleyan Church, and the pioneers of the German work in the United States. The same zeal and spiritual devotion are just as necessary in the present time as they were in those days. May the Lord grant to all his servants a rich baptism of fire on their entrance upon the new year! Dr. Freshman informs the *Guardian*, of Nov. 26, 1867, of new conquests, as follows :—

"'Last Sunday I was permitted to dedicate to the worship of the Triune God a new church, (or meeting-house, as we would call it,) in Erbsville, and to preach three times to very large and devout congregations. The house was crowded, and the Holy Spirit moved many hearts to tears during the proclamation of His word. This is the second German Church

which has been dedicated since Conference in this part of
our German work, and another is to be dedicated in Conestoga, on the 21st of December. But not alone are churches
being built, but souls are being converted, and arriving at a
saving knowledge of the truth as it is in Jesus. In Poole
and Heidelberg, where our young brethren have been holding a series of protracted meetings, the Lord has richly
blessed their labours, and at each of these appointments
classes have been formed. At the present time they are
making special efforts in Ellice and Erbsville, with the same
success. I may say that the German work on the field occupied by my son and his colleagues, has been crowned with
success, and promises still more. These young men labour
hard, very hard, and have many privations to endure, so
much so that I often wonder how they and their horses sustain it. But they are all courageous. Each of them labours
with one hand on the wall of Zion, and with the other grasps
the sword to defend the cause of God against its enemies.

"'What I have seen on this Mission, as well as on my late
journey to Ottawa fills *my* heart, and will no doubt the hearts
of *all* who love the Lord, with joy and thankfulness, and in-
spires me with fresh courage.

"'In conclusion, I may be permitted to say that I have
nothing to complain of in regard to the spiritual condition of
my Preston congregation. We are expecting an outpouring
of the Holy Spirit during the protracted meetings which we
intend to commence as soon as those on my son's field of
labour are finished.'"

Some time before starting on this visit to the Ottawa Mission, I was sent for to visit Paris and St. George, in which
places our German people were discontented with the Con-

ference appointments, as they did not get the amount of preaching and visiting to which they had been accustomed. I found the good people of St. George mourning over this state of things very deeply; but I preached to them, and also visited them at their homes, and finally succeeded in reconciling them to endure their fate until the end of the year. I had somewhat more difficulty with our friends in Paris, who especially complained of the neglect of pastoral visitation, but at last they too submitted, and peace and harmony were restored.

The Lutheran minister in Preston had, for a length of time, occupied a very equivocal position in regard to his doctrines. He wished the people to understand that the doctrines which he held were in no respect different from those of the Reformed Lutheran Church. By this means he had succeeded in gaining the confidence of some of the most intelligent and substantial men in Preston, who were of decidedly reform proclivities.

Some things however occurred which had a direct tendency to shake their confidence in him as a proper person for their spiritual adviser, and a series of well directed questions, in the form of a cross-examination, forced him to declare his true position, and he had to discover the cloven foot. Their confidence was at once destroyed, and they clamoured for a preacher after their own heart. Such an one was supplied to them in this manner :—

The Presbyterian Church not wishing to be behind other evangelical denominations in missionary zeal and enterprise had, some time before, engaged a young Swiss preacher, and sent him out to evangelize the Germans in Waterloo county. He took up his residence in Berlin, and commenced to hold forth in the Lutheran Church in that place. This he continued for more than a year, until finally he gave it up. He then began to make incursions in various other directions, and at length came to Preston, and asked permission to occupy our church for a service once in two or three weeks, on the Lord's-day. I thought if he were a sound evangelical preacher he might thus be able to reach some of the people in Preston, who would never come to a Methodist service; so I lent him the church, and gave him every facility to establish a cause here. I hope the Presbyterian minister will show as friendly a disposition towards our missionaries, if ever they have occasion to apply for a similar favour. I was somewhat amused at him when, on one Saturday evening I handed him our hymn-book, and requested him to select the hymns for the service on the morrow, to find him select a single hymn, saying that was all he would require.

"Well, but," said I, "do you only sing once during your service?"

"O yes," said he, "we sing three times, but we can divide this hymn into three sections, and sing a couple of verses each time."

Well, thought I, this is at any rate a novelty, if it is not a reform.

He preached a few times in our church—seemed earnest and zealous—but utterly failed in his endeavours to establish a cause in Preston. He has I have heard, since he took his departure from amongst us, been a little more successful in other localities.

The principal cause of his want of success among the German Reformers in this neighbourhood, I attribute to

the fact that he — as a Presbyterian — is a follower of
Calvin ; while the Reformers are nearly all followers of
Zwingle ; and these doctrines, I have no hesitation in say-
ing, do not completely harmonize.

I however do not approve of the entire doctrines of either
Calvin or Zwingle, but I believe they were both good men,
and I hope got safe home to heaven.   But I think the doctrines, as taught by either, much preferable to the perverted
doctrines of the old Lutheran Church, and hence I give their
dissemination every encouragement in such quarters as I
know are not yet prepared to receive the more elevated and
Scriptural doctrines of our church.   I believe all our ministers are of the same disposition, and this ought to acquit
us of the charge of bigotry, which misinformed people are
so prone to prefer against us.

There is no converted minister to whom I would not give
the right hand of fellowship, and no section of the church
which preaches the necessity of conversion, and a godly life,
to which I do not wish God speed.   But I know this vindication is unnecessary to those who are best acquainted with
us, and our doctrinal liberality.

But while I am no friend to bigotry, I am still less
friendly to latitudinarianism, which would teach us that it
is no matter what a man believes, if only his intentions are
good.   According to such, the sincere follower of Mahomet
is just as good a man as the sincere follower of our blessed
Lord and Saviour ; and the honest infidel as near salvation
as the believing Christian.   If they do not say so much in
as many words, certainly this is the tendency of their doctrine ; and to such a doctrine I pray the Lord I may never
become friendly disposed.

During the whole of the fall months, including December, I had occupied my spare time in assisting our young brethren on the Waterloo Mission in protracted meetings. At the New Year, I commenced in Preston; and although two weeks have yet only elapsed, we have encouraging signs of success. I believe the devil has always some hand in bringing about circumstances to retard our efforts. This year he broke the clapper out of our bell, which used, before this accident, to summon the worshippers to the house of God. This is but a small accident to mention, but it recalls another which took place last year at this time, when commencing similar services.

I had at the time I refer to, gone down to the railroad station, from which my daughter Rachel was starting to the Hamilton College, after her Christmas vacation; and in stepping off the cars, which were in motion, I severely sprained one of my ancles, so that it was with the utmost difficulty I could reach my home. But I had announced to preach in the evening, and I must not disappoint the people. In order to keep my appointment, I had to be carried into the church; and as I could not support the least particle of the weight of my body upon my foot, I had to preach with one foot resting on a chair. And this was repeated night after night, until my ancle was restored to its normal condition.

Notwithstanding this accident, the Lord vouchsafed us showers of blessings, which, I trust, will be repeated this year during the present series of services upon which we have entered. In a week or two, I expect to be reinforced by the assistance of my son and his two colleagues, who can in this manner pay back the assistance I rendered them on

previous occasions; and I see no reason why, with the help
of the Lord, we should not go up and possess the goodly
land which he as promised us in His word.   It is true, we
have this year influences to contend against of a particular
and trying nature—some of which may perhaps be referred
to in the following and concluding chapter.

CHAPTER XVIII.

Now that I have come to the last chapter of my book,
I cannot help feeling how incomplete the work will be after
all. The narrative detailed thus far is but a rough sketch —
an imperfect outline of what my entire life has been. The
interior life, composed of the thoughts of the mind — the
feelings of the heart — the outgushings of the soul — its
aspirations after God — its conflicts with the wicked one —
as well as those thousand sources of enjoyment with which
it has pleased God to bless me in my domestic relations, —
are things too sacred to be more than adverted to in these
pages. Their record would swell this volume into a large
octavo ; and, besides, could not prove of interest beyond the
circle of my personal friends and acquaintances.

But apart from this, I remember with regret that I have
omitted to mention in the proper place the names of many
of our brethren from whom I experienced a great deal of

13

kindness in my times of need.   There are others who have been intimately connected in various ways with some of the circumstances detailed in the previous pages.   Among the names thus omitted are some of the greatest lights in our Conference.   Before proceeding with the narrative, I hope I may be pardoned if I introduce a few of them.

Commencing with our own District, I select one, who, almost like King Saul of old, stands from the shoulders upwards higher than his brethren.   Who does not recognize the Rev. J. Potts ?   I became acquainted with him at the Grimsby camp-meeting, when he was still a young man, travelling under the superintendence of the Rev. S. Rose, who is now our Book-Steward, and who, I believe, deservedly enjoys the fullest confidence of his brethren.   His talents and piety, as well as his affable manner and gentlemanly deportment, at once stamp him as one of our first-class men. Mr. Potts and I both preached at the camp-meeting aforesaid ; and with that very laudable desire for information, so becoming in young men, he came to me after the services were concluded, asking me as a favour freely to criticise his style of preaching, and suggest anything I thought might be for his improvement.   I advised him to guard against the danger of becoming vain, or exalted above measure, if he should become popular ; for I already discovered in him a prospect that this would be the case.   The great Centenary Church in Hamilton, of which he is now the pastor, is a sufficiently important charge to show that I, at least, possessed penetration of character, and he possessed merit of no mean order.

In contrast with him, but only in so far as personal appearance is concerned, stands the Rev. Thomas Derrick. But if small in stature, perhaps he the more closely resem-

bles the Apostle Paul. He belonged to the Quebec District
when I was recommended to the Conference to be received
as a member, and has ever since been a warm personal
friend, to whom I am strongly attached. When my children first heard him preach, they were delighted with his
matter, his manner, his style, and delivery; but playfully
remarked, " What a pity it is he is not larger in stature !"
I know he has a large heart, and a large head also ; and
I hope he may long be spared to occupy similar positions of
usefulness to that which he holds at present, He visited
me in Hamilton shortly after I went to live there, and now
occupies the position of President's Assistant in Hamilton
Centre.

While lecturing in St. Catharine's, before my reception
into the ministry, I shall never forget the kindness with
which I was welcomed by the Rev. Mr. McCullough, who
was then stationed in that place. Besides his many tokens
of personal interest in the object of my visit, he introduced
me to several of the leading inhabitants of the place, and
endeavoured, by every means in his power, to elicit their
sympathies in my behalf—all of which I remember with
gratitude. In all my subsequent intercourse with him, I
have found him the same warm-hearted, consistent, devoted
Christian friend, which the early days of our acquaintance
gave promise he would become.

After commencing to labour as a German Missionary, I
felt it my duty to urge the claims of the gospel upon the
Germans wherever they were to be found. Among other
places I visited Brantford, where the Rev. Geo. Young was
then stationed. He immediately evinced a warm interest
in the object of my visit, and assisted me in opening an
appointment. I had the privilege of hearing him preach in

his own church on that occasion. I liked his sermon very much, and formed a high opinion of his ministerial ability ; an opinion which, I am pleased to observe, I only hold in common with my brethren—for they give him the most important stations in their power to bestow.

During the present year I have experienced much kindness, both from himself and his excellent lady, during some of my visits to Toronto, where he superintends the West Circuit, and presides as Chairman of the District. His noble self-sacrifice in accepting an arduous missionary appointment at Red River, for which place he is to start in a couple of weeks in company with the Rev. G. McDougall, shows that he is a man of the right stamp, willing to lay his all upon the altar of his Master : to sacrifice ease, position, and society, for the sake of extending the kingdom of the Redeemer into lands remote. May the pleasure of the Lord prosper in his hands !

Associated with him in Toronto is the Rev. George Cochrane, with whom I have enjoyed many seasons of delightful intercourse. He is one of the many examples of men who have risen by their persistent efforts in the pursuit of knowledge. He has an extensive and select library, filled with

"Many a quaint and curious volume of forgotten lore."

Encyclopædias of all kinds ; biblical and theological dictionaries, giving information on all possible subjects of enquiry which may arise to the mind ; lexicons, rare and valuable, of different languages,—form a prominent feature in his collection. He has made some progress in the study of the Hebrew language, and is availing himself of the facilities which his proximity with the University College in Toronto affords him, of further improving himself in this department. "*Labor omnia vincit*," says one; and I hope he may succeed in overcoming all obstacles, so that he may, in fine, learn to speak the language of Canaan.

While speaking of the language of Canaan, I am reminded of one occasion on which I was invited to Cobourg to lecture before the learned Faculty and students of our College there, on the Hebrew language. At that time I endeavoured to prove that it was the language which God taught to Adam, and which continued to be spoken until the confusion of tongues at the building of Babel. I am still of that opinion; and, more than that, I believe it is the language which will be spoken in heaven. The Rev. Dr. Nelles, the distinguished President of Victoria College, seemed deeply interested. In fact, the whole Faculty paid the most marked attention, which gave me much encouragement, as I felt I was addressing men of learning, who could appreciate the curious points which I started, and the delicate speculations in which I indulged. In conversation with Dr. Nelles afterwards, I was surprised at the variety of his attainments, and the extent of his knowledge; especially in that department which would in my country be called " Philosophical," but is here more frequently termed "Metaphysical." He, however, made no parade of his learning; but it seemed to come bubbling out spontaneously, as water from the spring. His conversation is, at the same time, so richly interspersed with anecdote, and real, genuine, lively humour, that he becomes immediately a most attractive person, and always improves the longer one is acquainted with him. I earnestly pray that he may long be spared to prove himself a workman that needeth not to be ashamed in the exalted position which it has been his lot now for so many years to occupy.

At that time I also became slightly acquainted with the Rev. W. H. Poole, who was then stationed in Cobourg. I have several times met with him since, and my slight acquaintance has ripened into warm personal friendship and sincere esteem. His commanding presence seems to qualify him for a leader among his brethren; and his affable manner uniformly secures him their good will. Without at all attempting the prophetic, I might predict for him the Chairmanship of a District at no distant day. No one doubts his qualification for this position; and the confidence reposed in him by his brethren will speedily secure it to him. I have uniformly experienced the greatest amount of kindness from him, and take this opportunity of expressing my gratitude.

While preaching to the Germans in London, I can never forget my indebtedness to the Rev. R. Jones, who was then stationed there. A veteran of the cross, he is still engaged in unfurling its banner with as much zeal and energy as when, forty-two years ago, he took up the standard and essayed to bear it. His gifts and graces have gained for him the highest positions in the gift of his ministerial brethren, not even excepting the Presidential Chair. Although there is only one now in the active work of the ministry in the Dominion of Canada who has been longer engaged than himself, still his eye can scarcely be said to have grown dim, or his natural force abated. The church may well pray that his efficient services may long be continued; for when at length he will have to lay his armour down, she will have lost a person whose efficient services, protracted over such an extended period, entitle him to the esteem of all who know him.

Among those who are not immediately engaged in the

work of the ministry, we have still very many prominent individuals who have raised for themselves monuments more lasting than brass.* Prominent among these stands the Rev. E. Ryerson, D.D., LL.D., Chief Superintendent of Education, which responsible and honourable position he has now occupied, by permission of the Conference, for a number of years. The history of this valued servant of the Church is in a measure the history of Canada, but especially of Methodism in Canada. Possessed of rare gifts as a writer and speaker, his talents procured for him, while still a young man, the most distinguished positions which the Conference had it in its power to bestow. Chosen, on more than one occasion, as our representative to the British Conference, he could not but secure their admiration and esteem, as he had already done that of ours. His tongue and pen have always been at the service of the Church, and have never failed to render it efficient aid,—especially in times of its greatest extremity. His educational system is the admiration of the world, and no doubt posterity will continue to bless him for it, till time shall be no more. His position outside of our regular work has prevented me from meeting him in the connection in which I have mentioned many others to whom I have had to acknowledge my indebtedness for favours conferred ; but I can at least boast that he is my friend, and I trust he will not consider this slight tribute to his worth out of place.

Associated with him on the Conference platform, no one could fail to notice the Rev. Anson Green, D.D., whose venerable appearance, and valuable counsels, would have

---

* The boast of the poet Horace, "*Exegi monumentum are perennius.* ' *Lib.* III., Carmen XXX.

rendered him an efficient member of the *Sanhedrim*, had he lived in the days when Judaism flourished. But Christians appreciate merit as well as Jews, as is readily seen by the deference which is paid him when he rises in Conference to express his views on any of the important questions which from time to time come up for deliberation. To enumerate his services to the Church would be to write out a list of the positions which he has occupied, from the President downwards, all of which require talent of the first order, and confidence unbounded on the part of his brethren. These, I am glad to believe, he possesses. Though he now occupies a superannuated relation, he has by no means ceased to be useful, nor has his light become dim, but rather resembles

"The bright setting sun, at the close of the day,
Which will rise in yet brighter array."

"But what shall I more say? for the time would fail me to tell of Gideon, and of Barak, and of Sampson, and of Jephtha, of David also, and Samuel, and of the prophets." All these were mighty men, men of faith; and the apostle meant nothing invidious by throwing them in, as it were, in a heap, or as a supplement to those already mentioned. In terms similar to those employed in reference to the brethren already mentioned, I might speak of the gentlemanly Howard, the laborious Scott, the pious McRitchie, the faithful Goodson, the good-natured Blackstock, the zealous Youmans, the philosophical Williams, the indefatigable Russ, the clear-sighted Madden, the studious Sutherland, the courteous Hunt, the devoted Grey, the venerable and respected Father Douse,* the theological Bishop; the rhetorical Stephenson, the affable

* See note * on page 317.

Berry, the indomitable Aylesworth, the persevering English, the self-denying Hugill, the modest Shaw, the devoted Mc-Fadden, the popular Griffin, the obliging Greener, the sympathetic Learoyd, the kind-hearted Adams, the hospitable Andrews, the accomplished Christopherson, the talented Fish, the pastoral McCollum, the retiring Preston, the cheerful Willoughby, the useful Clement, and the late lamented Spencer. All these brethren I am happy to claim as my friends; and to all of them I must express my gratitude for kindnesses, many and various, received at their hands,—as well as to the many excellent young brethren who were their colleagues on the occasions of my visits to them, many of whom have since risen to occupy important positions in our work. While expedience prohibits me from being more extended in my notice of them, gratitude and personal regard for these brethren claim that their names at least should appear in my "Autobiography." Another writer* is at present engaged on a work† which will no doubt do more ample justice to their merits.‡

Even while I write, the intelligence reaches me that the Rev. W. M. Punshon, M.A., has arrived in our Canada, and has already commenced his labours amongst us. I regret that I have not the honour of being acquainted personally with him; but I anticipate that pleasure before many weeks. No one can read of his doings without desiring to know more of him. Like a comet, or a meteor in the nocturnal sky, he already has become the cynosure towards which all eyes are attracted, and around which we lesser lights must be content

---

* Rev. J. Carroll.   † "Case, and His Cotemporaries."

‡ I must here mention that I am much indebted to a great number of our own laity, as well as to ministers of other denominations.

13*

to revolve. Among a nation proverbial for its great men, report awards him no secondary position. I look for his arrival to prove an epoch in our church. His presence will no doubt stimulate that principle of emulation in our ministers which the presence of a master-mind seldom fails to awaken. It is affecting to read, in the English newspapers, the accounts of the tenacity with which the people clung to him as he was about to leave them, and gratifying to hear of the substantial tokens which they have given him of their appreciation and esteem. But what must especially endear him to us is the modesty and diffidence with which, fame reports, he receives all his honours. We anticipate in him none of that aristocratic *hauteur* which would keep him at a distance from our sympathies, and continually endeavour to teach us, "Thus far shalt thou come, but no farther." We have not so learned to regard him. We rather expect he can sympathize with us as a man, like our venerable Dr. Wood ; and a brother, like Bro. Taylor, and reciprocate with us the sentiment of Terence :—" *Homo sum et nihil humanum a me alienum puto*,"—(I am a man, and I esteem nothing pertain ing to humanity as foreign to me). As a man and a brother then, we bid him welcome to our Canada, and devoutly pray for the blessing of God to crown his labours amongst us !

From this digression, which I trust is a pardonable one, I now resume my narrative ; and as I promised that this should be the last chapter, I must in some sort redeem my pledge, although in doing so I shall have to condense many things worthy of more extended notice, and omit others which deserve insertion.

I never like to expel a man from the church, and never do so, even in flagrant cases, while there is any hope that milder measures will correct his errors. In a few cases, however, I have had to exercise this prerogative, painful as it is to me. One of these occurred a few months ago.

On the complaint of ten of our members I had to bring a man to trial, during which the charges against him were so fully sustained, and his conduct at the trial so flagrant, that I saw no alternative but to expel him. From him I met with determined opposition, and he gave me a good deal of trouble—misrepresenting myself and my family as far as his influence extended. As regarded myself, I would never have taken any notice of his misrepresentations ; but where my family were concerned, I deemed it necessary to call those members together who had been instrumental in bringing the charges, and those who had been present at the trial. In the presence of my son and the English minister, I put a series of questions to these, calculated to elucidate the truth. Their answers were entirely satisfactory to the young brethren present, and some of them even volunteered to make statements in vindication of my course, not called forth by any questions asked. And thus, in spite of his effort to injure myself and my family, it only recoiled upon himself, and proved beyond question that he was no longer fit for a position as a member of our church. Strangely enough, neither he nor his wife seemed particularly aggrieved with those who brought the charges against them ; but I and my family must suffer the full weight of their vengeance,—while, in reality, I only acted in accordance with "Discipline," and could not have done other than I did, if I had been ever so willing.

In this manner I spent my "merry" Christmas and "happy" New Year. While my brethren in the English work were enjoying their fat turkeys and plum-puddings, as well as pleasant social intercourse with their friends, and delighting in the full confidence and hearty co-operation of all the members of their flocks, here was I with my troubles But I ate my turkey and pudding with my family, which is a little world in itself, into the sanctity of which I can always retire when the storm rages without. If our English brethren could. know what their German co-labourers have to suffer in comparison with them, they would readily admit that no pecuniary consideration is an adequate compensation for the conflict and strife, the trials and privations, which we are called upon to endure.

We commenced on New Year's-day, 1868, a series of protracted meetings, which continued a few weeks with encouraging tokens of the Divine presence. True, we only received six additions to our church; but that is saying a great deal for Preston. It is of the infinite mercy of God that we have any one at all even coming to our church, much more being converted there, when we consider the opposition with which every one of them has to contend! But the six additions were not the only result of these meetings; the membership were quickened into new life, the weak were made strong, the faint-hearted encouraged, the desponding cheered, the doubting removed from the clutches of giant Despair. I received valuable assistance from my son and his two colleagues, who, not only by their preaching, but also by their visiting from house to house, were the means of bringing the tidings of salvation to some who might not otherwise have heard it.

Of course opposition raged as usual. The more active we were in trying to get people to our services, the more diligent the enemies of our church became in persuading them from even entering such a "dangerous" place of worship, much less getting, as they termed it, "ensnared in our trap."

One family especially, who had been reclaimed from the Lutheran Church and brought under the influence of the gospel in its purity, suffered from the importunate visits of these, their so-called friends. But they knew in whom they had believed, and were always ready to give an answer to every one that asked them—a reason of the hope that was in them.

"How is it," they would say to those friends (?) who importuned them to go back to the Lutheran Church, "that you never cared to warn us of our danger while we were yet in our sins? Now we have found the Saviour; now we enjoy religion, which makes us happy; and we know we could no longer derive any benefit from listening to your preacher. And now we are resolved that 'nothing shall be able to separate us from the love of God, which is in Christ Jesus our Lord.'"

During the progress of these meetings, Bro. Schessar arrived one evening from Heidelberg, and informed me that the windows of our church in that place, which had only been erected during last summer, were smashed to pieces,—not only the glass, but the sashes. The deed had been done on a Saturday night, doubtless for the purpose of preventing the Sabbath worship; but in this their object was defeated, for there was to be no preaching service on that day, and the Sabbath-school alone was inconvenienced. But we accepted their good intentions all the same.

However, early on Monday morning my son attended to the matter, and the breach was repaired forthwith. I was not at all surprised at this little expression of their good-will; for a place which could be guilty of an attempt on my life a few months before, is quite capable of anything in that line. The German work must be of God, or we would not have a church, nor a member left to us, if He did not protect us, and restrain those who are opposed to His work.

But as an off-set to my discouragements of this kind, I am sometimes favoured with cheering evidences that the seed which I am permitted to sow, often falls in good ground, perhaps where least expected. As an instance, I may be allowed here to insert a letter which I received a short time since, from a boy who used to belong to our Sunday-school in Preston, but who removed over a year ago to Louisville, Kentucky. Evidently the impressions for good which he received while with us have been lasting, and have finally resulted in his conversion to God. He writes me the day after his conversion. But I will let him tell his own story, and I transcribe his letter *verbatim et literatim :—*

"Louisville K.y. 8th Fevery 1868.

"REV DR FRESHMENN—

"It is of my bleasure to take the pen and ride A Letter. we thank Gott that we are all Well, And i hope that yous are all Well.

"O Prother Freshmenn if you gout think what a happy Time we have got in our Savour our God. I got converted 7th Feberrey 1868 Soffia Forrell cot converted Last week I cand tell exact what tay. John Schmitt and his wife got converted. they youst to go to the Mettothiss Geurge and Fell back and went to the Lotheran Churge and God Leated them back to the our Churg and got convertet.

"In the time of three weeks 42 got converted and there is 14 on the Mornin Pench. and I hope that God will soon For give them there sins.

"In New Albney 40 got converted and 30 jound tho Mettothis Churge. there is 15 Mettothis churges in Louisville, and 11 catolick.

"there is more Mettothis churge in our town then eney other churges. 2 Paptis 2 Lotheran and so forth 65 churge In Louisville. Prother Schimmelfening is our Preicher.

"I Hope you will soon ride agane and Let us know how yous are geting allong in your churge.

"I send my re specks to all Frient. to all your Familey to William Maller, Conrad Diehl, to Mallers hole Family, Diehls hole Family. I woult Liked to be With you in Preston. if God will i think I com over to nex Chrismass.

"Il Stay your Frend

"WILLIAM SCHMIDT.

"Address William Schmidt
    "Louisville K.y.
  "Marshell St bet. Clay and Shelby
    "No 195
  "WILLIAM SCHMIDT

"I went to mornin Penche 2 weeks and I woutent give up till I Hat Found Geasus my Gott."

Apart from the orthography and style of this letter, which is calculated to excite a smile, it contains good news, and encourages me to labour on, not only among the adult portion of my charge, but in the Sabbath-school; and if ten thousand will conspire against it to destroy it, as long as I receive such intimations as the above of fruit "after many days," I will believe it is of the Lord; and if it be of God, men "cannot overthrow it," even though they are willing to be found fighting against God.

Preston is a peculiar place. It is large enough to furnish sufficient diversity of character, and small enough to admit of everybody knowing everybody's business better than everybody knows it himself.

The principal enjoyment of some is continually either to tell or to hear of some new thing. Hence, perhaps, it is that while I am here, they periodically avail themselves of "something fresh," which they are sure to cause to turn up to satisfy their desires. To show how this is accomplished, I might give an example :—

I had enjoyed a few weeks of comparative peace, and could actually walk to the post-office and back without hearing anything to my disparagement. I was beginning to dream of those "seas of endless rest," "flowery beds of ease," and that sort of thing, which sounds so nice in poetry, when my tranquility was disturbed, and my recollection restored to the fact that I had not yet been " carried to the skies," by an attempt on the part of the Preston Municipality to impose a tax on my horse and buggy. This they had never done before. I remonstrated with the Reeve, requesting him to lay my appeal before the Council, which he neglected repeatedly to do. In the meantime I consulted with several of my friends, ministerial and lay, all of whom advised me not to pay it, as it was an illegal measure. I accordingly demurred when payment was demanded. A bailiff was immediately sent to seize a portion of my furniture, and a large notice was placed in a conspicuous place in the post-office, informing the inhabitants that on a given day the following property belonging to Dr. Freshman would be sold by public auction at his house, viz., "a table, six cane-seated chairs, a rocking-chair, and other furniture ;" all of which were in due time sold for the very respectable sum of $3 45. The bailiff, who is a tavern-keeper, said he was authorized by the collector, who is the son of a tavern-keeper.

Perhaps this was the method by which they testified their disapproval of an exposition which I made of some of their pernicious doctrines, as taught in a catechism lately published by a Lutheran minister in New Dundee. I received a copy of the blasphemous little publication a short time after it was issued, and immediately sent a letter to the *Christliche Apologete*, published by Dr. Nast in Cincinnati. The little book is called, "Spiritual Food for Lutheran Schools and Families." As it contains many savory morsels, let me tempt the palates of some of my English brethren with a few of them

Question 109 reads as follows :—

What is the principal thing in Confirmation ?

Ans.—Holy Baptism.

Quest. 115.—What is a Lutheran if he leave his church ?

Ans.—A perjurer against God and his Word.

Quest. 138.—Can we then receive the Lord's Supper with other sects and churches ?

Ans.—No ; by no means.

Quest. 139.—Why not ?

Ans.—Because it would be a criminal hypocrisy and denial of the faith.

Quest. 159.—For what purpose is the Holy Sacrament given ?

Ans.—To be eaten and drunk.

Quest. 163.—When was the Holy Sacrament instituted

Ans.—On Green Thursday evening.

Quest. 170.—What is the duty of every Lutheran ?

Ans.—To learn Luther's Catechism, word for word, by heart.

Quest. 177.—What is confession?

Ans.—Confession comprehends two parts—one that a person confess his sins—the other that he receive absolution or forgiveness from the confessor AS FROM GOD HIMSELF.

This, then is the church, and these some of its doctrines, which vaunts itself as having already possession of the field, and entitled to be let alone in undisturbed enjoyment. I have no doubt that if some of our English brethren, who doubted the experiment of employing German missionaries, could know the present attitude and tendencies of the Lutheran Church,—if they have any love for the souls of the poor Germans at all,—they would be led to change their opinions. When I see an evil, I must expose it. When I see a man going to hell, I must tell him so ; and if it will result in persecution every day I live, I must do my duty, I must save my soul.

This being the normal state of affairs, it is not to be wondered at that I sometimes hail it as a relief when business leads me abroad. But, wherever I go, I cannot get rid of " Dr. Freshman ;" and although I am pretty well acquainted with him myself, I often meet in those excursions with people who know a great deal more about him than I do.

An amusing instance of this occurred a short time ago, during a visit to Hamilton. When about to return home, and while waiting at the station for the cars, a Mr. R——, a Jew, residing in Hamilton, engaged in conversation with me. On ascertaining that I was going to Preston, the following colloquy ensued :—

" To Preston !" said he; "then you are perhaps acquainted with Dr. Freshman of that place ?"

" Why, yes," said I ; " everybody is acquainted with him.
But why do you ask ? Have you a message to send him ?"

" Oh, no," said he; "the mention of Preston merely
brought him to my mind. When I was up there I went to
hear him preach."

" Indeed !" said I. " Then you are, of course, acquainted
with him !"

" Yes," said he ; " only too well !"

" How is that ?" said I. " Has he ever done you any
harm ?"

" Not to myself personally," said he. " But I take him
to be one of the greatest scoundrels that ever lived !"

" Indeed !" said I, "that is a serious charge to bring
against any man. You ought to have a good foundation
for it."

" I have," said he ; " it is sufficient, in my opinion, to
brand any man as a rascal who would leave the Jewish
Church ; and, as for him, I know him to be both a hypocrite and an imposter."

" Well, really," said I, " I am pretty well acquainted with
him ; I have heard him preach a number of times, and he
always seems to me to be sincere. I believe he is a truly
converted man, and preaches the pure gospel,—at least, if
I understand it. I know, as a preacher, he gives entire
satisfaction to his congregations ; and although some of the
people among whom he labours are not well disposed to
him, no one has ever been able to prove anything against
his moral character. I cannot help thinking, if you were
better acquainted with him, you could not say such hard
things as you do."

"I tell you," said he, "I am perfectly well acquainted with him. I have heard him preach; and although he passes for a learned man, I have a little boy who knows more than he does."

"Well, then," said I, "if you are perfectly well acquainted with him, I have nothing more to say, except that I am that Dr. Freshman, of Preston,—" that scoundrel, that rascal, that impostor, that hypocrite!" I am Dr. Freshman himself! And now, how dare you malign the character of a man whom you know nothing about, and whom, perhaps, you have never seen before? My Christianity teaches me not to lie, and to slander the character of no man. If your Judaism will tolerate such things, how long will it be before you learn the superiority of . that Christianity which you despise?"

If I ever saw confusion personified, that was the time! All the colours of the rainbow flitted in succession over his face, leaving a permanent pallor behind. If he could have vanished into a mousehole, I believe he would have done it. If he could have erected an adamant wall, or a thousand leagues distance between "Dr. Freshman" and himself, he would have done it. Just then Mr. Sumerfield, of Hamilton, came forward, and I acquainted him with the matter of our conversation; when Mr. R——, plucking up courage, tried to defend himself in the following manner :—

"You know me, Mr. Sumerfield," said he; "and you know I am not like other Jews, who delight to slander the character of Dr. Freshman. I believe he is a very good man, as well as very learned," &c.

"But stop, man!" said I. "You know it is scarcely two minutes since you said so many hard things against me; and now you do not blush to say the very opposite to ny face! Will you first tell me a lie, and then swear that you did not say it?"

"Yes!" said he; "I see the point, but I mis—, we mis—un—derstood one another! I meant—well, yes, I did say —but I am going to Preston some day, and will—"

"Poor fellow!" said I, "do you not see that you have no religion?"

At this point an acquaintance of his came forward and drew him away, and I saw him no more.

On my way home, I had a very interesting conversation with my old friend Mr. Hespeler. He is interested in the German work; and perhaps we may see our way clear to avail ourselves in future of the advantage of his good intentions. I believe, if Mr. Hespeler were fully to espouse the good cause of Christ, he would become a pillar in the temple of our God—a polished stone whose lustre would never become dim, neither in this world nor that which is to come. I hope he will remember—if his eye should scan these pages—that "without ceasing, I make mention of him in my prayers." My heart's desire and prayer to God on his behalf is, that he may be saved.

Neither I nor any of my family attach a great deal of importance to dreams; and yet, a short time ago, my wife and one of my daughters dreamed a peculiar and almost identical dream, about our second son, Edward, who is now in Cincinnati. We were startled the next day by the receipt of a letter, informing us of his dangerous illness, and how very near the gates of death he had stood. But we are thankful to God for his recovery so far, and we trust he will soon be perfectly restored. To Mrs. Dr. Weakly we would especially tender our most heartfelt thanks, for her very motherly attention to him during his illness.]

While speaking of dreams, a very strange circumstance was related to me a few weeks ago, which goes to prove that there may be "more things in heaven and earth than we dream of in our philosophy." A young man named Wait was killed near St. George a short time ago, while engaged among saw logs. This young man had a brother and a married sister, — a Mrs. Eastman, — who keeps a store in Owen Sound. On the night on which the young man was killed, his brother was asleep in the store in Owen Sound. A man came to him in his dreams, and told him, — "Mrs. Eastman's brother is dead!" He awoke, and finding it only a dream, composed himself to sleep again. Again the man came to him and said, "Mrs. Eastman's brother is dead." So vivid was the impression that he got up and went from the store towards Mrs. Eastman's house; but on the way thither, he met a man coming to tell him that they had received a telegram, stating that his brother was badly hurt. They started immediately for St. George, and on arriving found that he had died almost exactly at the time when his nocturnal visitor had first appeared. The spiritual messenger had made swifter progress, and conveyed more accurate information, than the telegraph.

As I belong this year to the Hamilton District, I was appointed on the Missionary Deputation to the Grand River and New Credit Indian Missions. I started on the 10th of February, and enjoyed my visit to both these stations exceedingly. It never was my privilege before to be among converted Indians, and I was thankful to God to see so many of them. I found that religion can educate and civilize an Indian as well as a white man. It seems as well adapted for the one as the other. I shall retain many pleasing reminiscences of my visit to them, and my intercourse with our ministers whom I met, and whose hospitality I shared; but it might prove tedious to particularize.

One thing I did want to satisfy myself regarding, and that was, whether, as some suppose, the Indians are descendants of the (lost) ten tribes of Israel. For this purpore I had a lengthy conversation with one of their chiefs. I enquired into their various traditions, but could find no similarity to those of the Jews. I asked him to repeat to me several colloquial phrases in his own language, but could discover not a single trace of resemblance to the Hebrew. This sub-ject I will endeavour more fully to investigate in my volume of "Lectures on Judaism," which I intend to publish.

(Extract from Diary, February 17.)

"Yesterday we had a most blessed day. Bro. C. Lavell, M.A., Chairman of the Guelph District, came up to admin-ister the Lord's Supper to Bro. Smiley's congregation. He preached one of his inimitable sermons: rich in thought, simple in style, lucid in exposition. Bro. Lavell is highly esteemed in Galt, and gives universal satisfaction to the brethren of his District. May God long spare his life to the Church!"

When I remember all the way in which the Lord has led me, I have very many special reasons to be truly thankful. Among other things, I may say, as it is somewhat remark-able, that not one of those who have been converted through my instrumentality, or that of my son, has ever backslidden; and not one of the many children whom I have baptized, has, to my knowledge, died. Some even, who were at the point of death, and supposed beyond the possibility of restoration to health, after being baptized by me, speedily recovered. These things may appear strange, but are nevertheless true. I say it not boastingly, but to the glory of God. I wish I could add that all whom I have married live happily; but if they do not, all I have to say is, that it is their own fault.

I have just received a letter from Bro. Schuster, stating that the new mission which I opened on the Ottawa last Fall, is doing well, and giving promise of success.

It will be eight years next Conference since I began the German work in Canada. Then there was not a single German Wesleyan Methodist. Now, thanks be to God! we have eight missionary labourers in the vineyard, several local preachers and class-leaders, and over two hundred members in the society—with a goodly number in heaven. Then we had not a single church or appointment; now we have twelve churches, and thirty congregations, among which flourish several very prosperous Sabbath-schools. Besides all this, other German churches, which were becoming cold and dead, have been awakened and quickened through our instrumentality. When we contemplate these facts, in the face of all the opposition with which we have had, and still have, to contend, how can we suppress from grateful hearts the exclamation, " What hath God wrought!" In the language of our sainted founder, we would ascribe all the glory to Him ; and surely we have a right to the same consolation as he used to derive from the reflection, " The best of all is, God is with us !"

And now my task is almost accomplished, my book almost finished, and yet a strange sort of fascination, or " *cacœthes scribendi*," keeps my pen in motion. Although I have thus come to the close of the record of my life, my life itself has not yet come to a close. It is somewhat saddening to think that perhaps some who read these pages, the Lutheran Church especially, would wish it had. It is not a very comfortable conviction to feel assured that you meet with people every day who hate you ; yet so it is with me. Even so, I am content for the sake of Him who said, "Ye shall be hated of all men for my name's sake."

"Yea, let men rage, since thou wilt spread,
Thy shadowing wings around my head ;
Since in all pain thy tender love,
Will still my sure refreshment prove."

In closing this record of my life thus far, I cannot forget that there is another record being kept in the book of God's remembrance, and that, finally, when my life-task is accomplished, I must be judged according to the things that are written in that book. What a solemn aspect does such a reflection give to life !

During the preceding pages I have had occasion to mention the names of many who are still alive ; some of these have merited praise, and some dispraise. Some, perhaps, may feel aggrieved ; but I can honestly say I have had no desire to injure any one. If that had been my object, to render evil for evil, the names of many would here have been inserted who are not. I feel that my Christianity enables me to forgive my enemies, yea, to pray for them ; and my heart's desire and prayer to God for each of them is that they may be saved. Even to those who feel aggrieved at any thing I have said about them, it will be manifest that I have said only what the integrity of history demanded. I would willingly have passed them by, and

14

allowed their efforts to injure me to be forgotten, could I have done so without mutilating my narrative.

I have little more to say. My heart is bound up in the German work, and although some of my spiritual children are ungrateful and wayward, I believe the work will, in time, become an important one. He who would ask for greater success as a proof of our ministry than that which has already crowned our efforts, little knows the nature of the field in which we labour. As I have before remarked, it is a mercy in view of all our difficulties, that we have even a "few names who have not defiled their garments." As the work lies near my heart, I feel jealous for its welfare, and if it cost me my life, I must defend its interests ; for in doing so, I feel that I am defending the cause of God. But I am satisfied that when our English brethren are fully acquainted with us and our work, they will see as we see, and assist us in protecting it from its enemies. May God hasten the time, and grant that the future may be as the past, only much more abundant.

Here, perhaps, I ought to write the little word

"Finis !"

and lay down my pen ; but as another important event occurred quite recently, which I neglected to mention in its proper place, it may not inappropriately be inserted here, and may be called a "P.S.," an "N.B.," an "Addendum," or anything else that suits the fancy of the reader. Those who have been wearied with the task of reading the preceding pages, may stop when they come to the word "Finis," if they please ; but if they do, they will never know

HOW I CAME TO GIVE UP SMOKING TOBACCO!

It occurred in this way. In the latter part of November, 1867, I was assisting at a protracted meeting in Heidelberg, on my son's mission. During one of the evenings I preached there, a good old lady, a Mrs. Weber, was powerfully awakened to a sense of her lost condition as a sinner. After the meeting, Mrs. Freshman and I went home with her to the house of her son, with whom she is living, and to whose kind hospitality we are always welcome. As she was in great distress of mind, we remained conversing with her, and pointing her to the Saviour who taketh away the sins of the world, till after midnight, when she found peace, and was made happy in God.

After this had been achieved, I thought I deserved to enjoy the luxury of a "good, comfortable smoke." While preparing the necessary materials, the following conversation ensued between myself and one of the young men, a grandson of the old lady I have mentioned:—

"Why, Doctor," said he, "do you smoke?"

"Yes," said I, "did you never know that before?"

"Well," said he, "your young men are not allowed to smoke, are they!"

"No," said I, "we would like our young men, if possible, to be in every respect an improvement on ourselves."

"Well," said he, "I was reading a short time ago in the *Apologete* an article, in which you were styled "The Father of German Methodism in Canada;" and it does seem to me rather inconsistent that a father will persist in doing what he will not allow his children to do."

That was about all he said, and the subject was dropped ; but never have I listened to a more powerful sermon than that contained in those few words of that young man. When I came home, I said to one of my daughters :—

"Search through my drawers, and pockets, and shelves— everywhere ; and wherever you find pipes, tobacco, matches, knives—anything I used in smoking, take it out of my sight, and out of my reach."

The command fell on no unwilling ear, and in less time than it has taken to write this, not a vestige of it remained —not a crumb if I had been starving, and scarcely an odor was perceptible in places formerly most infected.

From that day to the present, more than six months ago, I have never had a "whiff." To say that I gained the victory without a struggle, would be a simple untruth, and could serve no good purpose. For several days my old appetite would return with considerable intensity, especially after my meals. At such times I would pace the floor, sit down, try to read, get up again, and often could only find relief in prayer for sustaining grace. But I must say the victory thus gained was not such an *impossible feat* as I had always considered it. Now I not only have no desire to go back to my wallowing in the mire, but I enjoy a delightful sense of freedom from a thraldom which was worse than slavery. My appetite has improved ; some of my vests will now hardly button around me. My perceptive faculties are clearer ; my sleep more refreshing. I feel younger in years, and more vigorous in body. To all smokers I would say, —" If you don't believe it, try it !"

ADDENDA.

I BEG to acknowledge my great indebtedness to the Rev. E. Wood, D. D., for the invaluable assistance rendered by him to this little work, in correcting the proof-sheets prior to going to press; and also for the many judicious observations and suggestions rendered, from time to time, during the progress of the work.

THE AUTHOR.

---

* NOTE TO PAGE 296.

I became acquainted with Father Douse the first time that I visited Guelph. Among the pleasing reminiscences of that visit, is the introduction which Father Douse gave me to Jas. Hough, Esq., a prominent member of the Wesleyan Church in Guelph, who has from that time held a warm place in my heart. His son, now the Editor of the Cobourg *World*, was then at home; so that in one day I made two very valuable accessions to my already very long list of kind friends.

www.ingramcontent.com/pod-product-compliance
Lightning Source LLC
Chambersburg PA
CBHW020938030726
47496CB00005B/1244